CONNECTION

A GEORGINA VAN WYK MYSTERY

ROBERT PARKER

Matador
9 Priory Business Park,
Wistow Road, Kibworth Beauchamp,
Leicestershire. LE8 0RX
Tel: 0116 279 2299
Email: books@troubador.co.uk
Web: www.troubador.co.uk/matador
Twitter: @matadorbooks

ISBN 978 17846246 37

British Library Cataloguing in Publication Data.
A catalogue record for this book is available from the British Library.

Printed and bound by CPI Group (UK) Ltd, Croydon, CR0 4YY
Typeset in 11pt Aldine 401 BT by Troubador Publishing Ltd, Leicester, UK

Matador is an imprint of Troubador Publishing Ltd

Linda in 1969

For Linda

CHAPTER ONE

Wednesday 15th. January 1969
Cape Town, South Africa

Georgina Van Wyk was angry.

The trouble was, she was not sure what she was angry about.

She was only twenty, very good looking, she knew that, rich, she didn't know how rich, her husband took care of all that but she knew she had more money than she could possibly spend.

However, she was angry.

Driving home from the tennis club she was still wearing her short white skirt and top and white tennis shoes. Her new red Jaguar E Type was a wedding present from her husband of six months. She was driving much too fast along the narrow road towards her home in Constantia, a prosperous suburb of Cape Town.

Why was she angry?

At 20 years of age, when most girls her age were either still at home with their parents or at university, Georgina Van Wyk was mistress of her own home and what a home it was. It was the sort of place that appeared in magazines. With stunning views, superb gardens, swimming pool and five servants at her beck and call. It was all she could ever have dreamed of and more.

But she was angry.

Pulling up sharply in a shower of gravel outside the large double gates that led to her home, she impatiently punched in the four number entry code on the key pad located adjacent to her driver's window. Normally this would cause the gates to open automatically but today they remained firmly closed. Trying the sequence again without success Georgina angrily pushed the intercom button. There was no reply from the house.

Cursing under her breath she pressed the horn button so hard she thought it might break.

The horn blared.

She tried to release the pressure but couldn't. It was cathartic, she could feel the anger in her flowing down her arm and into the car. She noticed a neighbour drive by and look at her. She forced her hand from the hooter button and sat in embarrassed silence.

A moment later she heard the sound of the gate being unlatched and one half began to open allowing her a view down the hundred yard drive to her house.

It was not Amos the garden boy opening the gate but his ten year old grandson David. He was very small and the whites of his large eyes stood out against his black skin. She watched the boy struggle with the heavy gate, it was plainly too much for him to handle and at one point the boy slipped on the gravel and it started to close again.

Instead of helping him, she sounded the horn again which made the child panic. What a bitch she thought but couldn't overcome her again rising anger.

Suddenly, Amos appeared at his grandson's side and quickly opened both sides of the gate allowing the car to enter.

Georgina drove forward and stopped next to Amos who smiled down at her. Garden boy? He was well over fifty years and looked older, stick thin and dressed in the almost obligatory uniform of dirty white shirt, thread bare trousers and bare feet. His grey stubble contrasting to his black skin.

"Good afternoon, baas. I am very sorry but the automatic mechanism is broken, I didn't know you were outside until I heard your car horn," he explained apologetically.

He felt, due to his age and length of service with her husband, that he enjoyed a privileged place in the household. He could speak good English and Afrikaans after years of service in the houses of white employers. Georgina Van Wyk was in the mood to re educate him.

"Fast asleep more likely," she snarled malevolently. "You seem incapable of carrying out the simplest task and as for that brat of yours, I don't remember giving him a job here so as far as I'm concerned he is a trespasser and if I see him on my property again I'll call the police and have him arrested. Do I make myself clear?"

Amos was no longer smiling. He stood by the car door and looked down at his feet, avoiding Georgina's glare. She noticed that the little boy had disappeared into the bushes.

"Yes, Madam," he mumbled.

Georgina tried to hold her tongue but couldn't stop herself from verbally destroying this poor old man. She was enjoying his discomfort.

"I must warn you Amos, that I am seriously dissatisfied with your work lately and I'm considering replacing you with someone younger and more capable," she concluded dismissively.

Amos trembled.

He, like all blacks living or working in white areas, was legally required to carry a Pass Book. This needed Georgina's signature every month to remain valid. Without that signature he could be arrested and returned, under the Group Areas Act, to his designated homeland. This, in his case, had been decreed by the Government as Zululand, a place he had never visited and hundreds of miles away. It was an iniquity probably lost on Amos that to remain in the town where he had spent most of his life he needed the permission of a young woman who was not South African and had only come to South Africa seven years previously.

"And wash my car." she shouted as she engaged first gear and accelerated down the drive, the back wheels of the powerful sports car spinning as the tyres fought to grip the loose surface.

Arriving at the front of the large white painted double fronted house on two floors designed in what is called the 'Cape Dutch' style of architecture, she killed the engine and got out, leaving the keys in the ignition and the car door open. She walked up the three wide curving steps to the imposing double front door flanked either side by two enormous windows. The door was opened for her by Miriam the Xhosa housemaid who stood aside, her hand on the latch.

"Good afternoon, baas." she said in her broken English.

Her own language was Xhosa, which few white South Africans spoke. Most conversations between Mistress and servant were in 'Kitchen Kaffir,' a mixture of English, Afrikaans and Bantu.

Completely ignoring her, Georgina walked through the doorway and into the large square hall. She threw her jacket at the antique Dutch console table against the left wall, which matched it's replica on the right. It missed, hit the wall and fell to the floor. Without slackening her pace she crossed the elegant black and white marble tiled floor passing the two wide corridors leading off to the left and right that afforded access to the principal rooms of the ground floor. Each corridor was illuminated by a single large window at the end of the building. Ahead of her were a pair of double mahogany doors that led into the main lounge. Either side of these doors and projecting forward into the hall were double curving staircases leading to the first floor balcony.

A huge glittering glass chandelier hung level with the balcony, dominating the whole area of the hall and staircases. It was unlit at this time, the afternoon sun beaming through the floor to ceiling windows either side of the double front door, bathing the hall in soft reflected colours.

Today, all this elegance was lost on Georgina. When she had first married Hendrik she could not believe it was all hers. She would walk around the house, in and out of the rooms entranced by the opulence and beauty of her house. But not today.

She started to climb the left hand staircase. Halfway up she quickened her pace until she arrived at the first floor where the two staircases met in front of double doors matching those on the ground floor. These doors led to a minstrel gallery overlooking the spacious living room with stunning views across the garden. Georgina often had her breakfast here, avoiding the formality of the dining room and when it was too cold to eat outside. Duplicate corridors to those downstairs ran away to the left and right. She ran down the righthand, marble tiled corridor, lit as downstairs until she reached her bedroom. She entered, slammed the door behind her and threw herself on the bed. She burst into tears and cried deep sobs into her pillow. She could do nothing but give way to this overwhelming emotion that had been welling up inside her.

It was a full ten minutes before she could pull herself together. She stood up, wiped her eyes and walked to the window. Looking down, she felt a pang of guilt as she saw Amos busily leathering her car to a shine. Georgina realised the extra work she had caused him by leaving her car by the front door and not driving it round to the wash area equipped with hose, buckets and all the paraphernalia of car cleaning. It meant the poor old man had to carry buckets of water round to the front of the house. Georgina knew that he could not drive a car and even if he could he would not have dared sit in her driving seat.

She felt sorry for her behaviour, the gate security system was broken, nobody's fault. After all she was not a nasty person, she contented herself that she could easily make things right with him.

She walked back to the bed and sat down on the edge, it was time to confront her demons. No more kidding herself, something was seriously wrong in her fairy tale life.

She looked around the beautiful room, well it was more than a room, it was a bedroom suite. Off the bedroom was a dressing room, huge bathroom and shower, walk in wardrobe and a small sitting room with her desk and chair, two armchairs and an occasional table. All were expensive Dutch antiques. Of course, this was where the anger lay. It was her exclusive bedroom. There were no men's clothes in the wardrobe, no shaving things in the bathroom. Her husband of six months had his own matching suite on the opposite side of the corridor. This was his choice, claiming that his long hours and late nights working as a lawyer and now the additional pressure of trying to make his way up the slippery slope of South African politics as a member of the Cape Province branch of the National Party dictated this to be the best recipe for a happy marriage. Georgina had no problem with apartheid, but apartheid in the bedroom between husband and wife?

Georgina Van Wyk was surprised by the way her marriage was developing. This was not what she had envisaged, she expected her new husband, who was fifteen years her senior to have been all over her like a rash! It had to change and she would change it.

So far, nobody else was surprised by this state of affairs as nobody else knew. Georgina kept these things to herself.

*

The shrill ring of the telephone suddenly intruded into Georgina's thoughts, she picked up the receiver.

The familiar voice at the other end of the line dispelled her dark mood like the dawn dispels the night.

"Hello… Willy, Willy…it's you." she squealed.
"Where are you?… Cape Town?…Fantastic."

She lay on the bed with the receiver balanced on her flat stomach with the handset held to her left ear.

"When did you get back?…where are you now?…did you get the job? No, don't tell me, I just know you did."

It was her beloved cousin. She lived with him and her aunt and uncle when she first came to South Africa from England as a thirteen year old school girl, seven years ago. She was made so welcome in their home that she soon fell in love with them and all South Africa, and South Africa fell in love with her!

William Robinson had been away in Rhodesia on the first step of achieving his long held ambition of joining the British South Africa Police, an interview at the famous Morris Depot in Salisbury.

"I'm coming over" continued Georgina.

"No…you come here…no, we'll have dinner out, somewhere, anywhere, I just have to see you." she laughed.

"I don't care if you're meeting Angie, I'll come too." she giggled.

"Well, okay you beast, enjoy yourself this evening and give my love to Angie but you're mine tomorrow, do you hear?" said Georgina in a pretence of a petulant voice.

"I'll not take no for an answer, I'll pick you up at your place and we'll have lunch somewhere nice and you can fill me in about everything."

"Not one…twelve o'clock, I can't wait till one, what would I do all morning?"

"I don't need to, I'm already gorgeous as you well know."

"Okay, see you at twelve, and be ready! Bye darling, bye, bye." She blew kisses into the handset and replaced it on the cradle.

She hugged the phone to her body, feeling a warm glow as she thought about seeing Will tomorrow. She was happy.

★

A moment later she heard a car on the gravel drive as it pulled up at the front of the house. She replaced the phone on the bedside table and skipped to the window in time to see her husband Hendrik struggling to the front door with a bulging attache case in his left hand and half a dozen or more untidy brown cardboard files gripped under his right arm. In the distance the sight of Amos's grandson struggling to close the front gates was an unwelcome reminder of her explosive temper a few minutes earlier. She put it out of her mind.

Georgina ran from her bedroom and sprinted down the corridor to the staircase. She had a mind, such was her elation, to slide down the bannister but contented herself by daintily skipping down the stairs.

She ran up to her husband and threw her arms around his

neck. Startled, he dropped all his files and they scattered all over the marble floor.

"Hey, hey, Georgie" he said, "Careful."

He turned towards Georgina and his bespectacled face broke in a broad smile, surprised but delighted to receive such a welcome from his beautiful young wife. She gave him a long lingering kiss, full on the lips. Wow, thought Hennie.

Miriam, by this time, had scurried into the hall from the corridor that led eventually to the kitchens and domestic offices of the house. She immediately started to collect the papers and documents that were strewn all over the hall floor. From her crouching position she cast a quizzical glance towards her two employers. It was a long time since she had seen a show of emotion like this, especially bearing in mind the mood her young Mistress had been in not long before.

That was the trouble from a servants point of view, one never knew where one stood in this house.

"I've just had a call from Will, he's home and I'm having lunch with him tomorrow, why don't you take the day off and join us?" Bubbled Georgina.

"That's great darling but I'm in court all day tomorrow, I doubt if I'll even have time for a sandwich, you go and enjoy yourself and give young Will my best wishes." Apologised Hendrik.

He actually wondered why the boy couldn't get a profession under his belt and do a proper job like him and why travel up to Rhodesia. If he insisted on joining the police what was wrong with the South African police? At least he would be keeping his own family safe. Another thing, why were they called British when Rhodesia had broken its links with Britain in 1965 by declaring unilateral independence from Britain and why South Africa when that was the one place they certainly never set foot? He could never understand the British. Why not drop the pretensions and just call it the Rhodesia Police and be done with it?

However, after the welcome home he had just received he was genuinely sorry not to be able to join his wife for lunch tomorrow.

"Oh, Hennie, you never take a day off." Pouted Georgina with genuine regret but no great surprise.

"Darling, I'm devastated but there it is, I'm expected in court. Never mind though, we can at least have dinner together this evening."

"Fantastic, where shall we go?"

"No, no, I haven't time to get ready and go out, we can have a nice bottle of wine and eat in, just the two of us. It will be really romantic."

"Mmm romantic," said Georgina without much enthusiasm, "but I warn you, I'll look fantastic and you'll be sorry you can't show me off to all your friends."

Georgina gave Hennie another kiss and watched him stagger off with his bags and files towards the wide hall leading to his study door, Miriam dutifully struggling behind him burdened down with more files.

She smiled as she followed them along the corridor, passing the pair as they struggled into Hennie's study. Continuing to the far end, Georgina opened the last door on the left leading to the kitchen area, a place she visited infrequently. The door opened onto a short corridor that seemed in a different building. A stone paved floor and gloss painted walls in stark contrast to the opulence and comfort of the rest of the house. It was dark, lit only by a naked bulb hanging from the ceiling.

Georgina opened the door into the large kitchen and stood at the top of three steps leading down into the room. It was large, well lit with windows running the length of the opposite wall giving views onto an enclosed kitchen garden. Below these windows stood two large white sinks, one shallow like a butler sink and the other really deep. Large chromium plated hot and cold taps were fixed high up on the wall above each. Between the sinks was a stainless steel draining board piled up with several cooking pans. Against the wall on the left stood two gigantic refrigerators, each with double doors. Finished in grey stainless steel they looked more like the rear doors of delivery trucks than domestic appliances. In the centre of the wall was the door leading to the dining room.

On the right hand side of the room was a six ring stove in stainless steel with a double oven. Wisps of steam were rising from two covered pots gently simmering on the hob. Cupboards, both on the floor and walls filled the rest of the space. Pots, pans and all manner of ladles, knives and kitchen tools hung from wooden racks. Suspended from the white painted ceiling, between the two large strip lights was a slowly revolving electric fan.

In the centre of the room was a large scrubbed wooden table surrounded by half a dozen wooden chairs.

In one of the chairs, balanced on its two back legs sat Anan the cook with his legs crossed on the table, his head slumped forward, asleep. he was a tall slim African of about 30 years of age. As the cook, he considered himself to be a skilled employee and superior to the rest of the servants. After all, he had weekly meetings with Mrs. van Wyk about the food to be served during the forthcoming seven days and enjoyed giving his advice, usually unheeded, on what was fresh and good value in the markets. It was true enough that the success of his boss's famous dinner parties relied on his skills in the kitchen.

At one of the sinks, up to her elbows in soapy water stood Lena, another of the household staff.

A small radio set on a window sill quietly played African music.

Georgina smiled to herself as she surveyed the room.

Letting the kitchen door swing back with a crash on its self closing spring Georgina spoke.

"Ah, Anan, so this is how you spend your time when your working for me."

Anan's head shot back with a sudden jerk. He grabbed at the table with his left hand but it was too late. The chair leaned beyond the point of no return and Anan crashed backwards to the floor, arms and legs flailing in all directions.

Lena, wide eyed, swung round to face the room.

Scrambling to his feet, Anan picked up the chair, he was too shocked to realise how silly he looked.

"I was not asleep, Madam, I was simply thinking about tonight's dinner." he said with as much dignity as he could muster.

"And so you should, Anan, I would not have expected less from a chef of your excellence and reputation." She laughed as she entered the room.

Anan, realising he was being laughed at, decided, wisely to accept the complement in silence.

Still smiling, she walked across the kitchen towards the door to the garden.

"Just make sure dinner this evening is up to standard. It's just Mr. Van Wyk and myself so I think we will dine at the small table by the window."

Georgina couldn't abide eating at the long mahogany table that ran almost the length of the dining room. It was okay she supposed for dinner parties, being able to seat at least thirty, but when set for just two it was like sitting at each end of a cricket pitch. Georgina maintained that when she was sitting at one end and her husband was at the other she could see his lips move before she heard his voice he was so far away.

Leaving through the doorway she turned to Lena, still struck with horror at her employer's sudden appearance.

"How are you Lena, all okay I hope?"

"Yes baas."

Georgina had already left the kitchen and was in the garden as she called back.

"Good, that's all right then."

Still chuckling to herself, she stood and surveyed the neat kitchen garden. She couldn't remember walking here before, another part of Amos's gardening empire she supposed. Close by was a wooden door that she guessed lead to the servants accommodation. Georgina had never stepped beyond that barrier, all she knew was from chance remarks made by Hendrik. Apparently they had an electric light and a cold water tap. Feeling slightly uncomfortable she quickened her step, it must be safer than life in the townships she reasoned and after all, what more could they possibly need?

Walking along the narrow path between the neat rows of vegetables, she opened another wooden gate at the far end of the plot and stepped into the familiar acreage of well manicured gardens. Looking around she turned towards the house.

Her anger of earlier had now abated as quickly as it had arisen. She was certain her future happiness was in her own hands, her ego would not countenance for a moment the thought that her husband was having an affair, the idea was laughable. She knew he loved her and now she would seduce him away from his work and political ambition.

She entered the house through the glass sliding doors that formed one complete wall of the huge living room. Crossing this elegant room she made her way into the hall as the eighteenth century longcase clock struck six.

At the top of the stairs she met Miriam, the maid.

"Just run my bath." Georgina smiled, "and then I think you can leave the rest to me."

Miriam dutifully followed into Georgina's bedroom suite and went to the bathroom and commenced filling the bath, carefully adjusting the water temperature and adding the correct measure of scented oil. She then went to a cupboard and took two beautiful white Egyptian cotton towels and a similar bath robe to place by the bath. She breathed in the delightfully scented steam as it rose from the water. Testing the water temperature, she turned off the taps and quietly left.

Georgina opened the double doors of her wardrobe. The word wardrobe was misleading, it was a room the size of a double bedroom. Walking slowly along one side of the room she ran her hand along the dozens of dresses that hung in rows. Taking a perfectly plain black dress from the rack she held it up in front of her as she looked at her reflection in the full length mirror at the end of the room.

"Mmmm," she whispered to herself, "This will need some thought."

Georgina laid the dress over the back of a chair, undressed quickly, leaving the clothes where they fell and glancing in the mirror with satisfaction walked naked to the bathroom.

After washing her hair in the shower she tied a towel around her head and lowered herself into the bath sinking down into the scented water.

A full half hour later Georgina stepped out of the bath onto a thick white towel and put on the bathrobe, pulling the sash tightly around her waist.

Returning to the wardrobe she picked up the black dress

previously selected. Crossing to the other side of the room she selected underwear and accessories from the huge choice available. Taking these she laid them on the bed.

Smiling to herself, Georgina returned to the wardrobe and opened one of the many drawers along the right hand wall removing a new pack of sheer black stockings and a thin black suspender belt.

She rarely wore stockings or tights, she had no need but tonight she whispered to herself.

"These might be just what's required."

Georgina opened the packet and ran the sensuous nylon over the back of her hand before seating herself at her dressing table to commence the process of transforming herself into Aphrodite. She already held dominion over her beautiful home and everyone in it, now she would take control of her husband.

At eight o'clock she was ready. Georgina slipped on the plain three inch stiletto heeled black patent shoes she had selected and walked across to the full length mirror.

"Yes, I think that will do." She said to herself, turning and looking at her side view and smoothing down her dress. Her flawless complexion required very little make up, just enough to accentuate her big and startlingly blue eyes that contrasted with her short very dark brown hair. Georgina knew very well that she was the sort of woman men would die for and this gave her a natural confidence and elegance that could stop traffic!

She had a perfect figure, far from voluptuous, best described as athletic, almost boyish without a trace of fat. The hem of her plain black dress was six inches above her knee, slightly lower than she would normally wear but with sheer black stockings and high heels her legs looked stunning. As a finishing touch, to set off the plainness of the dress and to please her husband, Georgina wore the Van Wyk family diamonds, consisting of large solitaire earrings, necklace and a huge three carat solitaire ring. Personally, she didn't care for jewellery, however the diamonds had been in the possession of the Van Wyk family, since they had been mined in Kimberley in 1880. As an English woman, she was well aware that wearing them would always make a powerful statement of her ascendancy in this Afrikaner family.

Georgina picked up the telephone at the side of her bed. Using the intercom facility she dialed the kitchen and was answered by Miriam.

"Is my husband seated for dinner?" she enquired.

"Yes, madam, he is at the small table by the window as you instructed." Miriam replied.

With a little extra Chanel she left her bedroom, walked along the corridor and down the staircase to the hall. Intent on a grand entrance she opened the double doors into the living room, crossing the room to the further double mahogany doors that gave direct access to the dining room. Pausing for a moment, she pushed them open and entered.

She loved this house but of all its rooms this was the only one she truly disliked. It was huge and sombre. The walls were panelled in unremitting dark mahogany. The ceiling was ornate and heavily guilded. The left hand wall, as Georgina entered, contained five large windows giving views onto the gardens and beyond. In the centre of the opposite wall was a huge grey stone fireplace with a bronze French clock garniture on the deep mantlepiece. The room would not have been so bad had it been in a medieval English castle, Georgina thought, but in a house barely fifteen years old this was vulgar and fake ostentation.

But worst of all, in Georgina's opinion, was the painting hanging above the fireplace. It was of Andries Pretorius standing next to an ugly old harridan loading a flintlock rifle, with ox waggons in laager forming the background. Hennie however was proud of the picture. Apparently, Van Wyk ancestors had been among the five hundred Voortrekkers at the Battle of Blood River, when an army of ten thousand Zulus had been defeated by the Afrikaner settlers as they made their way into the Orange Free State to avoid living under British rule. A small brass plate screwed to the frame described the scene: 'Andries Pretorius at the Battle of Blood River, 16th December 1838'

Georgina thought the old girl could have seen off ten thousand Zulus all on her own and to make matters worse the painting had those eyes that seemed to follow one disapprovingly around the room.

She hated it.

Hendrik Van Wyk looked up as he heard his wife enter the dining room. As she approached, he pushed his chair back and stood. Gazing in awe at the vision before him, he stepped forward to meet her taking her hands in his.

Pulling her gently towards him, he paused for a second to look into her eyes. Savouring her feminine scent, he kissed her with almost religious reverence.

"Georgie, darling, you look stunning." He whispered.

"Thank you, Hennie," she smiled, "I always make a special effort for my husband."

He pulled her urgently towards him, this time holding her tightly in his arms and kissing her more passionately on her lips. She felt herself being lifted off the floor.

Georgina was secretly delighting that her plan for the seduction of her husband was exceeding all expectations, when the sound of the door to the kitchen swinging open caused a temporary conclusion to their embrace.

Recovering some decorum in the presence of Cato, the male member of staff seconded to waiting at table this evening,

Hennie pulled out the chair for Georgina to sit down, noticing how the hem of her dress rode up as she sat. He returned to his seat.

Cato, clad in a crisp clean white jacket with brass buttons up to his neck and resembling a ships steward, placed a bottle of Veuve Cliquot Champagne, wrapped in a white cotton napkin and immersed in a silver ice bucket on an adjacent serving table.

"Shall I open the Champagne, baas?" Enquired Cato respectfully.

"No, I will do that myself." Replied his boss, distractedly, still staring at his wife.

"Then may I serve the first course, sir?" He continued.

Hendrik looked up at Cato, hesitated and looked back to Georgina, before staring at the bottle of Champagne, finally returning his gaze to his beautiful wife.

Cato waited impassively, Georgina raised an eye brow, aware of her husband's indecision.

Suddenly, rattling the glasses on the table, Hendrik jumped to his feet. He looked at Georgina, then at Cato, then back to Georgina.

"I don't feel very hungry this evening, do you Darling?" He suddenly blurted out in a voice much too loud for the present circumstances.

"Errr, well, I…" was the most Georgina could muster in reply.

With that, Hennie picked up the two Champagne flutes, pushed them both down into the ice next to the Veuve Cliquot taking up the silver bucket in his right hand.

"Georgie, why don't we just skip dinner and take this Champagne up to your room?" Hennie spluttered.

"WOOO…HOOO! Hendrik, I'm shocked," laughed

Georgina in amazement. "Are you trying to seduce me Mr. van Wyk?"

"Yes, I suppose I am." replied a slightly embarrassed Hendrik.

"Yes, I thought you were." whispered Georgina with a delighted giggle.

Hendrik pulled out Georgina's chair, she stood and took his arm as he looked adoringly at her. She smiled back at him as they made their way together towards the living room doors.

A bewildered Cato, risked the question. "What shall I do with the dinner, baas?"

"You eat it," replied Georgina, over her shoulder.

Still smiling to herself she turned her head to look up at the painting of the old Afrikaner woman hanging over the fireplace, sticking out her tongue before turning back to her husband and kissing him.

As they walked from the dining room into the lounge a bewildered Cato stared after them.

Through the living room they entered the hall and climbed the staircase turning right at the top towards Georgina's bedroom suite. Hendrik opened the door and stood back to allow Georgina to enter. Passing him in the doorway she paused and kissed him. He followed her into the room, closing the door.

Georgina walked to the large double bed, kicked off her shoes, slipped out of her dress and sat on the edge. Twisting slightly she brought up her feet, leaning back against the fashionable velvet quilted headboard. She watched her husband as he placed the ice bucket on a bedside table.

In the short time since she had left the room to go down to dinner Miriam had tidied the dressing table and picked up Georgina's discarded clothes and towels, the room was again immaculate.

"Well, you've made me miss my dinner, Darling, at least you could offer me a glass of Champagne," she smiled.

Saying nothing, Hendrik took the bottle and removed the gold foil, unwound the wire and eased out the cork. At no time did he take his eyes from his beautiful wife. Taking the two glass flutes he filled them slowly, waiting for the bubbles to subside. He knelt by the side of the bed where Georgina lay, handing her a glass. Raising it to her lips she then lowered the glass, keeping eye contact with Hendrik. He leaned across and kissed her lips, then turned his head and bent to kiss her thigh just above the top of her stocking.

Georgina now moved with more urgency. Without taking her eyes from her husband she took a generous mouthful of the Champagne, placing the half empty glass on the bedside table where it toppled and fell, spilling its contents and breaking the delicate stem. Ignoring this mishap, she roughly gripped her husband's shirt and pulled him up towards her. As he stretched onto the bed, Georgina slid down towards him and kissed him passionately. Starting to move his body across her she deftly slipped from under him. Before he realised what was happening he was on his back with Georgina's modest weight on his chest. She was in control and intended to remain so, shifting her weight, she undid the top of his trousers, slipping her hand inside.

Quickly removing their remaining clothing, they made love.

After their passion they lay in each others arms. For Hendrik, the last hour had been quite simply the most wonderful experience of his life, even better than their wedding night. He loved his wife with all his being, he was happy.

As for Georgina, it was true that she had planned the whole evening, but the blissful happiness she was now experiencing was nonetheless as real as his.

She was not even annoyed that Hendrik was asleep. Slipping from his embrace, Georgina took a cigarette from a packet on the bedside table. She rarely smoked but this evening was special. She lit up and walked back to the window. Inhaling deeply, she stood naked looking out over the distant lights of Cape Town. She felt warm and at peace within herself. All was well, she loved her husband and he clearly loved her. She would ensure they did not sleep separately again.

After a few minutes she flicked her cigarette end through the open window and returned to bed. Lying there in the darkness, listening to her husband breathing, she fell asleep.

CHAPTER TWO

Thursday 16th January 1969

Hendrik awoke, it was already light and he had a long day in court ahead of him. As he got out of Georgina's bed he looked lovingly across at his beautiful wife. He didn't notice that she was also awake and looking at him through half closed eyes.

Georgina lay feigning sleep as she watched him moving around. She had to restrain a giggle as he struggled into his boxer shorts. Why? she thought to herself, he's only going to the next room. Mustn't shock the servants, I suppose. She watched him hurry to the door, muttering to himself under his breath. But then, he turned and walked back to the bed. Georgina closed her eyes as he kissed her gently on her cheek.

"I love you," he whispered.

As her husband walked back towards the door she watched him pick up her dress, discarded last evening. He buried his face in the material before carefully placing the dress on a chair. He left her room, quietly closing the door behind him.

Georgina had the best confirmation she could possibly need of what she already knew.

"Mmm," muttered Georgina to herself as she noticed the bedside clock indicating 7.00am., "still the middle of the night."

She went happily back to sleep.

★

Georgina awoke for the second time that morning at 8.30am.

She quickly went over in her mind the events of the previous evening and declared herself very well satisfied. A few minutes later there was a knock on the bedroom door and Miriam entered without waiting for a reply.

"Good Morning, Madam." she said placing the tea tray she was carrying on the bedside table. She noticed the broken wine glass. "I will clear this away, baas."

"No, just leave it while I drink my tea, you can clear up later, I'll have my breakfast at nine o'clock in the Minstrel Gallery."

"Thank you, Madam." murmured Miriam as she hurried from the room.

Georgina took a couple more sips of tea before getting up and taking a shower.

By nine o'clock she was dressed in a white blouse and tight, flared bottom blue jeans, she was ready for the day. Making her way along the first floor corridor towards the staircase, she turned right and opened one of the double doors leading to the gallery, overlooking the living room and out onto the gardens. A small table was already laid with cereals, milk, toast, butter, marmalade and The Cape Times. As she sat, Cato entered with a pot of fresh tea.

"Thank you Cato," she said, looking up, "I'll pour it myself."

Cato gave a nodding bow and left.

For the next twenty minutes Georgina busied herself between breakfast, being quite hungry, having missed dinner, and the cryptic crossword in the newspaper, she did both justice. Sitting with her second cup of tea she felt satisfaction in entering the last crossword clue. She was acknowledged as a crossword genius and if she had lived thirty years earlier would probably have worked on cracking the Enigma Code, she had that sort of brain. Tossing the paper aside, she looked absently out onto the garden noticing Amos weeding one of the flower beds.

Replacing her cup in its saucer she jumped up, wiped her lips on the napkin and turned towards the door, running down the stairs to the hall below. Crossing the living room she skipped out though the glass doors into the garden. She could see Amos some fifty yards further down the immaculate lawn. Jogging effortlessly across the grass Georgina was only a few feet away when Amos looked up from his work and saw her, a worried frown appeared on his old face. After yesterday's interview he dreaded what might be coming next.

"Hello Amos, I saw you from the house and remembered that I wanted to speak to you." she said, smiling.

"Good morning, Ma'am." he muttered, rankled at her casual manner when she was about to sack him.

"Amos, you keep these gardens so well and the pool is always sparkling, it must be a lot of work so I was considering your grandson as an under gardener. He could be your apprentice. Do you think he would like the job" she laughed.

Amos looked puzzled.

"But yesterday baas, you said…"

"…That was yesterday…today's another day." she interrupted sharply, the smile fading from her face.

Embarrassed, she noticed tears well up in the old man's eyes but that was the furthest she was prepared to go in apologising to a servant.

"Thank you, Thank you, baas. I am sure he would love to work here. You have made me very happy, I was very worried and I didn't want to leave. You will not be sorry, I will work very hard."

Georgie smiled at him again as she replied in a soft voice. "I know you will, Amos and get those gates fixed."

"Yes, baas, the engineers are coming today."

Taking some folded bank notes from her pocket she handed them to him.

"Good and here, buy yourself some of that dreadful tobacco I forbade you from smoking in my garden."

Before Amos could reply, Georgina, still embarrassed, walked away.

After a few paces she stopped and turned, Amos was staring after her, still holding the money in his hand.

"Buy some chocolate or something for that grandson of yours."

Satisfied at having set things straight, she hurried off to enjoy her day. After all, she was not a nasty person.

★

Georgina parked her car with the usual difficulty. She needed a space about the length of a bus, although she enjoyed the admiring glances the sparkling red Jaguar attracted. Leaving the car with the hood down she walked the short distance along the busy pavement towards Luigi's Italian Restaurant. Looking back she was amused at the sight of several men crowding admiringly around the car, almost as many as those staring admiringly after her. The car's my only rival she thought. I'll get rid of it and get a Mini, much easier to park.

Her cousin Will had telephoned just before she left home to say that he was already in Cape Town and which restaurant should he meet her at.

She looked up as someone called her name and was delighted to see a tall, slim, good looking young man running across the road towards her.

"Hello Georgie," beamed Will as he picked her up in a bear hug that lifted her off her feet. "You're a sight for sore eyes, you look fantastic."

"And you look pretty good yourself," she laughed, pushing him away so that she could look at him. She hugged him again, kissing him on both cheeks. Taking his hand she continued. "Come on, let's eat, we used to come here when I was home from Grahamstown, remember?"

William held the door open for her and they entered the small cosy Italian Restaurant.

"Of course I remember you idiot, it was only last year but I thought you would be much to grand now to set foot in a place like this."

"Not fair, Will, I'm still the same person, still your cuz, you know."

"I know you are, Georgie, but you have to admit, you do have a smart car," Will kissed her again, laughing.

"Ja, ja, okay, I've got a nice car…and you're jealous," she laughed, punching him playfully on the arm.

"Can I have a go then?"

"Certainly not," smiled Georgina.

Luigi, the proprietor, and head waiter came to meet them.

"Ciao." beamed Luigi, the short, fat, bald headed proprietor of the little restaurant. "A table by the window perhaps?"

Georgina allowed William to take the lead. "Yes, that will be fine."

Luigi led them to a small secluded table in the corner of the restaurant next to the window, pulling out a chair for Georgina to sit. Will sat opposite and looked around.

It was quite crowded and only a couple of tables were still unoccupied. Most were young couples, a few business people and a table full of tourists. The noise of a dozen conversations, some Italian, created a vibrant and cosmopolitan ambience. The walls were hung with cheaply framed prints of Italian scenes and squat, empty Chianti bottles in their raffia baskets with carefully preserved candle wax, adorned each table.

"Hasn't changed much," said Will.

"I used to love this place, shall we order that spaghetti dish we used to enjoy?" said Georgie, looking at the menu.

"Fine with me, the food is secondary, it's you I came to see."

William caught Luigi's eye and the rotund Italian hurried over.

"Signore, signora?"

Will pointed to the menu card, "Luigi, we'll both have the Spaghetti Carbonara…"

"…But with no cream or butter, just plain yoghurt, hey," interrupted Georgina.

"Of course, signora, and to drink?"

"No alcohol for me, just a bottle of Pellegrino, okay for you, Will?"

"Fine"

"Grazie," said Luigi as he scuttled away.

"I can't believe it's nearly three months since I last saw you, Georgie."

"Well, you chose to go charging off halfway across Africa to join the BSAP," she laughed, "Hendrik sends you his best wishes, but privately, he cannot understand why you're intent on going all the way up to Rhodesia."

"Well, your husband is an Afrikaner, Georgie, he wouldn't understand. I know us whites have to put on a united front to the blacks and the rest of the world and all that but you know as well as I do, there's not much love lost. They resent the English speaking whites like us. They can't get over the Boereoorlog, the Boer War I suppose."

"William Robinson, how dare you, I love my husband, Afrikaner or not."

"Do you Georgie? I hope so," Will looked serious as he took her hand.

"I won't deny I was worried when you married Hendrik and I know that Mum and Dad were too. After all, it was such a whirlwind romance. You dropping out of university when you were doing so well. All we could see in him was a stuffy Afrikaner fifteen years your senior. Oh, he's rich enough, that's plain to see but tell me you didn't just marry him for his money."

Georgina smiled back. Had she been asked this question twenty four hours previously her answer might have been less than truthful, but after last night she had no further doubt.

Gently squeezing Will's hand she replied, " I know everyone was worried about me and at times I did wonder myself if I had done the right thing, but now, after six months marriage, I can assure you that I love Hendrik and he loves me, my life is perfect."

"And you do have a fabulous car."

"Yes..., I do have a fabulous car, don't I?"

"So...can I drive it?"

"I knew that was coming," she laughed, "absolutely, categorically, NO. Not a chance, don't ask me again."

Luigi appeared with the Pellegrino and filled their glasses. He was followed by another waiter carrying the two steaming plates of spaghetti.

"Buon appetito," Luigi smiled as he turned away.

"I'll tell you something though, I love Hennie, but his family are the absolute pits. That sister of his, Brunelda du Plessis, what a monster, all twin set and pearls. She's five years older than Hennie, so she's old enough to be my mother, made it quite clear she thought I was after the family loot. Hasn't got a car, goes everywhere in a waggon pulled by a span of sixteen oxen," Georgina giggled, "If they were good enough for the Voortrekkers to cross the Orange River then they're good enough to take Brunelda out to lunch! And she has a shambok stuffed down the back of her skirt ready to deal with any disrespectful blacks."

"You do make me laugh, South Africa has been pretty good for that shy little thirteen year old English girl who arrived on our doorstep nearly eight years ago."

"Yes, South Africa and a wonderful cousin and auntie and uncle, who made me so welcome," she said in a more serious tone, keeping her hand in his. "I'm really grateful you know."

Before William could reply Georgie started to laugh again. "Of course, being stunningly beautiful, having a captivating personality and being brilliant at everything I do, has also helped my success,"

"Eat your spaghetti, big head."

"Yes, mmm baas!" replied Georgie. They both laughed.

A moment later he re-started the conversation. "I was really sorry to miss your mother when she was over."

"Yes, it was a shame, but she saw plenty of auntie Olga and uncle Frank, she really enjoyed the month she spent here, I loved seeing her and she loved the house. We did have a few heart to hearts, she had the same fears as you, but I put her mind at rest. You know, Willy, people think there is a rift between mum and I but she sent me out here for the best. She was trying to build up her aerial photography business and she thought I would be better off in South Africa, but I had the final decision and I chose to come."

"And the business is still doing well?"

"Seems to be, she's bought a new 'plane, a Beagle I think. But that's enough about my family, tell me all about Rhodesia."

William took a sip of water.

"Well, you know I always wanted to do something exciting. Ever since I was a kid and I used to read comics about the Mounties in Canada always getting their man and cowboys in the States, Stanley and Livingstone and Selous in Africa. Even the Great Trek is exciting to read about. Churchill in the Boer War, it all fascinated me." William began to warm to his subject and became animated.

"Georgie, Rhodesia is now the front line against the communists. With us and the Portuguese in Angola and Mozambique they are the last white strongholds in Africa. That's where the action is, on the Zambezi. As for Hendrik saying I should do my bit back home, what he has to realise is that if Rhodesia falls, then the front line won't be the Zambezi it will be on the Limpopo, the commies will be knocking on South Africa's door. The rest of the world is against us so we must look after our friends."

She thought for a few moments, raising an eyebrow.

"Perhaps, but what about the interview, was it tough?

"Well, I had to have a medical first at Morris Depot in Salisbury, that was…"

"…I've been there, Will, Morris Depot, I played Hockey there for Cape Province Ladies when we were touring Rhodesia in '66."

"And of course you won."

"Of course and I scored both goals."

"There's a surprise," smiled William resignedly.

"Well, go on, the medical, you must have passed it okay?"

"Yes, of course, no trouble there. Then I had to take a test. That was okay as well, quite simple really, just a few sums, some tick box questions, that sort of thing. There were about ten of us applying. Most were Rhodesians, a couple of British lads and another South African. He came from Pretoria. They all seemed good chaps, we had to sit about most of the afternoon waiting for our turn for interview." Will took his last mouthful of spaghetti. "That was a good meal," he said, wiping his mouth on a napkin.

"And the interview?"

"That was fine as well, there was a Superintendent and an Inspector, the BSAP has English police ranks mostly, not military ones like our police. They asked me all the usual questions and I told them pretty well what I have just told you. Well, they seemed satisfied, so I'm in."

"Come on, the training, when do you start?" asked Georgie.

"They said they would write to me with a starting date, give me plenty of time to get up there and settle in. I think the training is about six months, lots of spit and polish and marching about. I don't mind that, I knew there would be, but there's lots of interesting stuff as well, horse riding, shooting, rock climbing, everything. They're like the army but much better paid!"

"So I'll have to get used to calling you constable Robinson."

"No, it's not like here, all the constables, sergeants, those sort of ranks are raised from the African population. They train at Tomlinson Barracks, up the road. When I finish my training I will be a Patrol Officer."

"Quite right too!" laughed Georgie. "Are there any lady police, if it's a nice uniform, I might join."

"You, join the BSAP?" roared Will, incredulously. "That's a joke. You'd spend a month's salary on one lunch and I can just see you bulling up your boots."

"Not fair again, I could do it, I can do anything I set my mind to, and I'll have you know I look very good in shiny black boots."

"Yes, of course you could, but you're not going to are you?"

"Probably not this week, no. Anyway, let's get the bill and go to your place, do you think anyone will be in?"

Will caught Luigi's attention and he came over with the bill on a little silver tray.

"Mother is sure to be there, she'll love seeing you," said William, looking at the bill. "I'll pay this."

Georgina had the good sense to just say "Thanks." She knew the cost was modest, that's why they came here and did not want to dent Will's dignity by offering to pay herself.

A beaming Luigi stood at the open door as they left. They complimented him on the meal and walked slowly back towards the car hand in hand.

As they approached the resplendent Jaguar, Georgina was amused to see that she now occupied second place in Will's attention.

Standing admiringly by the passenger door, he ran his hand lovingly over black leather seat back. He crouched to get a better view along the car's long, low bonnet. Men and cars, hey, thought Georgie as she brushed past him, dropping on the seat the ignition key attached to it's red leather Jaguar fob.

"Here, you drive the thing."

"Thanks, Georgie, I love you," he laughed, racing round the back of the car to the driving seat.

Climbing into the passenger seat, she glanced across at the excited driver. "And take it easy, remember this car is at least five years salary for a BSAP Patrol Officer, including overtime."

William Robinson was not listening. Georgina had been temporarily replaced in his affections by a new red Jaguar 'E' Type drop head.

Will started the engine and it instantly roared into life. Slipping the short, stubby gear lever into first he gingerly eased the car out of the parking space and into the traffic flow. Georgie smiled to herself, covering her eyes in embarrassment at Will's excessive engine revving. Then, as soon as the opportunity presented itself they hurtled off in the direction of Wynberg.

Georgina burst out laughing at the ecstatic expression on William's face as he gripped the stylish wooden steering wheel.

CHAPTER THREE

The same day
Fairoaks Aerodrome, near Woking, England

Joyce Browne got out of her car and stared at the Beagle A109 Airedale monoplane that was parked on the tarmac among a group of perhaps a dozen other light aircraft of varying designs, makes, colours and sizes.

She felt no pride of ownership at the sight of her new possession. The only emotion she could identify was one of silent dread, the same feeling one might have if suddenly confronted by a dangerous wild animal.

The aircraft, bought as a more modern replacement for her previous Auster, represented the biggest single purchase she had ever made, even more expensive than her house in Chiswick, that she had bought with her late husband many years before.

It wasn't even new, being one of the last of this type built in 1965, so it was already four years old.

She walked a few paces closer to the machine, almost expecting it to roar at her. When her husband had died she had invested all her money in a partnership in an aerial photography business. The owner had welcomed the cash input enabling him to buy improved cameras and equipment.

There was no doubt that Joyce had brought some welcome dynamism to the company. Her partner, an experienced pilot with RAF credentials, was sadly no business man.

With Joyce managing the business on the ground, her partner Richard Wilding was able to restrict his activities to flying, a state of affairs in which he delighted. She had even taken the huge decision of sending her teenage daughter to live in South Africa, to enable her to dedicate all her time to building the company. So it was a terrible shock when Richard was diagnosed with hypertension that would, in the not too distant future, prevent him from flying.

With every penny both of them possessed invested in the business and considerable loans to be serviced, the obvious remedy of employing a pilot and paying him a salary would have pushed the little firm over the edge into bankruptcy.

Joyce had no real alternative to taking the previously unthinkable decision of learning to fly herself.

This had been four years ago and with dedication from both partners Joyce, in her mid forties, with no experience of flying had shown great aptitude and miraculously qualified as a pilot. Richard, with great regret contented himself to flying a desk in the office and taking the photographs. However, Joyce now found herself running the business and flying the plane. Richard, although assiduous in his duties, was little more than the office clerk. His heart was still in flying. Joyce, however, though qualified and competent, remained apprehensive!

Nevertheless, the business was doing well and on the strength of a contract to produce the aerial photographs for Hobson's Holiday Villages' new brochure, they had taken the plunge and bought this new plane.

Joyce, having no deep knowledge of aircraft, had left the selection of a replacement machine to Richard, contenting herself to managing the finance. She doubted they could afford it, but there was really no alternative, so here she was, face to face with the new business tool.

Feeling no great desire to go any closer, she noticed Richard emerge from the nearby office that was attached to the large hangar. He waved a sheath of documents at her as he approached. He was looking excited.

I suppose I've got to fly the bloody thing now, she thought, biting her finger nail and eyeing the four seater monoplane with some alarm.

★

17th January 1969.
Chiswick, west London, England

Robert Simmons walked around the old BSA Gold Star motorcycle for the umpteenth time. He had seen it advertised in a newsagent's window at only two hundred and fifty pounds. He wanted it badly. His chief concern at present, of which the vendor was blissfully unaware, was an unfortunate lack of cash. One of the chief reasons for Robert's lack of finances was his passion for photography, having just bought a beautiful new Voigtlander 35mm camera.

He had recently resigned his clerical job with Martins Bank, a post he had disliked with all his heart. The recent amalgamation with Barclays Bank had prompted his decision and he was just a little dismayed by his employer's eager acceptance of his resignation. It was clear that the bank shared his doubts of achieving a successful career in the financial industry.

In his jeans pocket were one hundred and fifty pounds in five pound notes. There was no more available and even this modest outlay would seriously inhibit his social life for the foreseeable future.

As well as being unemployed, Robert was also reeling from the shock of having the door closed in his face by his latest girlfriend. The love of his life so far had informed him that she was searching for a more meaningful relationship, meaningful in this case being a Spanish waiter she had met on holiday and had followed her back to England.

That left Bob with an opportunity of pursuing his other passion, motorbikes. In his case that meant British bikes. They were usually cheaper, easy to repair (and they often needed it) but above all, they enjoyed great street presence.

Now, without a girlfriend, he was free to invest.

Pulling back his shoulders he squared up to the young man who claimed to be the owner.

Bob had immersed himself in the lore of vehicle negotiations and commenced in well rehearsed, good style.

"I think there's a bit of movement in the steering head bearings and the brakes need attention, I'll take it away now for a hundred and fifty."

Well pleased with his opening gambit, Bob fixed the owner with a steely glaze.

"Okay, done," was the unexpected reply.

The cash was handed over and counted in exchange for the Log Book and Test Certificate. There were no keys, Bob supposed that people must have been very honest back in 1958 when the silver and black Goldie rolled off the production line in Birmingham.

With that, the vendor, with Bob's money in his pocket, was gone.

Bob's satisfaction with his new acquisition was slightly blunted by the thought he might have achieved the same result and still had fifty pounds left in his pocket. But it was done, the bike was his.

In his new joy of ownership, the technicality of insurance had surprisingly, not yet occurred to Robert. He was torn between risking the one mile journey home without insurance, or pushing the bike around the corner to the little insurance brokers in Devonshire Road. Deciding on the latter option, he obtained a twenty eight day cover note in exchange for a cheque drawn on an empty bank account. He would worry about that later.

Now to the fun!

Bob had passed his motorcycle test when he was seventeen but he had never ridden anything this big.

Right, gears in neutral, yes.

Petrol on by pushing the little brass knob under the tank.

Retard the ignition just a bit, using the big lever on the handlebars.

So far, so good.

Now the clever bit, astride the bike and balancing on his left leg Bob eased the large kick start lever down with his right foot until he felt the engine compression. Ease the kick start past the resistance. Open the throttle slightly and give it a big swinging kick.

The old five hundred single started up first time with a satisfactory window rattling roar. The bike still gave the famous Goldie 'twitter' from the exhaust when revved, a delight to motorcyclists and an anathema to everyone else.

Well satisfied, Robert snicked the bike into first gear and hesitatingly roared off towards home.

Parking the BSA in the unruly front garden, Robert opened the communal front door of the house in which he lived. He examined with great interest a white envelope addressed to him that was waiting on the hall table.

Mmm, looks promising, he thought as he mounted the stairs two at a time to his small attic room.

Putting his helmet and gloves on the table Bob sat on the edge of his bed and opened the letter.

Wilding Photography
Hogarth Parade
Chiswick High Road
London
W4
01 994 8234

16th January 1969

Dear Mr Simmons

Thank you for your recent letter and CV seeking employment with our company.

Together with our wedding, studio and general photographic departments we are intending to extend our successful operations in the field of specialised aerial photography.

In view of this I am happy to invite you to attend our Chiswick office for an interview, in support of which I would expect you to bring along a portfolio of your recent work.

Please telephone this office to arrange a time and date that is mutually convenient.

Yours sincerely
Joyce Browne (Mrs)
Director

"Fantastic." shouted Bob at the top of his voice, punching the air. He lay back on his bed and read the letter again. What a result, he thought.

Robert had sent off his CV speculatively to every photographic studio in west London. He had received a few disappointing replies but most of letters had gone unanswered, however, this made it all worthwhile.

Jumping up and kissing the letter he opened his room door

and ran down the stairs, three at a time to the pay 'phone that hung on the wall in the communal hall.

More good luck, he got through to Mrs Browne straight away. She sounded really nice and he arranged to attend for interview the very next day at 10.00am. It couldn't be better he thought.

Returning to his room, and forgetting to eat, he spent the rest of the day preparing with infinite care a portfolio of his photographs for the all important interview. He knew he had not got the job yet, but there must be a chance he thought with unbridled enthusiasm.

The next morning, Bob was up in plenty of time. He prepared himself with great care. Suit, shirt, tie, shiny shoes, his own mum wouldn't recognise him. Too excited for any breakfast he checked his portfolio again and set off much too early for his interview.

He left the house at 9.15am to walk barely a mile to Wilding Photography in the High Road. Well, he reasoned, he must leave extra time in case he broke a shoe lace, got knocked down by a bus, have to help an old lady across the road, give directions or get lost. Whatever happened, he could not be late.

Needless to say, 9.25am found him staring at the window display of Wilding Photography, a full thirty five minutes early.

The photographs in the window were well known to him, as he was in the habit of examining the display whenever he passed the shop. He was paying particular attention to a large, new picture in the centre of the window of a Beagle Airdale aircraft, when the door of the shop opened.

"Mr Simmons?" enquired a pleasant, smartly dressed lady of about forty five years.

"Err, yes, that me." replied Robert in surprise.

"I thought it might be you," laughed Mrs Browne, "We

don't get many young men paying so much attention to the shop window you know."

"I'm sorry, I'm much too early, I know," said Bob, with some embarrassment. "I just didn't want to be late."

"Please don't apologise," smiled Mrs Browne, "I'm impressed, better than being late. Come in and have a cup of tea."

From there on the interview was a dream. Far from being tongue tied as he feared, Bob couldn't stop himself from talking. As Mrs Browne sat behind the desk in her small office at the rear of the studio, Bob bombarded her with his opinions of everything from cameras, film types, and flash arrangements, to the benefits of various shutter speeds, readily using his own photographs to support his arguments.

"Your aircraft looks fab," continued Bob with enthusiasm, "I have to admit that I don't know much about aerial photography but it must be really exciting."

"Oh, I'm glad there is something you're not an expert on," smiled Mrs Browne.

"Who flies the 'plane?" continued Bob.

"I do," replied Mrs Browne, with some pride.

"Wow!" said Bob.

"Wow!" laughed Mrs Brown.

Glancing at her notes, she continued.

"Look, Mr. Simmons, I have a partner I must talk to but I will let you know our decision as soon as possible. If you should be successful we would only be able to pay you a moderate wage. However, we would be willing to teach you the whole range of our business. In return we would expect you to be flexible in working hours, meal breaks and days off. Would you be satisfied with those arrangements?"

"I'll sleep in the shop if you like."

"I don't think that will be necessary, well not often."

Showing Robert to the door, Mrs Browne shook his hand. "I promise I'll let you have a decision as soon as possible, but while you're waiting I think you can be quietly optimistic."

Robert was floating at least a yard off the pavement as walked away from the studio on his way home. He stopped to admire the new Triumph Bonneville in the window of the motorcycle shop. £885. I might have one of those, he thought.

Two days later, a letter arrived from Mrs Browne, his new boss. Could he start next Monday?

"Yes," he shouted in delight.

CHAPTER FOUR

Saturday 18th January 1969
Cape Town, South Africa.

The morning was already hot as Georgina sat at a small, white wrought iron table on the sun terrace of her home. She wore only a very brief, black bikini with a fluffy white towel around her shoulders, having just enjoyed a swim in the large rectangular pool that glistened below her in the garden. Behind, the glass doors that formed a complete wall of the living room were fully open. She heard the antique Dutch bracket clock strike eleven.

On the table in front of her was a white china coffee pot and two demi-tasse cups. Georgie refilled her's and took a sip, the other cup and saucer had yet to be used. Where was he? It was a Saturday morning and her husband Hendrik had promised to join her for coffee. He worked hard all week so surely he could relax on this beautiful summer's day. After all, they hadn't even had a holiday this year.

She smiled to herself as she quickly dispelled the embryo of a sulky mood by picking up a handful of gravel from a potted palm that stood nearby. Walking down the steps to the garden and along the gravel path at back of the house, she started to aim well directed stones at her husband's ground floor office window.

After three or four attempts a puzzled looking Hendrik peered through the glass before opening the window.

"Are you coming out to play, meneer? It's Saturday, it's supposed to be your day off," she teased. "The pool is warm and the coffee's cold."

"Ja, ja, I'm on my way, I just stopped for a moment to make a note in a file I need for Monday. If I don't do it now I'll forget, two minutes, get some fresh coffee."

Georgina made her way back to the sun terrace, stepping just inside the living room to press a brass bell on the wall.

Returning to the table she had been sitting for a few moments when Miriam the maid came hurrying from the house.

"Bring me another pot of coffee and take this away, it's cold," said Georgie, indicating her half empty cup.

"Yes, mevrou." said Miriam, clearing the cup, saucer and coffee pot onto a tray before hurrying off.

Sitting in the sunshine, Georgina caught a faint, acrid smell on the air, a reminder of the recent fire in the fynbos that grew on the slopes of nearby Table Mountain. Her attention was drawn to the lazy buzzing of a small light aircraft. She shielded her eyes against the sun as she watched the plane making its way across the cloudless sky.

Thinking of her mother back in England she had difficulty imagining her at the controls of an aircraft, incredible but true. She was very proud of her mum.

Georgie always referred to England as home, but to be honest, she had no desire to return to the cramped little houses in Chiswick, preferring to cling to a secret ambition of enticing her mother to join her in Cape Town. That seemed unlikely now, as mum was doing well and making a success of life in England. An uncomfortable thought occurred to Georgie, that her own film star lifestyle was the result of someone else's hard work.

Recovering from her thoughts she decided to quickly dress and collect Hendrik in person from his office on her way back to the terrace.

Making her way through the living room and into the hall she was at the foot of the staircase when the front door bell rang. Thinking it was one of her friends from the tennis club Georgina crossed the hall and opened the door to be confronted by a tall slim black man, dressed in a clean, cream coloured suit, white shirt, tie and shiny black shoes. He was carrying a brown leather brief case.

The man smirked at Georgina and stepped forward offering his hand and looking her up and down appreciatively.

Surprised and with a degree of alarm, Georgina uncomfortably pulled the towel closely around her shoulders. Damn, she thought.

"Who are you, how did you get in here?" she demanded coldly, ignoring his outstretched hand.

"I have an appointment with Mr. Van Wyk."

"I asked you how you got in here?"

"A Picanin let me in, he was sweeping outside. I am simply a messenger." He raised the brief case. "But I should have realised I was addressing the beautiful Mrs Van Wyk."

"How dare you speak to me like that. Wait there, I will see if my husband wishes to speak to you."

She closed the door in his face.

"I'm very sorry baas, I came as soon as I heard the bell, but we were in the kitchen," apologised Cato, Miriam standing behind him.

"It doesn't matter Cato, I was by the door, but wait here with me. Miriam, go and fetch my husband immediately"

"Yes, ma'am."

Miriam hurried away in search of Mr. van Wyk.

Georgina was keen to see Hendrik's reaction. This facetious black man might be many things but he was certainly not a messenger, not with a Rolex watch on his wrist, even if it was a fake, Georgie was certain of that.

She was intrigued.

Hendrik hurried into the hall, closely followed by Miriam. Frowning, he looked at Georgina and Cato standing by the door.

"Well, who wants me?"

"Hennie, there's an unpleasant African outside the door demanding to see you, says he's a messenger and has an appointment with you. I don't believe it."

"Open the door Cato and we'll have a look at him then,"

Conscious of still being underdressed for the present circumstances, Georgina had positioned herself behind Cato. She had no wish to be further mentally undressed by this leering black man who had appeared unbidden at her door.

As Cato opened the door all eyes except Georgie's were on the man waiting on the doorstep. Georgina's stare was firmly fixed on her husband. The cream suit slid round the door and into the hall.

Georgina was alarmed to see the look of shock on Hendrik's face as the visitor confronted him. He seemed to physically shrink within himself. Something was very, very wrong.

"Good morning, Mr Van Wyk," said the visitor stepping forward and again holding out his hand with confidence. "Thank you so much for seeing me sir."

After a slight hesitation, Hendrik returned the handshake.

"Good morning, Sibanyoni, I'm very busy, but I can give you five minutes, come along to my office." Hendrik replied.

Glancing nervously towards Georgina he was dismayed that she held eye contact with him until he looked away in embarrassment.

Well, well, thought Georgina, we'll be inviting this man to lunch next.

As Hendrik hurried his unwanted visitor towards his office, Sibanyoni turned towards Georgie and smiled malevolently, "A pleasure to meet you, Mrs Van Wyk."

Georgie looked away without replying and shuddered.

As the two men left the hall, Miriam broke the silence.

"Your fresh coffee is on the terrace, baas."

Walking quickly towards the staircase, Georgina, murmured, more to herself than in reply to Miriam, "All I want at present is to get some bloody clothes on."

Changing into white shorts, flip flops and a white silk blouse she left her bedroom, closing the door quietly and walked silently down the corridor until she was standing at the top of the staircase looking down into the hall.

Listening carefully, she could hear Hendrik's voice coming from his office. If this wasn't unusual enough she could clearly here Sibanyoni's voice raised in argument. However, try as she may Georgie was unable to make out was was being said.

Feeling a bit like a spy in her own home, Georgie, tiptoed halfway down and sat on the stairs. The heated conversation was now even louder but she was still unable to make out the conversation. What was certain, in Georgina's mind, was that this man Sibanyoni was no messenger but had the confidence to come to the house and argue with her husband.

Puzzled, she knew almost certainly that Hendrik's law firm had no business with Africans. What was going on? Who was this man?

Her brain raced, seeking a plausible solution. Perhaps he

was some sort of witness, or a private detective in one of the townships, hardly likely though.

Suddenly, the voices became louder as Georgina heard her husband's office door open. Scrambling back up the stairs she crouched against the further wall of the balcony, away from the balustrade. She judged that here she would be best able to hear any conversation without being seen as the men crossed the hall to the front door.

"My mind is made up, Sibanyoni," said Hendrik, trying unsuccessfully to keep his voice to a conversational level. "The plan has not been successful, we have moved on."

"It is not that easy, promises have been made, my people have expectations. I will tell them what you say Nkosi, but they will be disappointed."

Georgina raised herself very slightly so that she could just see the men standing by the front door. To her dismay her husband appeared agitated and tense, she could see that his fists were clenched.

"No promises were made," hissed Hendrik, trying to control his rising anger as he opened the front door. "There is nothing more I can do."

Sibanyoni stood in the doorway looking at the lawyer, "We will speak again."

Hendrik watched his visitor for a few moments as he descended the steps and walked steadily down the drive towards the gates of the house, the gravel crunching under his receding steps. Closing the door, Hendrik returned to his office.

Georgina hurried back to her bedroom, where from the first floor window, she was able to see Sibanyoni approaching the gates at the end of the drive. She watched as David ran from the direction of the house, arriving in plenty of time to open half of the gate. Sibanyoni paused and appeared to speak to the boy before leaving. David closed the gate carefully. He took his duties very seriously.

Stepping away from the window, Georgina sat on the edge of the bed. She had never had any reason to doubt her husband, but something was clearly amiss. Hendrik's business was with multi-national companies, not impertinent Africans in cheap suits.

Walking thoughtfully back down to the hall, Georgina was confronted by Cato.

"Madam, David let that man in through the gate without asking any permission, I will give him a thrashing he will never forget," offered Cato, keen for Georgina's approbation.

"No, No," replied Georgie, raising her hand and frowning, suddenly aware of what Cato was saying. "Don't hurt the boy, he's only a child, I will speak to him myself."

Opening the front door, she stood at the top of the steps looking down the drive, uncertain of what to do next. She was determined to have an explanation from Hendrik but first she needed to get her thoughts in order.

While she stood thinking to herself she noticed David busying himself with something near the front gates. "Well, let's talk to the boy." she murmured under her breath.

Since David had officially joined the staff, he attended school in the morning but could usually be found helping his grandfather in the gardens in the afternoons. A gate security system had been installed by Hendrik during the nervous weeks after the Sharpeville massacre in 1960. Georgina was amused that the boy seemed to have appointed himself as the gatekeeper and whenever he heard the gate bell ring would run headlong to be first to open the gates before anyone could answer the intercom, so Georgina was not surprised to see him loitering in this locality.

David looked up as she approached and placed on his head a large black object that was laying on the grass. The boy ran across and stood to attention in front of her giving a very smart salute with his right hand.

Georgina had great difficulty in suppressing a laugh as she realised David was wearing on his head a very large and very battered black peaked cap. He had been in the process of stuffing his prized possession with grass in an attempt to make it fit and now looked for all the world, with his little thin body, like a carpet tack.

"Very smart indeed, David."

"Thank you, Miss Georgie," replied the boy, delighted with the praise.

"Miss Georgie? Miss Georgie? How dare you. Who said you could call me that?"

"Sorry, baas," David replied looking a little less confident, "Mr. Hendrik calls you Georgie."

Forgetting the worrying events of the morning Georgina could not stop herself from laughing. She was secretly pleased that the little boy was no longer frightened of her.

"Mr Hendrik may call me all sorts of things, but that doesn't mean you can young man but hey, as a reward for your cheek, you and only you can call me Miss Georgie, that's only when you're wearing that hat." She could hardly speak for laughing at the sight of the delighted little boy.

Trying to control her giggling she continued.

"Now David, this is very important. I'm not cross with you, but you must promise me never to open the gate to anyone until the intercom has been answered. You can answer the 'phone yourself, but you mustn't open the gate unless you know who it is." Georgina spoke gently to the boy, "If you're not sure then fetch one of the grown ups, you can even come and find me, hey?"

Oh! yes, Miss Georgie, I understand, I will always answer the telephone first." beamed David.

"All right David, you can go now." smiled Georgina. Up to now she had only regarded the servants as functionaries to do her bidding, but she had to admit, she liked this boy.

David gave another smart salute that started her giggling again. She playfully returned the tribute and as the boy turned away Georgina couldn't resist reaching out and tipping the cap over the boy's eyes.

Pushing his hat back into place David ran off laughing.

That small matter dealt with satisfactorily, Georgina had turned back towards the house and her thoughts returned to her forthcoming confrontation with Hendrik, when David appeared again in front of her.

"Miss Georgie", he said excitedly, not forgetting to salute. "I know why you spoke to me, it was because I let in that man in the smart suit. But I did know him, he's been here before and he told me he had an appointment with Mr Hendrik."

Georgina was suddenly all attention.

"You say that man had been here before, when?"

"He's never been in the front gate before, Miss, but I have seen grandfather talking to him at the garden gate."

"What did Amos, I mean your grandfather say to him?"

"I don't know miss, grandfather and the man were talking quietly and when they saw me grandfather told me to go away and get on with my work."

"Well, did they seem like friends?" She snapped with impatience.

Beginning to fear that he might be in trouble after all, David remained silent, fidgeting from foot to foot.

Remembering she was talking to a child, Georgina took a deep breath and continued slowly and quietly.

"David, as I said, you're not in trouble but this is very important. You must tell me everything you saw, did your grandfather shake the man's hand, did he seem pleased or was he cross? You must have heard something, try and remember."

"I don't think grandfather liked the man, he told him that there were no jobs here, I think he wanted him to go."

"When was this?"

"Don't know, Miss," muttered David, staring at his feet.

Georgina, not at all sure what sort of a grip on time the boy had did not press the question further.

"So he was looking for work, no I don't believe that for a moment," said Georgina thoughtfully, more to herself than the boy.

David began sniveling to himself. "I thought he'd come to see Mr Hendrik about a job."

Lost in thought Georgina was unaware of the boy's discomfort until a huge sniff reminded her of his presence.

"Stop crying, David," she said, with a little more impatience than intended, "You must tell me straight away if you ever see that man again. Do you understand?"

"Yes, Miss Georgie." David replied followed by another huge sniff. Georgina winced as the boy wiped his nose on his arm.

"Off you go then."

She looked down at the dejected little chap. As he started to turn away, Georgina forced a smile.

"What about my salute?"

David sniffed again smiled and gave a smart salute. His employer returned the salutation and the boy ran off.

I must have a quiet word with Amos thought Georgina, continuing her way towards the house but first, let's find my husband.

Back in the house, she made her way to Hendrik's office, opened the door without knocking and entered the room. Hendrik, sitting at his desk and speaking on the telephone appeared flustered by his wife's sudden appearance.

Placing his hand over the receiver, he smiled weakly at his wife.

"This is an important call, darling, I'll see you on the terrace in ten minutes."

"That's okay, I'll wait here," replied Georgie, defiantly, sitting herself purposefully in the green leather armchair on the opposite side of Hendrik's desk.

"But darling this is a confidential call."

"Confidential from your wife, who is also a partner in your firm. How can that be?" She smiled sweetly, raising a quizzical eyebrow.

As he continued to stare at her across the desk his expression reminded Georgina of a rabbit caught in a car's headlights. Much to Hendrik's discomfort she picked up some papers on the desk and casually flicked through them.

Tacitly admitting defeat, he replaced the receiver.

"Of course, Darling, I can have no secrets from you, Was there something?"

Georgina did not reply, but stood up from the chair and crossed slowly to the bookcase on the far side of the room. She ran a finger languidly along the mahogany top, picking up and examining a photograph in a silver frame. Replacing it, she turned and looked with disdain at the rather moth eaten Zulu shield that hung in company with two rusty assegais on the wall behind Hendrik's head. Aware that he was watching her intently, she crossed to the side of Hendrik's desk and perched herself on the corner, one foot on the floor and the other leg swinging slowly and seductively next to Hendrik's arm.

She picked up a photograph of herself from the desk, looked at it and smiled.

Just as Hendrik was about to speak Georgina said quietly, still looking at the picture.

"Who was that man?"

"Just a messenger, darling."

Georgina replaced the photograph on the desk and looked at her husband. "I'll ask you again," she said quietly, "and this time I would be grateful if you would do me the curtesy of telling the truth, Who was that man?"

"Darling, he is just that, a messenger," Hendrik sighed deeply and took Georgina's hand. "The truth is, some months ago I was approached by a couple of black law students, they were graduates of Fort Hare University, you know, the black college at Alice in The Cape.

They wanted to be taken on as trainees in the firm. Well, that was impossible and I told them so, but I thought it might be a good business move to fund a completely independent black legal firm. Our company could take a cut of the profits and nobody would know we were involved.

"Well, I don't think even the blacks would be likely to trust that man, Hennie", Georgina scolded gently. "He's a crook. What were you thinking, darling?"

Hennie looked up at his wife and sighed again. "That was the trouble, at first I was dealing with a few genuine black law students, no trouble I thought. Then this Sibanyoni appears on the scene and says he is appointed to negotiate for the others. The real students all seemed frightened of him. It soon became obvious that he was a political agitator, ANC or communist or something."

"They're illegal, Hennie," said Georgie with alarm. "What have you got yourself into?"

"I know, I've put a stop to it all, it was never an option from the start, it's not our line of business but he won't take no for an answer. I suppose I will have to sack him or even go to the police."

"Yes, I think you may have to," she replied thoughfully. Kissing him again, she smiled and stood up from the desk. "Don't worry, darling, we're in this together."

"I'm sorry I was so bad tempered," said Hendrik, grateful for his wife's support.

"Shhh, this evening you can take me out to dinner, somewhere expensive and we can discuss this further."

"Well, of course darling, anywhere you care to choose."

Georgina left Hendrik's office, quietly closing the door behind her.

CHAPTER FIVE

Tuesday 4th February 1969

Georgina awoke and peered at the clock beside her bed. Six-thirty and the sun was streaming through the gaps around the heavy curtains. Turning over, she put out her hand to touch her husband's sleeping body. He looked so peaceful, in fact, Georgie smiled to herself, it was one of his greatest assets, he didn't snore. He slept soundly and peacefully, like a baby. It must be all that hard work making money, she thought dreamily.

A knock on the door announced Miriam, the housemaid as she entered carrying a tray laden with tea and coffee pots, milk jug, cups and saucers.

"Good morning, meneer, mevrou."

She put down the tray on the table at Hendrik's side of the bed before crossing to each window in turn opening the curtains.

Georgie put her arms around her husband's waist and leaning across started to nibble his ear. "It's six thirty, time to get up, darling."

Hendrik had offered to sleep in his own bedroom suite next door when he had an early start to save disturbing his wife, but Georgina wouldn't hear of it. Things were so much better between them now that they shared the same room and besides, Georgie enjoyed pouring her husband's coffee, it was what a wife should do.

Hendrik rolled on to his back, yawning and scratching his head.

Georgie kissed him, "Morning, darling, you were late last night."

"I'm sorry, Georgie, did I disturb you?"

It was an election meeting with the local party committee, after all there is a General Election next year and I am the National Party candidate."

"I heard you come in but I was soon asleep again. You know, I'm really looking forward to being South Africa's First Lady."

"I'm not even an MP yet."

"Foregone conclusion."

Miriam had by now opened all the curtains and was about to leave when the telephone rang.

"I'll get it," said Georgina, dismissing Miriam with a wave of her hand. She reached across her still dozing husband and picked up the receiver.

"Hello, who's this," she said in a rather bored voice.

"Speak to me, I'm his wife." Georgina sounded suddenly alert. "Well, he is, if you must, hold on."

Georgina put her hand over the mouthpiece and turned to look at her husband. "It's the police, they say they need to speak to Mr. van Wyk urgently."

Hendrik, propping himself up on one elbow took the 'phone from his wife.

"Hello, Hendrik van Wyk…Yes."

Listening to the telephone, he sat up on the side of the bed next to his wife.

"Good God," exclaimed Hendrik, staring wide eyed at his wife. He put a hand over the mouthpiece, "Johannes is dead."

"What?" mouthed Georgie.

Hendrik held up a hand for silence.

"I don't believe it, where, who found him, where is my sister, is she okay?...Yes, of course, at the house?... Yes, right away... Yes, my wife will go. Thank you." he replaced the receiver and took his wife's hand.

"Darling, Johannes has been found dead and the police say he was murdered," said a shocked Hendrik.

"Murdered," gasped Georgina. "Where, what happened, how do they know it's murder?"

"Apparently he was in his office at home. Brunelda woke up and wondered why he wasn't in bed and found him in his office – dead !" Hendrik repeated what the police had told him.

"Poor Brunelda," whispered Georgie almost to herself.

"She's collapsed," continued Hennie. "She's in Wynberg Hospital, I told the police you would go and see her, bring her here when she's discharged."

"Me," gasped Georgie. "But Brunelda hates me, thinks I'm the devil's spawn."

"Look, Georgie," said Hendrik sharply. "We're all the family she has, you're just going to have to get on with it. Sort it out, please."

"Of course," replied Georgina, a little chastened, a hand to her face. "I'll go straightaway."

Hendrik, already in the bathroom called out. "The police want me at the house, a Captain Adendorff."

"Did they say why they thought it was murder?" quizzed Georgie, joining her husband in the bathroom.

"No, they didn't say, they just want me over there. I'll ring you as soon as I know anything."

"God, Hennie, I can't believe this is happening."

Hendrik dressed quickly, not bothering to shave. He kissed

his wife, promising again to call her as soon as he had any news and left the room pausing only to take a gulp of the coffee Georgina had poured for him.

Taking a little longer to get herself ready, she followed him a few minutes later.

★

Within ten minutes, Hendrik was turning into the drive of his sister and brother in law's large and comfortable single storey house on the other side of Constantia. His Mercedes – Benz was stopped by a uniformed police officer at the gate. Hendrik identified himself and was directed onwards, towards the house.

Three marked police cars were parked outside, together with two unmarked cars that Hendrik supposed were detective vehicles. Another uniformed police officer stood by the open front door.

Hendrik parked his car a short distance behind the police cars and got out. The constable on duty at the front door, watched him as he approached.

"Good morning, constable, my name is Hendrik van Wyk, Mr. du Plessis was my brother-in-law, your Captain Adendorff asked me to come."

"Please come with me, meneer," the constable replied, entering the house.

Although Hendrik knew the inside of his brother-in-law's home well, the sight of police officers, portable lighting and the unfamiliar equipment of crime and forensic investigation left him feeling strangely disorientated as he crossed the threshold into the entrance hall.

A young man dressed in white overalls, crouched in a corner retrieving items from a large open case. A uniformed constable and a sergeant stared intently through the open doorway of a brightly lit room on the opposite side of the hall. The constable accompanying Hendrik spoke to the sergeant, who in turn, spoke to someone unseen within the room.

A few seconds later, a large figure appeared in the doorway, silhouetted against the light within the room. The two uniformed men separated and he passed between them, closing the door behind him.

Crossing the hall towards Hendrik, the large man held out a hand.

"Mr. van Wyk, thank you for coming, I am Captain Adendorff of the criminal investigation department. I am in charge of this case."

Hennie shook Adendorff's hand automatically. "I came immediately, of course, I'll do anything I can to help, Captain, but can you tell me what happened?"

"All in good time, sir. Perhaps we could have a chat, first."

Hendrik was ushered into the living room.

Captain Marius Adendorff was a very large man by any standard. More than six feet tall, probably sixteen or seventeen stones and rather too much of it around his waist. He wore a crumpled navy blue suit that had, like its wearer, seen better days. Adendorff had a large bald head with a fringe of light grey hair. A grey straggling moustache completed his lugubrious appearance. Hendrik guessed his age at about fifty, but he might have been younger.

"Sit, please," Adendorff gestured with a large hand towards one of the comfortable chairs.

Hendrik accepted this invitation from a stranger in the familiar house and sat stiffly on the edge of the seat. Adendorff sank heavily into the chair opposite, relaxing and crossing his knees.

"When did you last see your brother-in-law?" opened the officer without further preamble.

"Well, around five yesterday afternoon, he was in his office at our business premises in Loop Street in the centre of town. He was getting ready to go home and I was staying on for a meeting we were hosting in our conference room."

"And how did he appear, was he agitated, did he seem upset?" continued Adendorff, almost disinterestedly.

"No, he seemed perfectly normal." Hendrik replied, cautiously.

"And your meeting, sir, what was that about?"

Hendrik felt a little childish as, even in these circumstances, he was unable to resist a slight display of pride. "As a National Party candidate in next years General Election I was hosting a very important discussion on the disturbing crime statistics we are experiencing here in The Cape. Your own Brigadier Geldenhuis was one of the speakers, in fact I had dinner with him afterwards." Hendrik continued, warming to his subject. "In my capacity as a prospective National Party Member of Parliament, I have offered the Brigadier my full support in the fight against crime. We are great friends, you know."

Unsuccessfully attempting to stifle a smile, Adendorff replied. "Yes sir, I had heard that. How long did the meeting last?"

"Until gone ten, then we had dinner and the Brigadier was kind enough to drop me home in his car."

"And what time was that?"

"It was a quarter to midnight, I remember looking at the hall clock which was chiming as I opened the front door. Can I ask you why you need to know all this?"

"Of course sir," replied Adendorff, looking absently out of the window. "Mrs du Plessis retired to bed early last night but she remembers someone coming to the house around midnight. Her husband let him in, so we must assume that he knew the visitor."

Adendorff smiled at Hendrik. "It clearly wasn't you."

"Well, I know it wasn't me, officer," exploded Hendrik. "As you know very well I was with your Brigadier all evening. Anyway captain, may I ask a question of you?"

Adendorff nodded, placing his fingertips together and looking steadily at Hendrik.

"How did my brother-in-law die, and how do the police know it was murder?"

"I was coming to that, sir. In fact it will be necessary to ask you to make a formal identification of the body. This is merely for routine administration as your sister was the first person to find her husband. However, she was understandably too shocked to complete the formalities. If you would like to come over to the study I am hopeful that the photographers and forensic boys will be finished. Then we can think about getting the body moved."

Crossing the hall to the closed study Captain Adendorff opened the door just enough to look into the room. Hendrik nervously waited behind him.

"Are you finished now?" Adendorff asked of someone unseen within the room. "Good, then I can bring in the brother-in-law, okay?"

Turning back towards Hendrik, he closed the door behind him, leaving his hand on the door knob. He gave a slight smile, placing his left hand lightly on Hendrik's elbow.

"Now, you must understand, Mr van Wyk, that this is a murder scene, nothing has been touched and I must ask you not to touch anything. Are you quite ready?" said Adendorff quietly, and with what appeared to be genuine empathy. "It's not a pretty sight."

Hendrik swallowed deeply and nodded.

"Right then," said Adendorff as he pushed open the door and steered Hendrik in by his elbow.

The familiar office was still brilliantly lit by two large tripod lamps positioned on each side of Johannes's large, antique desk in the centre of the room. Two men in white overalls were packing photographic equipment away into metal camera cases. They glanced at Hendrik with interest as he entered the room, accompanied by Captain Adendorff.

However, Hendrik could see only the dreadful apparition before him as his brain struggled to make sense of the appalling scene. He felt his knees begin to buckle when he felt the strong supporting arms of the police captain.

"Take your time sir, try some deep breaths."

"Thank you Captain, I'm okay, it's such a shock." replied Hendrik, his voice quavering.

There, laying on his back on the desk was his brother-in-law, Johannes du Plessis. From his position it looked as if he had been standing with the desk behind him and had been pushed backwards, his legs hanging over the front. He was clothed in the same white shirt and grey trousers he had been wearing during the previous day. A huge dark, almost black stain spread across the front of his shirt and beyond onto the desk and surrounding papers and documents.

The centre of his chest was pierced by a Zulu assegai that was so deeply embedded in Johannes's torso, that it was clearly impaling him to the desk. What looked like a colour photograph was also sliced through by the blade.

The sight of his poor brother-in-law reminded Hendrik for all the world of a butterfly, pinned down in some monstrous collection.

As Hendrik began to recover some composure he became aware

of Captain Adendorff's intense stare. The photographers switched of the bright lights and began dismantling them from their tripods.

Hendrik broke the silence.

"My God, murder obviously, but who would do this?" said Hendrik, returning Adendorff's stare. "It's almost..."

"...A ritual killing?" interrupted the Captain, raising his eyebrows. "Yes, that thought had occurred to me. What is interesting, is that the assegai was not the murder weapon," Adendorff continued, darting a glance at Hendrik's astonished face. "When the police surgeon made his preliminary examination, he discovered another, much smaller wound, in the left side of the victim's abdomen, up and under the ribs, inflicted by some small thin instrument. The doctor will discover more when the PM is performed, but he feels certain that this was the cause of death. It was probably inflicted by a right handed, upward thrust as the victim was pushed back over the desk. The doctor also remarked that there were no cuts or blood stains on the victims hands."

"What is the significance of that?"

"Well, if your brother-in-law was still struggling when the assegai wound was inflicted he would have instinctively clutched at the blade, damaging his hands, but when the police arrived they were stretched out to each side of his body in the form of a...," Adendorff hesitated, "...a crucifixion."

"Then why that dreadful assegai?"

"Why indeed! It's apparent to me that the suspect wanted to make a clear statement about this murder. Either to claim some perverted hubris for himself or, as a warning to others, or to identify an organisation or individual by the manner of this death. But as you can see, the room has been searched, locked drawers forced, documents everywhere. What was the murderer looking for? Money, "

"The MK, Umkhonto we Sizwe, The Spear of the Nation," blurted out Hendrik.

"Could be, Mr van Wyk, a high profile murder by the illegal military wing of the terrorist African National Congress, the ANC. But why? You must also remember that the assegai and the knobkerrie are traditional, ceremonial weapons associated with the Zulu. Another point to consider, is that if the murderer intended to make such a symbolic statement by using an assegai, he would have needed to know that this office had two such weapons on the wall. In other words, he must have been here before"

Hendrick glanced up at the Zulu shield on the wall behind the desk, the marks where two ceremonial assegais were mounted on the wall could clearly be seen.

"And of course," Adendorff continued, "You will notice that both the assegais are missing, one is here," indicating the blade embedded in the corpse, where is the other? Is the murderer intending to commit a further offence? Another interesting point, is the photograph impaled on the assegai blade. It shows three people, Mr Du Plessis, yourself… and your wife."

"Captain Adendorff," said Hendrik, excitedly, "We have a Zulu messenger in my legal practice, Dingani Sibanyoni, he is a law student from Fort Hare University and has been pestering me to help him and some colleagues set up a legal practice to represent blacks in the townships. I did consider the proposal but when I refused to help, he became quite abusive, visiting my home demanding I help him financially. He was even discourteous towards my wife. I had meant to sack him, but it takes a long time to teach a new messenger and I regret I let the matter slide."

"Discourteous to the beautiful Mrs van Wyk," murmured Adendorff. "A crime indeed."

"You know my wife, Captain?"

"Alas, no sir, but I have often admired her pictures in the newspapers."

Hendrik always felt uncomfortable when men mentioned his wife and could never be sure whether to be flattered by the complement, or feel threatened by the attentions of other men. A condition, he suspected, was common to the husbands of beautiful women.

"Sibanyoni, you say, that is interesting," mused Adendorff, rubbing his chin and examining his note book. "One of our uniformed patrols did a pass book check at ten past eleven last night on a male named Sibanyoni, not five hundred metres from this house. I think we had better have Mr. Sibanyoni in for a chat."

Hendrik nodded, feeling a sense of panic rising inside him.

"I don't think I shall need to take up any more of your time, Mr. van Wyk." said the captain, concluding the interview. "We need to detain this man Sibanyoni, and we will speak to the servants here. It will also be necessary to interview any staff who came into contact with your brother-in-law at work. These are all routine matters generic to any murder investigation."

"Of course, Captain, I will ensure that facilities are made available for your officers."

"Thank you sir, your co-operation is appreciated of course," continued Adendorff with a nod counting the various points off on his fingers, "We will also need to speak to Mrs. du Plessis, but I think that can wait until she is discharged from hospital. It may also be necessary to speak to your servants and possibly your wife as well. It all depends how quickly we can pick up Sibanyoni."

"My wife should be at the hospital now and will take poor Brunelda back to our house when she is discharged, she cannot possibly return here," said Hendrik, feeling the need for some fresh air.

"Good, excellent. Then, if you will give my sergeant your contact 'phone numbers for the next few days, I need detain you no longer, sir." said Adendorff, holding out his right hand.

"Of course, captain, I am at your disposal," Hendrik concluded, returning the hand shake.

Hennie returned thoughtfully towards his car.

⋆

Georgina made her way along the corridors of the Wynberg hospital following the signs for Ward W4. The hospital receptionist had advised that Brunelda had been transferred to this ward following her examination in the Casualty Department on arrival by ambulance that morning.

Although still shocked by the horror of the morning's news and full of sympathy for her sister-in-law, Georgie was apprehensive of the reception she was likely to receive. After all, Brunelda disliked her intensely, principally for having the impertinence to marry her younger brother Hendrik, for being English and not speaking Afrikaans as her first language. For being young, good looking and the only other full partner in her brother's legal firm when her own husband was merely the salaried chief accountant, never having been granted partner status.

Arriving at Ward W4, she spoke to a nurse and was directed to Brunelda's room. The hospital was apparently pleased for Mrs du Plessis to be discharged into Georgina's care at the earliest opportunity.

Crossing the corridor to Brunelda's room, she peeped through the small window in the door and saw her sister-in-law sitting in an armchair at the side of the bed. She was wearing a shapeless hospital gown and had a white blanket draped around her shoulders.

Taking a deep breath, Georgie knocked and entered.

Here goes, thought Georgie as she bent over the chair, putting an arm around Grunelda's shoulders and kissing her on the cheek. Continuing to hug her, Georgie was surprised to feel Brunelda's arm around her own shoulders pulling her more tightly into the embrace.

After several moments, Georgie released herself and sat on the edge of the bed, still holding Brunelda's hand.

"Thank you for coming, Georgina," said her sister-in-law in a whisper, "It's so good to see a friendly face."

It must be the medication, thought Georgie, she's delirious.

"You poor darling, I still can't believe what's happened, it must have been a nightmare for you," she said soothingly in Afrikaans.

"It's just a daze, Georgie, the doctors have given me something to calm my nerves and to make me sleep but I can't go back to the house, not now Johannes is…," Brunelda started to cry quietly.

"Of course, you can't go home," said Georgina, continuing in a language she understood well enough, but had made a stand since her marriage into an Afrikaner family, of refusing to use. She squeezed both Brunelda's hands. "That's why I'm here, You're coming back to our place to stay for as long as like."

"What about poor Johannes, who could have done such a terrible thing?" sobbed Brunelda.

"Hendrick is at your house now, he will take care of all the arrangements so don't worry," said Georgie with genuine sympathy. "Let's just get you back home, have a nice hot drink, make you comfortable and you can have a long sleep. When you wake up Hendrik will be back."

With the help of two very willing hospital porters, Brunelda was soon sitting in the passenger seat of the large Peugeot estate car that was kept for airport runs and holidays.

"Let's get you home," said Georgie, as she drove away from the hospital.

During the journey through the suburban traffic, Brunelda sat silently staring out of the window. Georgina darted an occasional glance in her passenger's direction but apart from regular enquiries as to her comfort and welfare there was little conversation.

It was just that Georgie, for probably the first time in her life, was truly lost for words. There was bad history between her and her much older sister-in-law. So bad that meetings between the two would often descend to almost comic exchanges of insults but today that was all forgotten. She desperately wanted to do something to take away Brunelda's pain.

Gently stopping the big Peugeot in front of her Constantia home, Georgina tapped the four digit security code into the keypad and waited for the gates to swing slowly open before driving in, the gates closing behind her.

Having telephoned ahead from the hospital she was not surprised to see Miriam and Cato standing by the front door.

As she stopped the car, the two servants hurried to the passenger door.

"Get her inside as quickly as you can," ordered Georgie, getting out and hurrying round to the passenger side.

"I've prepared the blue guest room as you instructed, madam," said Miriam, placing a large, tartan, travelling rug around Brunelda's shoulders as Cato assisted the still sedated woman from the car.

"Good, you two help her upstairs, I'll bring her things," said Georgina, opening the rear door and picking up a large hospital carrier bag containing Brunelda's clothes and handbag.

Within five minutes she was comfortably tucked up in bed, supported by three enormous white pillows.

Georgina sat in a wooden arm chair next to the bed as Miriam entered carrying a cup of tea but Brunelda was already asleep.

"Let her sleep now," said Georgie, as they both left the room, quietly closing the door behind them.

Back downstairs, Georgina was just crossing the hall when she heard a car pull up outside. Opening the front door, she saw her husband getting out of his Mercedes that was parked next to the Peugeot. Hendrik looked tired and pale as he kissed his wife at the front door.

"What happened?"

"It was awful, darling," confided her husband, putting his arm around her shoulder as they crossed the hall. "Let's go into the living room."

Closing the door behind them they sat together on a chesterfield by the window. "Did, you see my sister?" asked Hendrik, taking his wife's hand.

"She's here, darling, asleep upstairs, she's still sedated, but bearing up remarkably well, let her sleep while she can."

Hendrik kissed his wife, "You're wonderful, thank you."

Sitting alone together on the sofa, Hendrik described his interview with Captain Adendorff and under pressure from Georgina, he went on to describe the murder scene in graphic detail.

Georgina sat listening, wide eyed, with a hand covering he mouth.

"So it looks like that horrible Sibanyoni is the murderer, the bastard,"

"Well, the police seem to think so, they're looking for him now. They think that after I refused to support his scheme any further, he may have gone to try his luck with poor Johannes."

"But why should he think he would have any more luck with Johannes, after all, he's just the accountant?" puzzled Georgie. "And why kill him?"

"How should I know?" snapped Hendrik, angrily. "He's a black, I don't know how the blacks think, do I? I need a drink."

"I'm sorry, Hennie, I was just thinking aloud, let me get you that drink, whisky? I think I need one as well."

Walking to the drinks cabinet she poured a very large whisky for her husband and an even larger gin and tonic for herself. Returning to the sofa, she handed one of the exquisite lead crystal glasses to Hendrik. Silence followed as they both savoured the restorative properties of alcohol.

"I didn't mean to snap at you, Georgie," whispered Hendrik, taking her hand. "It's been a terrible day."

Georgina bent forward and kissed him. "Do me one favour, darling."

Hendrik looked at his wife.

"Get rid of those bloody spears from your office wall, they always gave me the creeps, but now…"

"Of course," replied Hendrik, trying to smile.

CHAPTER SIX

Friday 7th February 1969

"I cannot understand why they haven't caught him yet." grumbled Georgina over top of her cup of Rooibos tea, "After all, it can't be that difficult, they know who he is, we've all given good descriptions. They'd catch me quickly enough if I was speeding."

Hendrick, gave his wife a private little kick as he reached forward to place his cup and saucer on the coffee table. Georgie glanced at her husband.

As a concession to her sister-in-law, Georgina was speaking in Afrikaans, a language she did not enjoy using. She was aware that Hendrik spoke Afrikaans as his language of choice during the working day, but reverted to English at home in compliance with his wife's insistance. However, the gesture had been tacitly, but very well received by Brunelda and was perhaps the principal reason for the recent and almost miraculous harmony between the two women.

It was now three days since that dreadful day when Johannes du Plessis had been found murdered. Georgina, Brunelda and Hendrik were in the living room, seated comfortably around a large coffee table near the windows. Nothing out of the ordinary but this was a special occasion. It was the first time that Brunelda had dressed and descended from the seclusion of her first floor room.

"He's most probably gone to ground in one of the

townships, Langa perhaps," said Hendrik, "You know what they're like, acres and acres of shacks and tin sheds, one area indistinguishable from another. It must be near impossible to find one black man among so many thousands."

"Well, actually I don't know what they're like," said Georgie with heavy sarcasm, "I doubt if the restaurants are quite to my taste and where would I park the 'E' Type?"

"Good God, Georgie, grow up," hissed Hendrik.

"Of course, the old Voortrekkers would have known how to deal with him," piped in Brunelda, joining the conversation for the first time. "Strung him up from the nearest tree, they would have done."

Georgina lent across and gently squeezed Brunelda's arm. "I'm sorry, darling, you're right but let's change the subject and talk about something else."

After a moments embarrassed silence.

"What's the gossip at the tennis club, darling?" asked Hendrik, instantly regretting his words, after all what other gossip could there be.

"For heaven's sake Hennie, surely you don't think I've been spending my days playing tennis when poor Brunelda is recovering from…"

"…No, sorry, should have thought," replied Hennie wretchedly.

"My cousin William will be going up to Rhodesia soon to join the police," said Georgie, trying again after another short silence. "How about we have him and his girlfriend, what's her name? Angie something, over for a few drinks."

Georgie looked enquiringly at Hennie and Brunelda, especially Brunelda.

"I don't know Georgie," said Hennie doubtfully. "It's not fair to expect my sister to be up to entertaining."

"No, Hennie, it's okay," replied Brunelda, "Nothing can bring back my Johannes but life must go on. I think I would enjoy seeing some young people and I could always go back to my room if it was too much for me."

"In that case, if you are quite sure, I'll invite them over on Sunday," said Georgie, secretly pleased with the progress. "Nothing special, perhaps we could have a game of tennis if the weather is nice, you could come down and watch, Brunelda, some fresh air will do you good."

"I don't suppose I shall be much company."

She patted Brunelda's hand.

"You're doing great, darling," whispered Georgie, with real feeling. "I'll make the arrangements."

Saturday 8th February 1969

The next day, Georgina was sitting in the living room having just concluded a booked long distance telephone call to England. To save causing alarm, she had decided not to inform her mother of the dreadful events of the last week. Newsworthy it no doubt was in South Africa, but she doubted it would make the British newspapers.

Georgina was satisfied that for the time being at least, there was no likelihood of her mum flying in on the next South African Airways jet.

Replacing the telephone handset, she walked out to the terrace and down the steps to the garden. She made her way past the swimming pool, along the path between the immaculate flower beds and across the lawn towards the tennis court at the far end of the property.

Sliding the bolt across, she opened the gate and entered the hard court and looked around. Her own tennis court had received little use recently as Georgina preferred the social scene and plentiful opponents at the local tennis club. However, all seemed in good order, the lines were crisply white and the surface was good without any cracks. Amos had clearly been doing his job. Even the adjacent equipment shed had recently been painted.

She looked back at the house, so far away across the huge garden and saw Amos hurrying in her direction. Georgina watched as the old man opened the gate and joined her on the court.

"Good morning, baas," said Amos respectfully, "Will you require the tennis court today, madam, I can have it ready in a few minutes."

"Yes, I think so, Amos," replied Georgina, looking around the court, "We are expecting a couple of guests tomorrow and we may well have a doubles match. You have kept it very well, it looks good."

"Thank you madam," murmured Amos, pleased with the praise.

"I haven't played for nearly a week so I might have a knock up on my own this afternoon but for tomorrow, please make sure there is a comfortable chair for Mrs du Plessis, I'm hoping she will come down and watch the game."

"Of course, ma'am, do you want me to send David down as ball boy for you?"

"No, leave him be, I think a little running around will do me good,I feel a bit rusty." smiled Georgina, opening the gate and strolling back towards the house.

"I'll get on with it straight away," said Amos, hurrying towards the tennis shed.

"Thank you," said Georgina without looking back.

★

An hour later, Georgie was back in the tennis court, warming up with some gentle but accurate serves. She was not surprised that after a few minutes the sound of racket striking ball had attracted the boy David. As she continued serving the six balls from each end, she was aware of being watched as the boy peered through the green wire netting fence.

"I can collect the balls up for you Miss Georgie."

"It's okay, David, I shall start hitting them really hard soon and if one hits you it will hurt."

"I don't mind, let me, please."

Once again, Georgina had to admit to herself that she liked this little boy and his eagerness to please.

"Come on in then but if you get hit it's your own fault," she smiled and waited until he was inside the court. "Crouch down there by the net and don't move until I've served all six."

Now thoroughly warmed up, Georgina began to serve faster and faster until she had used all six balls, nodding to David to recover them.

A player of near professional standard she now began to serve with breathtaking ferocity and accuracy. It mattered not to Georgina that tomorrow's game was merely a family get together, she knew only one way to play and that was all out to win.

Inevitably, she served a super fast delivery that was fractionally off line and struck the crouching David with tremendous force in the side of his head. Georgina watched as the boy silently rolled on his side clutching his head in his arms.

Walking to the centre of the court, Georgina looked down at the boy as he lay on the ground still holding his head.

"Are you all right David, I didn't do it on purpose. Come on, let's have a look."

David slowly sat up, leaning on his left arm, his right hand still held to his face. Georgina noticed that his eyes were full of tears, but he wouldn't cry.

Crouching down, she put a hand on his shoulder.

"I bet that stings."

"I'm okay, Miss Georgie, it doesn't hurt,"

"You're very brave David," said Georgie with genuine admiration for the boy's pluck. "Perhaps that's enough tennis for today."

"I'm all right," insisted the boy, standing up with great determination.

Georgina looked at him for a few moments. "Have you ever played tennis, David?"

"No, miss."

"There's another racket on the seat, go and get it."

David soon forgot the pain, as for the next half hour Georgina went through the basics of tennis with her eager pupil, ending with some gentle back and forth serves and returns.

"Come on, that's enough," she smiled.

Closing the gate, David ran off excitedly. "Wait 'till I tell Grandfather that I've been playing tennis with you, Miss Georgie."

"You're welcome, David,"

As she walked back towards the house, she was still smiling at the little boy's antics. For probably the first time she realised, with surprise, that David's happiness and good opinion were important to her.

She stopped and looked round just in time to see the little lad dart through the open gate into the kitchen garden and then, presumably to the servants' accommodation where he lived with his grandfather. Georgina prided herself that she wasn't a bad employer, certainly not a slave driver. Provided the house and gardens were maintained to a high standard, as she conceded they were and someone was always there to do her bidding, then she was not too concerned how this was achieved. That said, there was little communication between servant and mistress other than the giving and receiving of instructions. She was sometimes amused by Miriam's idle gossip, but little more than that.

Georgina was not ill disposed towards her staff, but gave them little thought, they were merely functionaries after all.

The servants, for their part would studiously avoid their young mistress if they possibly could. Her temper was often unpredictable and any chance encounter would usually incur extra work. "Ah, Lena, give the dining room floor another polish." "Amos, I think the shrubs in front of the house could do with a trim." Yes, the mistress was best avoided if at all possible.

But the boy was different. If he saw Georgina by the pool, in the garden or on the tennis court, he would run up to greet her. Arriving home in her car, as often as not he would run alongside to be able to open the door for her. She was always pleased to see him. She took pleasure from the self evident fact that he liked her and it was mutual. She had even started to notice the time when he should be back from school and would look out for him.

Sunday 9th February 1969

"First up, and I own the place, must be doing something wrong." muttered Georgina as she left the silent house and made her way down the garden towards the tennis court. She glanced at her wristwatch, it was only eight o'clock.

As she approached the tennis court the morning silence was broken by a dreadful scream. Georgina stopped and listened, someone or something was in real distress, perhaps it was an animal, she wondered. A moment later she had her answer as the boy David came into sight, moaning in a pitiful manner and staggering from side to side, his hands over his eyes.

"David," shouted Georgina. "What on earth…?"

David saw his employer and started to run towards her shouting incoherently and crying. As the small boy reached Georgina he seemed to lunge at her, throwing his arms around her, his momentum causing her to lose balance and stagger backwards under his weight.

Startled, Georgie angrily snatched at the collar of David's shirt, pulling him away from her.

"Get off me," she shouted, as she pushed him to the ground. "What on earth do you think you're doing, are you mad?"

As David lay on the grass sobbing uncontrollably, he looked up at Georgina, "Grandfather" he managed to articulate between deep body convulsing sobs, pointing towards the tennis court.

Her anger now abating, Georgina left the boy and ran the remaining distance towards the tennis court. At first glance all seemed well, the gate in the fence was open and a broom and wheel barrow stood just inside the court. Amos had clearly started preparing the court for play, but where was he?

Looking up, she saw the door of the wooden equipment shed was standing open. Georgina approached the hut with a feeling of impending dread in the pit of her stomach. Gingerly peering into the confines of the small dark wooden store room, she stepped over the threshold. As her eyes became accustomed to the lack of light, she was aware of several rolled nets standing against the back wall together with tins of white lining paint and a white lining machine. Looking cautiously around, on the right hand wall were shelves with boxes of new tennis balls and bags of old ones for practice. In the far corner was a stack of green folding chairs. The sight of these familiar items began to restore her confidence and, there being nothing untoward, she turned to leave.

Suddenly her whole body convulsed, she was unable to breathe, it felt like being punched in the stomach. She crashed backwards into the shelves on the wall behind her, scattering tennis balls in all directions. Georgina felt her heart pounding in her throat. Desperately trying to scream, she was only able to produce an animal gurgle.

Terror gripped her as she tried to regain her feet, forcing herself to look at the horror that was emerging from the darkness.

The body of Amos, the gardener hung before her eyes in the half light. He was pinned to the opposite wall by an assegai in his chest.

As she looked at the macabre sight, the spear gave up it's struggle to support the weight of the corpse. The body, now detached from the wall, lurched forward towards her, a deathly sigh issuing from Amos's open mouth as he crashed to the ground. This time Georgina managed a full blooded scream and with a supreme effort staggered to her feet throwing herself through the open door. Fighting for breath, Georgina saw David standing on the grass, trembling and crying.

Grabbing the boy more roughly than she intended, Georgie pulled him towards her, glad of contact with another human being. She kicked closed the shed door so that he could not see inside.

"Come on, quickly, we must call the police," said Georgina, her voice shaking, trying to pull the boy towards the house.

David resisted with all his might, digging his heels into the path. "But Grandfather," he cried.

"For God's sake boy, do as I tell you."

Instantly regretting her aggressive manner, Georgina mustered all her self control and knelt next to the terrified little boy.

"David, the best thing we can do is call the police, come and help me."

Together, they ran back towards the house.

*

The early peace and quiet of Sunday morning was now well and truly broken. A marked police car arrived within five minutes of Georgina's first frantic telephone call and within half an hour, the full impedimenta of another murder investigation was in full swing.

Detectives and forensic experts swarmed all over the garden, with a concentration in the vicinity of the tennis court and the equipment shed.

The police had confined Hendrik and Georgina to the living room. It had been impossible to keep the truth from Brunelda and she had been taken to bed, her fragile self control shattered, she was close to hysterics. The doctor had administered strong sedatives and thankfully, she was now sleeping, with a private nurse in attendance.

The servants had been instructed to stay in the kitchen with the exception of the boy David who remained with Georgina in the living room.

Georgie would have been the first to admit that she was woefully ill prepared to offer sympathy and support to a small, traumatised black boy of ten years of age.

When they first got back to the house, Georgina, in shock herself, had found David almost uncontrollable in his grief. Ideas of racial superiority had need to take second place. Simple humanity decreed that she could do nothing other than envelop the sobbing child in both arms, hugging him tightly. Apart from David's crying, the room was in silence.

There was a knock at the door, Hendrik and Georgina looked up as Captain Adendorff entered the room.

Hendrik rose to greet the police officer with a hand shake, introducing him to his wife.

Sitting on a sofa, Georgina continued to hold David tightly in her arms.

Captain Adendorff addressed them, "Meneer, Mevrou, I will need to ask you a few questions,"

Hendrik spoke first but Georgina interrupted, ignoring her husband. "What do you want to know, Captain, I got up to play tennis this morning in my own secure garden and I find my gardener has been brutally murdered. All the evidence is in that shed by the tennis court and if you have no idea who did it, then I'll give you a name."

"Darling, please, let the Captain do his job." said Hendrik, with some embarrassment.

"I wish he would do his job," continued Georgie, on the attack. "We've given the police a description of Sibanyoni but they can't find him. Perhaps they'd do better to get into the townships and look for him there than tramp about my garden asking pointless questions."

"Mrs van Wyk," said Adendorff, stepping towards her, "This must be terrifying for you and I do understand your concerns but..."

"...I don't think you have any idea what we are going through. First my brother-in law is brutally murdered and now this poor old man, I don't think you've got a bloody clue."

"Madam, I must ask you to co-operate with us as your husband has done. I think it may be best if the little boy joins the other servants in the kitchen where they are giving their evidence."

"Do you think it best, Captain? Well, I don't, the victim was this child's grandfather and his guardian. The boy is in a state of shock, as are we all, or has that escaped your notice. "

Adendorff raised his eyebrows, passing a hand across his forehead, "Nevertheless, Mrs. van Wyk, I must ask you some questions."

"Get on with it then," snapped Georgina, removing one of her arms from the boy so that he could sit up next to her.

"Madam, do you think the child has seen…err…inside the shed?"

"From the state he was in when I found him, yes, I'm sure he has."

"Then I am afraid I must insist on speaking to you in private, Mrs. van Wyk, it's a matter of continuity of evidence, your husband will explain."

"That's quite correct, darling." said Hendrik, lamely.

"I'm not stupid, Hendrik," Turning to Captain Adendorff, she continued. "Very well Captain, you can interview me in the dining room."

Georgina removed her arm from around David's shoulder and walked through into the dining room, indicating the policeman to follow her.

Closing the door behind him, Adendorff looked around the room. Georgina had seated herself at one of the small tables near the windows and lit a cigarette.

"A beautiful room, Mrs. van Wyk."

"You think so? I hate it," sneered Georgie, "An opinion that will be even further confirmed by any time spent here in your company."

"Ouch !" winced Adendorff, raising his eyebrows.

Georgie exhaled a long stream of cigarette smoke.

"That wasn't fair, please sit down and ask your questions."

Captain Adendorff sat at the table and with some prompting, Georgina gave a full account of the morning's events. She resisted, with difficulty, her desire to direct the police investigations to arrive at what she considered obvious conclusions.

"Captain, we both know who the murderer is but what I can't understand is, why? Why kill that poor old man? He had been the gardener here for years, long before I married Mr. van Wyk. All he was doing was sweeping the tennis court as I had asked him to."

"Well, Mrs. van Wyk, I have yet to complete my investigations but I will admit that we need to find Sibanyoni, it is only a matter of time before we catch him."

"You're like a bloody gramophone record, do you know that?"

"But for what it is worth I think your gardener may have disturbed the murderer," continued the Captain, choosing to ignore Georgie's insult.

"Disturbed him from what?"

"Burglary, perhaps."

"Then why this assegai, stuff, why nail him up in the tennis store, what is the point of all that?" challenged Georgina, becoming heated.

"The murderer may be trying to make a statement, to link this crime with the other. There may also be some ritualistic element in the crime. I think I can tell you that the assegai wound did not cause death. The murder weapon was almost certainly a long, thin blade, pushed up under the ribs, in a similar manner to the killing of your brother-in-law. I first thought it would have been impossible for one man to support the corpse against the wall of the tennis store and force the assegai through the chest and into the wall."

"Then he must have had an accomplice," suggested Georgina, who had not foreseen these developments.

"No, I don't think so," continued the Captain showing satisfaction. "There were several hooks and brackets on that wall and I think the murderer simply looped Amos's trouser belt over a convenient projection while he tied the corpse's arms to other available brackets. Then, with the body secure, he hammered the assegai into the victims chest. Later, the weight of the body detached itself from the wall in the terrifying circumstances you refer to in your statement."

"It was the most frightening thing I've ever seen," shuddered Georgie. "But why all this effort?"

"I think it may have been a warning. He is trying to frighten you by clearly identifying this murder with the one of Mr. du Plessis. He may have come here with burglary in mind but something went wrong, your gardener disturbed him and paid for it with his life and once dead was used to create a link with the previous murder."

"Captain, I've just thought," interrupted Georgie in alarm. "My husband had a pair of those assegais on his office wall, the same as poor Johannes, I always hated them but after the first murder I asked Hendrik to get rid of them but I don't know if he did."

"I will speak to your husband about that but of the two spears in Mr. du Plessis's office, one we recovered in the room and the other was still missing. I can confirm that the spear used to kill your gardener today is identical to the one used in the previous murder and fits the marks on the wall of your brother-in-law's office."

"Who's next, then Captain?" said Georgina, raising her

voice. "It must be my husband, you must realise that. You have to catch this lunatic before we all go bloody mad."

Before the Captain could reply, one of the double doors to living room opened and a uniformed constable stepped half into the room.

"Excuse me sir," said the young officer nervously. "The servants, sir, they've all legged it."

"Legged it, what do you mean legged it?" demanded Adendorff, standing up from his chair at the table.

"Lieut. Swart and the boys have been in the kitchen taking the statements of the three servants."

"Yes, I know that." said Adendorff, impatiently.

The constable swallowed, "Well, sir, Lieut. Swart sent them back to the kia. When we went back to get some signatures, they were gone, sir."

"What do you mean, bloody gone?"

"Errr… gone sir, taken all their belongings, the place is empty."

"Wasn't there someone on the back gate, for Gods sake."

"Smit, sir, but he said no one told him not to let anyone out, sir."

"Then God almighty, get 'em back." shouted the captain.

"Sir," muttered the young constable, glad to get out of the room.

By this time Georgina was already on her feet and as the constable shut the door behind him she crossed the room and stood in front of Captain Adendorff.

"What sort of fucking joke is this? she shouted stabbing a finger in his direction. "Two murders, no arrests, now you lose all my staff, are you some kind of fucking idiot?"

Losing her temper completely, Georgie did not wait for an answer but flung open both the double doors and entered the living room like an avenging angel.

"They've let the servants go, gone, belongings the lot, it would be funny if it wasn't so bloody serious," shouted Georgie to her husband, slapping both hands on her thighs in exasperation.

"What's happened, darling?" asked Hendrik, standing up and moving towards his wife.

"Ask that bloody idiot," shouted Georgie, spinning round and pointing an accusing finger in the direction of Captain Adendorff who was standing shamefaced in the doorway.

Any further embarrassment of the unfortunate detective was prevented by the ringing of the telephone. Georgina was nearest and snatched up the handset.

"Yes!" she said angrily.

"Oh hi, Will," said Georgie, softening her tone, "No, we're all okay, Is Angie with you?…Come on up to the house and I'll explain what's happened."

"Who won't let you in?" Georgina spoke into the phone, her anger returning, "Hold on."
Holding the telephone against her body, she looked across at Captain Adendorff,

"I don't believe this, you let all my staff out then you have the bloody cheek to stop my guests from coming in." shouted Georgina.

"Mrs van Wyk, you must understand, your whole house and gardens are still a crime scene and…" replied Adendorff lamely.

"…Don't you dare, don't you dare to tell me who can come into my own house," screamed Georgie, stabbing her right index finger in the direction of the detective as an emphasis to her words.

"Darling, please," said Hendrik.

"No, Hennie, I won't be quiet," she replied furiously,

turning back to the detective and holding out the phone, "Tell that cretin you've put on the gate to let my cousin in or so help me I'll go up there and…"

"… I see no reason why your guests should not come up to the house, provided you don't wander about the garden until my men have finished their work." replied the detective, submissively, taking the telephone from Georgina.

"Just fuck off, will you," said Georgie, contemptuously, "I have done nothing wrong and I'll do whatever I like in my own home. I might have a braai if I feel like it, trample all over the garden."

"If you will excuse me, I must go and speak to my officers." said an embarrassed Adendorff, closing the door behind him.

Georgina sat down next to David who had stopped crying and curled himself into a foetal position on the sofa, his face buried in a cushion. She looked at the boy but said nothing.

A few moments later the front door bell rang.

"I'll go," said Hendrik, jumping up, glad to escape the room.

Entering the living room, Georgina's cousin, Will and his fiancée crossed to where Georgie was sitting and kissed her. They looked at the boy David, curled up next to her. Georgina gave the visitors a short precis of the mornings events.

"Poor little sod," said Will, lightly putting a hand on the boy's shoulder.

"Poor all of you," repeated Angie. "What a terrible shock for you all, I don't know what to say."

"How's Brunelda?" asked Will.

"In bed sedated, out for the count, there's a nurse with her," replied Hendrik, "Look, sit down you two, let me get you a drink, we could all do with one."

"We should go, you don't want us here now," offered Will, taking Angie's hand.

"Please, stay, I really need you, please stay to lunch, after all, we have to eat," pleaded Georgie.

Hendrik prepared drinks for everyone while Georgina continued with her graphic account of the day's events. With occasional gasps from William and Angie, she was uninterrupted for nearly thirty minutes.

"So, there you have it," finished Georgie as Hendrik refilled their glasses. "This dreadful man seems to be stalking us, I'm sure it was Hendrik he was after, and why? Revenge we suppose because Hendrik would not support his stupid scheme for black lawyers."

Hendrik accidentally poured whisky over Will's hand.

"Hey, don't waste it," said Will, licking his fingers. "And what do the police think, Hendrik?"

"I think even they have come to the conclusion it's this Sibanyani but with all their resources they can't find him, they can't even keep our staff in one place," replied Georgie.

"So what are you two going to do now, tonight I mean?"

"We shall have to stay here, I suppose," said Hendrik, "My sister is upstairs, we cannot leave her alone, even with a nurse."

"I hadn't given it any thought," interrupted Georgie. "But I hate the idea of staying here all alone with no staff and a murderer on the loose. I suppose we will have to tonight, but I want to go somewhere else tomorrow. We won't sleep anyway."

"The Captain says that he will arrange for officers to be in the gardens all night," offered Hendrik.

"Why doesn't that fill me with confidence," mused Georgie holding her quickly emptied glass out towards her husband for a refill.

"Do you know what I think we should do?" said Hendrik, as he replenished her drink. "Get away for a few days. I have to go up to our Pretoria offices soon anyway and there is a three bedroom apartment there. We can take Brunelda with us, if she's okay and if you and Angie wanted to come too we could go on up to Salisbury, stay at Meikles hotel and check William in for his training."

Georgina jumped up and hugged her pleasantly surprised husband, "Hennie, that's why I love you," she smiled, giving her husband a lingering kiss on the lips. "What a fantastic plan." Spinning round she looked at William and Angie. "Please, please say you'll come, Will, you have to be in Salisbury next week anyway."

Will hesitated. "Well, it would be no problem for me but…"

"…I would like to come, let me ring my boss tomorrow and see if I can get a few days off," said Angie, squeezing Will's hand.

"How about us staying here with you tonight," suggested Will, looking at Angie, who nodded her slightly blushing agreement. "We can keep each other's courage up."

"Fantastic," beamed Georgina, getting up and looking around at the others. "Let's have some lunch."

"But darling," questioned Hendrik. "The cook's gone."

"I might not do it often but I think I can still cook," said Georgie, "But you can all come with me. I'm not cooking while you lot are up here drinking so we'll eat in the kitchen for once, hey?"

Everyone agreed, the two men collected the bottles and prepared to follow.

However, Georgina turned to look at the one person they had all forgotten. David was sitting up, looking around and rubbing his eyes. She realised he had never been inside the house before. The boy willingly took her outstretched hand.

"Come on, David," she said in a soft voice. "You're eating with the white folks today."

Down in the kitchen, Georgie hunted through the refrigerators and cupboards for suitable ingredients while the others sat at the table with their drinks, all offering to help. The boy David forgot his grief as he stared in amazement at his employer busying herself with the paraphernalia of cooking, he couldn't believe his eyes.

After a while, with the smells, noise and heat of the cooking beginning to permeate the kitchen and with a few more drinks, the ambience of the room became more lighthearted. The others couldn't help laughing at Georgie's antics at the stove, she had learned to cook years earlier at school in England but lack of practice ensured much cursing and swearing from the mistress of the house. Even David was now running about fetching saucepans and implements as Georgie called for them.

Within thirty minutes, the adults and David were sitting together at the table with a very acceptable meal, although, as Georgie admitted, it resembled a breakfast rather than a lunch. The child was finding the whole situation incomprehensible as he sat with all these bosses, watching in awe as Miss Georgie, placed a plate of food in front of him that she had actually cooked herself. Then, as if wonders would never cease, she went to the refrigerator and placed a whole bottle of ice cold Coca Cola in front of him, stroking his head as she walked away.

"Had I known you could cook so well, darling," said Hendrik, smiling. "We could have saved a fortune by not employing a cook."

"Ja, right, enjoy it now, Hennie, you won't see it often," smiled Georgie. "I could probably clean floors as well, but don't hold your breath."

As they began to eat, the door opened and a surprised looking Captain Adendorff entered the kitchen.

"You're too late for lunch, Captain," said Georgina in a conciliatory manner. "But sit down and have a drink."

"Sir, Madam, I will need to interview the little boy as soon a possible."

"Well, let him eat his meal first, Captain," said Georgie. "So have a drink, while you wait."

"Just a small one then."

"You'll have a big one the same as the rest of us," smiled Georgina.

"Whisky, Captain?" asked Hendrik, pushing the bottle and a glass across the table towards the detective.

"Thank you," said Adendorff, nervously pouring the single malt into his glass. He looked around the room and his eyes rested admiringly on Mrs Georgina van Wyk, his formidable adversary of half an hour ago. She smiled and raised her glass to him as she caught and held his embarrassed stare. That woman is magnificent he thought.

"Have you finished your enquiries Captain, did you find anything?" enquired Hendrik.

"I think we have done as much as we can today, sir, with the exception of speaking to the boy. Our forensic team didn't find any fingerprints, but there is enough to link this crime to the murder of your brother-in-law."

"Well, I think we could all have guessed that, Captain," said Hendrik, mildly.

"By the way, sir," continued Adendorff, taking a gulp of his drink, "Do any of you know the whereabouts of the boy's parents?"

Glancing across the table at David, who was busily eating and drinking his Coke, Georgina replied in a theatrical whisper. "We know the mother is dead and the father is in one of the miners' hostels near Jo'burg, more than that, we've no idea."

"Mmm…I would like to take the boy down to the station, we have women officers there who are trained to deal with children. May I ask what plans you have for the child?"

"None, Captain," replied Georgie, with some surprise. "He was living here with his grandfather without our permission, but we gave him a job. I think he attends school in the mornings and we see him about the gardens in the afternoons. I like the boy, but apart from that, I've no plans for him."

"If you wish it, I could arrange for the child to be taken into the care of the City," he proposed.

"I think you must, Captain, with no staff here we intend to go up to Pretoria for a few days with Mrs. du Plessis and then on to Salisbury to see my cousin checked in for his BSAP training," said Georgina, looking at the boy, who seemed unaware of being the topic of discussion. Adendorff nodded his acceptance of this responsibility.

"Come along, David," said Georgina in a kindly but authoritative voice, "If you've finished I would like you to go with this officer for a ride in his police car, there are some nice ladies like me who want to ask you some questions.

"Will I come back here, Miss Georgie?"

"I don't think so, David, you are going to stay for a little while with some other children. I promise you will be well looked after."

Without saying any more, David got down from his chair and looked nervously at the detective. Hesitating, he turned back towards Georgina and ran towards her holding out his hands to her.

"No, David," said Georgie sharply, stepping back, "Go with Mr. Adendorff."

David was visibly taken aback by Georgie's sudden change of manner towards him. In the eyes of the small boy it was like the link with safety being suddenly withdrawn. She had changed in an instant back into the scary white lady of a few weeks ago. He didn't understand what was happening.

Everyone was silent as Captain Adendorff, taking the boy by the hand, opened the door to leave.

"David," said Georgie, quietly, as the boy looked back towards her. "How about my salute, then?"

He smiled and raised his right hand in a smart salute that was returned by a silent Georgina.

After the door had closed behind them, Georgina returned silently to her seat, blinking back tears.

"Darling," said Hendrik, taking his wife's hand, "Would you like me to ring Janet, my PA in the morning and ask her to make arrangements for the boy to go to one of the Missionary boarding schools for African children? He will be well cared for and will get a good education. We can foot the bill. At least it will give him a chance."

"Please, I would like that very much," smiled Georgie, kissing her husband's cheek. "And could Janet let me know what school he is attending?"

"Of course."

Georgina finished the remainder of her gin and tonic in one gulp.

"Let's go back to the living room folks," said Georgie, smiling at her guests, "I need another bloody drink."

★

The combined effects of the alcohol, the companionship of friends and the possibility of escape from the house in the morning managed to keep spirits up during the afternoon and evening. There were a few alarms and diversions that took the four scurrying to the windows to peer out in panic only to glimpse a police officer patrolling through the grounds.

The telephone rang at about seven o'clock in the evening. it was the officer posted at the front gate.

"Hello,...Oh yes, send her along and we'll let her in," said Hendrik in answer.

Hendrik left the room to admit the night duty nurse and show her to Brunelda's first floor room. He waited respectfully outside the room as the two nurses discussed their patient for a few moments before showing the off duty nurse through the house to her car parked outside the front door. Apparently, Brunelda was sleeping peacefully.

By ten-thirty, thoughts turned to sleeping arrangements and the four companions made their way upstairs. Georgina and Hendrik would occupy their own bedroom suite. Georgie took delight in showing William and Angie into Hendrik's old room.

"Well, you should be okay in here," smiled Georgie, seductively winking at William as she bounced up and down on the bed. Turning to Angie, she showed her the bathroom and dressing room stocked with beautiful white Egyptian cotton towels and gowns.

"If you need any girly things just pop next door."

Angela's embarrassment was saved by Hendrik entering the room. All conversation ceased and even an ebullient Georgina looked shocked as Hendrik placed a Browning 9mm Hi-Power automatic pistol on the bed.

"Just in case, Will. It's old but serviced and loaded, there's a thirteen shot magazine don't forget, I have one the same." Hendrik produced a matching firearm from his back pocket. "One could start a small war with that."

William picked up the gun with something approaching reverence. "Crikey," he said.

"Is this a good idea, Hennie?" asked Georgie, nervously. "Considering all the drink we've had. If Sibanyoni turns up in the night you'd better get to the thing first because if I get my hands on it I'll blow the fucker's head off."

"Oh, Georgie, you don't think he will do you?" said a genuinely scared Angie, holding Georgina's arm.

"Don't be silly," said Hendrik taking his wife's hand. "The police are outside, the alarm is on and we are armed. Now lock your door and have a good night."

As they left the room, Georgina turned towards William and Angie, "Sleep well," she said suddenly giggling for no obvious reason.

*

The night had been quiet except for a minor melodrama around three in the morning when Hendrik thought he heard someone moving about downstairs. Quietly tapping on the door of the next room he aroused William for moral support and they crept along the corridor to the top of the stairs, brandishing their firearms.

Whilst whispering between themselves about what to do, Hendrik somehow managed to drop his gun. To the horror of the two men it clattered down the marble staircase bouncing three times before sliding across the hall floor.

A tremulous Georgina and Angela, following the pair of heroes along the landing and deciding that the element of surprise had now probably been lost, turned on the lights.

The gun had slithered to a halt at the feet of a rather surprised looking nurse who was returning from the kitchen with a pot of coffee.

Retrieving his gun and enquiring politely from the nurse after Brunelda's health, Hendrik and the others, shamefacedly returned to their rooms.

By seven everyone was up, Georgina was in the kitchen preparing some breakfast. Will and Angie, having swallowed a very quick cup of coffee were preparing to return home to pack for the forthcoming trip.

"Will, I'll let you know the travel arrangements as soon as we hear," said Hendrik, sitting at the table with a cup of coffee.

"I do hope you can make it Angie," said Georgie. "I've just been in to see Brunelda and, thank heavens, she is well and agreeable to coming with us. The nurse has promised to speak to the doctor, she's sure it will be okay."

"I don't suppose my boss will mind, he knew I would be going up to Salisbury soon anyway," replied Angie as they were about to leave.

By seven forty-five, Hendrik was in contact with Janet, his long suffering PA, requesting her to book five air tickets for Pretoria. Additionally, if that was not enough, to arrange for the boy David to be located, equipped with new clothes and enrolled, at the van Wyk's expense in the best missionary boarding school to be found near Cape Town.

With that done, Hendrik and Georgie hurried upstairs to help Brunelda and pack their own cases.

"We will have to call in at Brunelda's and get her passport," said Georgie.

"Yes, okay, and I suppose I had better let Captain Adendorff know our plans, then as soon as we hear from Janet, we'll be off," replied Hendrik.

CHAPTER SEVEN

Monday 10th February 1969
Pretoria, South Africa.

Three in the afternoon found a chartered Learjet 25 flying north east towards Pretoria. On board, in addition to the pilot and co-pilot, were Hendrik and Georgina, William and his girlfriend Angie with Brunelda sitting alone.

Hendrik's personal assistant, Janet Steyn, had done a good job in a very short time. Enquiries with scheduled airlines having proved unsuccessful she had contacted a small charter company they occasionally used in such circumstances, Capital Law, the van Wyk law practice having offices in Cape Town, Durban, Pretoria, Bloemfontein and Jo'Berg. In happier circumstances Georgina would have delighted in this expedition. Even now, she was secretly enjoying the boost to her ego of this executive travel.

There was no such secrecy from Will and Angie. This was a new and thrilling experience and they loved it.

After an hour or so of excited chatter the conversation slowly died away as the drone of the twin jet engines and the events of the previous night combined to bring sleep to the five passengers. The aircraft continued to hurtle across South Africa at four hundred and fifty miles per hour.

Shortly before six they were wakened by the instruction to

fasten their seat belts as the small jet aircraft began it's approach to Wonderboom airfield on the outskirts of Pretoria.

Georgina looked idly out of the window as she heard the engine notes change and watched the flaps and tabs operating on the wings. Listening to the voice of air traffic control she could see, at about one thousand feet, individual buildings as they circled round from the north. Suddenly, Wonderboom airport, just north of Pretoria came into view. Everyone braced themselves as the runway raced up to meet them but the Learjet touched down with only the slightest bump before quickly decelerating and turning towards the airport buildings.

"This is definitely the way to travel," said an appreciative Georgie to the others. "Although I think we should have our own aircraft, Hendrik, don't you?" she continued, laughing. "Just think, we could have the number 'GVW1' on the wings and tail."

"I don't think you can choose the number, darling, it depends on where the 'plane is based," explained Hendrik, with great patience. "Anyway, we can't afford to keep a jet aircraft just for you."

"Of course you can, Hennie," scolded his wife.."Anyway, how else am I going to learn how to fly?"

"Oh, no," grumbled Hendrik, as the others laughed.

"Well, it can't be difficult if my mother can fly a 'plane."

Two taxis were waiting nearby as the five passengers descended from the sleek Learjet. Hendrik, Georgina and Brunelda took the first cab while William and Angie followed in the second. They were soon heading south, towards the centre of Pretoria.

The offices of 'Capital Law' occupied the ground and first floors of an imposing nineteenth century building in Paul Kruger Street, off Church Square in the centre of the city.

Standing on the pavement with their suitcases, the front door was already open and a uniformed security guard hurried down the steps to greet them.

"Good evening baas," he said, approaching Hendrik. " The executive apartment is ready for you, sir."

"Thank you, please help the ladies with their luggage."

"Of course, baas." replied the guard, struggling with Brunelda and Angie's cases in each hand and Georgie's Louis Vuitton bag under one arm.

Hendrik and his sister had visited this building often, Brunelda accompanying her husband on business trips. However, this was the first time Georgina and the other two had seen the Pretoria office.

"Not bad," said Georgie, looking around as the group followed the security guard through the mahogany panelled and brass trimmed reception area toward the elevator at the far end of the hall. There was a strong aroma of furniture polish and stale cigar smoke.

"Solid and dependable, but a bit old fashioned," teased Georgina. "A bit like you, Hendrik."

"Such praise."

Arriving at the door of the first floor apartment, the security guard placed the cases inside and stood respectfully as the others entered.

"Are you on duty here all night?" enquired Hendrik.

"Oh yes baas, until seven tomorrow morning when the day man arrives."

"Thank you," said Hennie dismissing the guard.

Georgina was very pleasantly surprised by the apartment. Although in an old building, the flat had been recently re decorated in a contemporary style. The living and dining rooms were large and comfortable, the drinks cupboard full. Three luxurious bedrooms, each had en suite bathrooms. Georgie was aware there were no staff available except daily cleaners, however she was pleased to see that the kitchen was very well equipped and the cupboards all full. Anyway, she resolved, they would be eating out every day.

Georgie had soon allotted bedrooms and returning to the living room, clapped her hands.

"Well, I don't know about anyone else, but I need a drink. Come on, Hendrik, before I die of thirst."

Very soon they were all sitting comfortably with their chosen tipples.

"What shall we do tomorrow," said Georgie brightly.

"You must all enjoy yourselves but I have to work," replied Hendrik. "Someone has to earn some money."

"If one is in Pretoria, there is one place that one must not miss," piped up Brunelda to everyone's surprise.

"We must see the Voortrekkers Memorial," she continued, breaking into Afrikaans, "It is dedicated to the Afrikaaner Nation and is very impressive."

"Yes," replied Georgie, raising an eyebrow, but respectfully speaking in Afrikaans in deference to Brunelda. "We certainly mustn't miss that."

"Are there any night clubs, do you think?' she giggled, winking at the others before walking to the window and peering out. "After we've visited the Memorial, of course,"

William and Angie stifled their smiles.

"Behave, Georgina," said Henrik, frowning, but returning the wink.

The companions continued in good spirits until Brunelda announced that she would like to go to bed.

"I think that may be a good idea for all of us," agreed Hendrik. "After all I have to work tomorrow."

"Yes, we were up at seven, and have travelled half way across Africa," chimed in Angie. "All this excitement has made us all tired."

Georgina smiled at William as he eagerly agreed.

"We'll say goodnight, then," said Georgie, taking her husband's hand.

With a last round of 'good nights' and 'sleep wells' they departed to their respective rooms. Soon, all was silent with the exception of the occasional car passing by outside.

Tuesday 11th February 1969

Georgina awoke at eight the next morning to feel slightly disappointed at finding Hendrik's side of the bed already empty. He hasn't got far to go to work she thought as she got out of bed and put on a dressing gown.

Angie and Will were already in the kitchen making tea and coffee.

"Sleep well?" enquired Angie.

"Like a log, thanks," replied Georgina, sitting at the table and yawning. "I didn't even hear Hendrik go out."

"Well, what's on today, then?" asked William, rubbing his hands together.

"I suppose, we should go and have a look at this Voortrekker thing," suggested Georgie, "Brunelda, is really into all that Afrikaaner stuff and she has been through a lot."

"It's actually very good you know," enthused William as the two girls looked at him doubtfully. "It's huge, you can see it for miles and although it was only finished in 1949 it's in a sort of 'art decco' style. The wall around the outside is carved with lines of ox waggons as if they were in laager, just like the real thing. There are great gardens as well.

"Mmm," said Georgie, unenthusiastically.

"But no, this is real South African history," pleaded William, warming to the subject, "I know they were against the British and made the trek to get away from us but they were tough you know. Hundreds of Afrikaaner men, women and children going off into the unknown with all their possessions in waggons, fighting pitched battles with Zulus, really great stuff."

"That rotten picture in our dining room is all about the Battle of Blood River," remembered Georgina. "You know, the one with great great great grandmother Grizzly van Wyk or whatever her name was."

"You should be proud that the van Wyk's were a real part of the history of South Africa, Georgie," encouraged Will.

"I am, Will, truly I am," conceded Georgie, raising both hands in a gesture of surrender. "And I propose we speak in Afrikaans today just for my sister-in-law."

With that a sleepy looking Brunelda appeared at the kitchen door.

"Goeie môre, Brunelda," enquired Georgie, in her best Afrikaans. "Het jy goed slaap?

"Ja, dankie," replied Brunelda in surprise. "It's so nice to hear you speak in Afrikaans, Georgina. If you would only persevere with the language you would soon be as fluent as us."

"Then it's Afrikaans today at least, especially as we are going to the Voortrekkers Memorial," continued Georgie, smiling. "As soon as we are all ready."

Georgina had to concede that the visit was interesting and enjoyable. Brunelda was the most animated she had been since the death of her husband and took it upon herself to personally escort her English sister-in-law around the memorial. Georgie congratulated herself that the decision to converse in Afrikaans was the catalyst to a much improved relationship with Brunelda.

In fact she privately regretted her insistence on first marrying into the van Wyk family of only English being spoken in her new home. That one act, she now admitted to herself, had caused the animosity between the two women.

They returned to the Pretoria apartment in the late afternoon to find Hendrik sitting in the living room. He looked exceptionally tired.

It had been agreed that they would all dine out that evening and so the others retired to their rooms for a rest and then to prepare for the evening.

Georgie sat next to her husband. Kicking off her shoes she pulled her legs up under her.

"You look tired, darling," said Georgina, kissing Hendrik on the cheek and slipping her hand through his arm. "Do you know this is the first time I've spoken in English today?"

"That's great, dear. How was my sister? I really appreciate the effort you have made to be friends with her. Did you have a good day?"

"Hennie, she was great, she really seemed to be enjoying herself and the place was much better that I had expected. Will and Angie had a good time but they always will so long as they're together."

"That's good," said Hendrik, rubbing his eyes. "But I really need to talk to you, Georgie,"

"Save it for dinner, I'm going to have a bath."

"No, this is private, between you and me, darling."

"Wooo! Hennie."

"It's serious, Georgie," said Hendrik, speaking in a whisper. "There's something I need you to do for me."

"Not dress up in tight black leather, with boots and a whip, again," laughed Georgina out loud.

Hendrik smiled, but the grin soon faded from his face. "I need you to go to England."

"No problem, when do we go?"

"Not us... you, and you need to go tomorrow, the next day at the latest."

The smile faded from Georgina's face in an instant, she sat up and took both her husband's hands.

"What's wrong, Hendrik?" It must be something serious."

Hendrik was silent, looking up at the ceiling he took a deep breath and exhaled.

"It's very serious," commenced Hendrik, speaking quietly, his face only a few inches from his wife's, "I have...I have taken up some business partnerships that at the time appeared to be sound, but that I now fear may have been unwise. I really need you out of the country while I try to set matters right."

"Hennie, you're talking like an attorney, I'm you wife, and a partner in the firm, tell me what's going on."

"Look, the less you know, the better it will be for both of us."

"Is there another woman?"

"Of course not!"

"Don't tell me it's a man?" said Georgie, wide eyed.

Hendrik looked shocked and they both suddenly burst into stifled laughter.

"Thank goodness for that, I could have coped with another man but having an affair with some office tart would have been intolerable, what would I have said at the tennis club?"

They both stifled a renewed fit of giggles.

"This is getting us nowhere," frowned Georgie, serious again. " If you want me to leave you and go abroad on some wild goose chase I am at least entitled to an explanation. If you won't tell me the truth you force me to make assumptions and my first is that you have been avoiding tax. You are forever grumbling about the tax paid by better off whites in this country. Is that it?

"If it was only as simple as that," muttered Hendrik holding his head in his hands.

"Then what is it?...have we lost the business?... the house?... all our money?

"Not yet, but it could come to that,"

"God," said Georgie, turning Hendrik's head to face her she placed her forehead against his. "Right, the full story please."

Hendrik sighed, "I had no chance of keeping anything from you, did I? You know that I have been selected as National Party candidate in the General Election next year?"

"Go on."

"After my selection, I was introduced to some high ranking government officials, not the sort of people who's names appear in the newspapers, but influential in government circles none the less. Please don't ask me their names because I won't tell you."

"Why not."

"I'll tell you the story, but you will be safer not to know the names."

"You're worrying me but go on."

"Well, it was suggested that once in Parliament, which I was told would be a foregone conclusion, it might be possible that a chap with my opinions, who remained loyal to those who had helped him could find himself a minister within a couple of years."

"Okay, what was going to be the cost of this meteoric rise in your political fortunes?"

"Ah, Georgie, you're ahead of me as usual. There were a couple of ways in which it was suggested that I might be able to help them."

"Who's them?"

Hendrik ignored his wife's question and continued.

"The first was through my business connections. They knew that our practice involved being the legal representatives of some of the biggest corporations in South Africa and international companies doing business in South Africa. It was suggested that I might be able to pass on confidential information on how these companies were likely to react to renewed calls from the United Nations for anti apartheid sanctions."

"But Hendrik, that would be unprofessional."

"Yes, I know, but it was suggested that loyalty to my country would exonerate me from any malpractice and I would not be damaging their profits merely being patriotic."

"That's one way of looking at it and did you comply with their wishes?"

"Sometimes, when I really felt that the odds were against the country."

"And the other way?"

"Other way, what?"

"The other way they thought you might help them."

"This is probably the more serious. You remember that the ANC, the African National Congress was made illegal along with the South African Communist Party in 1960."

"Go on."

"It was explained to me that a secret police department called 'Operation Slapelose' existed to keep these organisations under surveillance using members of the 'Umkhonto we Sizwe', The Spear of the Nation, the military wing of the ANC as informants, 'Askaris' they called them."

"Terrorists, in fact."

"Yes, I suppose you could call them that, but now informing our security services and the police, of the activities of the ANC, very dangerous people, certainly. Operation Slapelose also paid them for information about the internal politics of the townships."

"And your involvement?"

"These payments were all, by necessity, cash transactions. The police had no means of doing this through their accounting system."

"Don't tell me, 'Capital Law' are the paymasters."

"Yes, darling, I would invoice the government for work we hadn't done and then use that money to pay the people on their behalf."

"Please tell me I'm wrong, Hendrik," sighed Georgina. "But Johannes, found these discrepancies and challenged you over it, didn't he?"

"Yes," whispered Hendrik shamefaced, " I went to my friends at 'Operation Slapelose' and told them that my chief accountant had found the irregularities and I wanted to get out of the arrangement. They said not to worry as they would deal with it. The rest you know." His voice tailed off.

"The murder, it was an assassination?" gasped Georgie.

"It may have been," replied Hendrik avoiding his wife's eyes.

"Of course it was," snapped Georgie.

"I suppose so. That's why I'm going to see the head of 'Slapelose' at the Union Buildings tomorrow and I will explain to him the situation and insist he closes this operation."

"And do you think he will?"

"I don't know, they just say – keep calm, you'll be a minister in three or four years but two people have been murdered already."

"Then come with me, we can leave together, tomorrow and you can deal with it from the safety of England."

"No, Georgie, I would love to, but the only chance I have is to extricate myself from this whole dreadful mess and that means me staying in South Africa and trying to convince the top people to let me out."

"Then I'll stay with you, I think you've been an idiot but you're my husband and I love you. We can fight this together," said Georgina in desperation, her voice rising barely beyond a whisper.

"Shhhh darling," said Hendrik placing a finger on her lips. "I may have to threaten to go public in which case I could be arrested. I could see them trying to sequester the business assets, that could mean the house, everything. I need you to build a power base in England."

"God, we're in trouble."

"Thank you for saying 'we', darling," said Hendrik kissing her.

"What do I need to do?"

"Go up to Salisbury with William and Angela tomorrow, after all, that was always the plan, you are just going a day earlier. I still have the Learjet here at Wonderboom. I have arranged for it to take the three of you up to Salisbury. When you arrive, drop Will and Angie off as we had planned and they can get a taxi to Meikles, I've brought the booking forward a day, but you stay aboard and fly on to Nairobi. Will and Angie will be surprised but if you tell them that, as a partner in the firm, you have to sign some papers in Kenya I don't suppose they will question the change in arrangements. To set their minds at rest, tell them to enjoy themselves on the business account and we will all join them in a couple of days. Meanwhile, you have a British Passport and I've booked you first class on a BOAC scheduled flight from Nairobi to Heathrow.

"I'll need money."

Opening an attache case on the table, Hendrik handed Georgie, US dollars 2000, a similar value in Rhodesian and a large quantity of Rand.

"You've got all this planned," she whistled.

"You will also need these," continued Hendrik, opening a black velvet bag and shaking the van Wyk diamonds onto the coffee table.

"I can't take them, they'll be stolen at the first baggage search."

"Not if you wear them. Nobody would ever believe you are wearing priceless diamonds on a flight out of Nairobi. When you get to England, put them in the bank. They are worth hundreds of thousand of pounds."

"Phew, it's a terrible risk."

"I think it will be okay, Georgie. I wouldn't put you in any more danger than I possibly have to so I have arranged for the two charter pilots to stay with you until you board the flight to London. I know them well, they are both ex South African Air Force and very good men in a tight situation. They have agreed, in fact they insisted on looking after you."

"Then what?"

"Then I will join you if I can. If I can't, you will be able to locate, should you need to and that decision must be yours, information that will compromise the police and government. You may need that to try and plea bargain my release. I have also arranged for a lot more money to be available to you. This cash, indicating the money on the table, is just to keep you going in the short term."

"Then where will I find all this loot? I'll need to know."

"I will get that information to you when you are in England. If I tell you now, and you were arrested the information could be extracted from you. I cannot tell you how all this will develop."

"Oh my God, Hendrik," gasped Georgie. "Torture?"

Hendrik took his wife in his arms, with tears in his eyes

he whispered. "These are serious people, darling, big players, they are ruthless and have access to anything they need. I was thinking of Sodium Pentathol."

"The truth drug, Jesus. And I thought life with you might be boring."

"You see, Georgie, the less you know, the less you can tell. That is why I have bought you this."

Hendrik reached once more into the attache case and produced a small leather wallet. He handed it to her and she opened it. By now nothing would surprise her.

"That's beautiful," smiled Georgie, looking at a ladies gold Cartier wristwatch. "Is it for me?"

"Of course. Wear it and don't lose it, whatever you do. When you are in England you may need it, that's all I can tell you now for your own safety, but I know your clever brain will soon work out it's significance. "

To be honest Georgina was thoroughly frightened but was determined not to show it to her husband.

"What an adventure Hendrik, I can't wait to start," she smiled, kissing him. "Now, dinner, I need a bath."

As Georgina closed the bathroom door she dropped to her knees and started to cry.

Twenty minutes later Georgie appeared from the bathroom clad in a white toweling gown. She crossed to where Hendrik was laying fully dressed on the bed, apparently dozing. Stooping to kiss him, he opened his eyes and smiled, only to receive a playful slap on his stomach.

"Come on, darling, get in that shower and stop feeling sorry for yourself," smiled Georgie, looking at her reflection in the dressing table mirror. "You need to look good if you're taking out to dinner the best looking woman in Pretoria."

Hendrik got up from the bed and looked admiringly at his young wife.

"I don't deserve you do I darling?" said Hendrik choking on his words as he stood behind her and gently kissed her neck.

"You probably don't, but you still won first prize when you married me," whispered Georgie as she turned her head to receive an increasingly passionate kiss from her husband. Pushing him away she slapped his backside.

"That's enough of that, now go and get ready." scolded Georgie, as lightheartedly as she could manage.

"I'm so sorry I've got you into all this, if only I could turn the clock back."

Georgie reached up and put her arms around his neck.

"Look, darling, when I married you I walked into a fairy tale life, I have the most beautiful home, cars, clothes, money and most importantly yourself – the man I love. I have done nothing to earn any of this...shhh" Georgie put a finger on Hendrik's lips to stop his protest. "...Apart from being stunningly beautiful, witty and intelligent of course. Now I am going to prove to you what a wife I can be. We are in this together and I shall do everything in my power to get us out of it, trust me. So let's forget our problems and have a good evening out with our friends."

"I love you."

"And I love you too."

By seven-thirty everyone was assembled in the living room of the apartment and all seemed in good spirits. The decision on where to eat had been left to Hendrik as he had the best knowledge of Pretoria.

"After all the fresh air and walking we've done today, I'm absolutely starving," said Will, still speaking in Afrikaans.

All echoing agreement, Hendrik suggested they waste no further time, he had already ordered two taxis and if they made their way down to the street he had no doubt the cabs would be waiting.

Eight o'clock found them seated at a large table in a small restaurant that specialised in genuine South African food and fine Cape Wines.

"What an excellent choice, Hendrik," said Georgie, looking around the comfortable restaurant, before picking up the menu.

"After all that South African history today," suggested Hendrik, 'I think it only right that we should have some good chargrilled and marinated steak."

"I like the sound of that," said Brunelda. "I have an appetite for the first time since…" her voice trailed away.

"I agree," said Georgie, hurriedly squeezing Brunelda's hand. The others nodded in agreement.

"What a carnivorous lot we are," laughed Angie.

Hendrik called the waiter and placed the order.

"Monsiers, Medames, quelle cuisson votre steaks?" asked the rather pompous waiter.

"This is good," laughed Hendrik, turning to the others. "We are all speaking Afrikaans in a restaurant in Pretoria and we get a French waiter!"

Everyone joined in the laughter, much to the dismay of the maitre D.

"If they speak in French it makes the bill bigger," said Will.

"Looks like a rooinek to me and I should know," said Georgie, joining the fun.

Hendrik held up his hand for silence.

"Saignant, s'il vous plait."

"Le vin, monsieur?"

"I've had enough of this," laughed Hendrik. "I see no reason for ordering good South African wine in French. We'll have the Rustenberg Cabernet Sauvignon, all the way from

Stellenbosch, and bring two bottles, we're in the mood."

"Merci monsieur." Glad to escape, the waiter hurried away with the order.

"Let us hope this will be a memorable meal," said Hendrik, looking around the table at his four companions. "Because tomorrow morning we must part for a few days."

Angela and Brunelda looked up in surprise, Georgina and William already had some idea of Hendrik's plan but only Georgina was aware of the reasons.

Hendrik held his tongue for a few moments as the waiter returned with the bottles of Rustenberg. Showing the bottle label with dignified ceremony he poured out a small quantity. Georgina's husband was clearly irritated by this interruption but resigned himself to the ritual tasting as the others watched in amusement. Swirling the ruby coloured liquid around the glass he raised it to his nose in time honoured tradition and breathed in the aroma. Smiling at his companions over the top of the glass he took a slip.

"Thank you, that will be fine," said Hendrik, impatient for the waiter's absence.

Glasses were then charged, the nearly empty bottle placed on the table with it's replete companion and the waiter finally retired.

Lifting his glass to eye level, Hendrik looked around the table making eye contact with Brunelda, Will and Angie in turn and finally with his wife.

"To us."

"To us," responded the others, taking their first sips in unison and chinking their glasses together.

There followed general words of praise for the quality of the wine as Georgina reached across and squeezed her husband's hand.

"As I was saying," continued Hendrik. "Tomorrow we must part for a few days. I have more business to complete in Pretoria and I am hoping my sister will stay on to keep me company."

A smile from Brunelda confirmed her agreement, she was clearly pleased at the thought of having her brother to herself for a while.

"Meanwhile, Georgina, William and Angela will pave the way up to Salisbury for us older ones," said Hendrik.

"Why don't we wait and all go together?" interrupted Angie.

"The rooms are already booked at Meikles Hotel," snapped Hendrik, quickly. "And I think that if none of us show up they might just be rebooked and we wouldn't want that."

"It's a bit like 'The Lord of the Rings'," said Georgie, glancing at her husband. "You know, Gandalf and the Hobbits setting off on an adventure."

"Mind who you're calling a Hobbit," smiled Will, raising his glass.

"I've no idea what a Hobbit is or what you young people are talking about," said Brunelda, who had never read Tolkein. "But I will be happy to stay behind for a couple of days with my brother, while you youngsters go dancing in Salisbury."

"So that's decided," continued a relieved Hendrik. "And you Hobbits will be pleased to know that at enormous expense to the company, I have managed to keep the chartered Learjet at Wonderboom, so you will travel in style."

A cheer went up from Will, Angie and Georgie at this news.

"We've had the thing so long Hennie, you might just as well buy it," laughed Georgie, keen to keep the conversation upbeat.

Hendrik wagged a finger at his wife in mock disapproval as he refilled all the glasses.

"Georgina, behave," he smiled.

Glances exchanged between husband and wife showed a

private satisfaction that the change of plan had been accepted without any awkward questions. Now, as the waiter returned, all thoughts turned to the food now being placed before the diners. Hendrik felt assured that with the assistance of a few more bottles of Rustenberg, he could now relax and forget about the future for a few more cherished hours.

For the next few minutes all was silent as the hungry diners attacked their meals.

"Just replace the wine as the bottles are emptied," ordered Hendrik, catching the waiter's eye.

The little dinner party progressed very well, the meal was declared excellent by everyone and the wine kept flowing. Every once in a while Georgina's eyes caught her husband's and he would wink at her and smile. Georgie could not help but acknowledge to herself the irony that on the eve of her secret departure from South Africa to an uncertain and possibly dangerous future, she couldn't at this moment be more happy and content.

"And another thing I thought was wonderful at the Voortrekkers Memorial," declared Brunelda, in a voice that was slightly too loud, betraying the two, or was it even three glasses of Rustenberg she had consumed and interrupting William, who was giving his opinions of the threat from communist terrorism, "Was the beautiful polished marble cenotaph in the centre of the building with it's simple and touching inscription, 'ONS VIR JOU SUID AFRIKA' 'We for Thee South Africa'."

Everyone, including Georgina, nodded in agreement.

"Our next toast then," said Georgie, raising her glass, "Ons vir jou Suid Afrika."

Brunelda beamed as everyone stood and raised their glasses.

"Ons vir jou Suid Afrika."

"The amazing thing is," continued Brunelda, as everyone resumed their seats and enjoying the attention of her captive audience. "Every year on the 16th of December, the anniversary of the Battle of Blood River in 1838, a shaft of sunlight beams down through the roof and exactly strikes the centre of the cenotaph, isn't that wonderful?"

Brunelda smiled at each of her companions in turn, everyone agreeing that it was truly wonderful.

"Unless it's cloudy," muttered Georgie into her glass, struggling to subdue a grin.

"I'm sorry, darling, I didn't catch that," enquired Brunelda.

"I was just thinking of that beautiful painting of our van Wyk ancestor loading a rifle in the heat of the battle that hangs in my dining room back in Cape Town," replied Georgie, thinking fast.

"Oh yes, I do envy you that picture," replied Brunelda, taking another sip from her glass.

Georgina stretched her hand across the table to touch Brunelda's fingers. "Would you accept the picture, darling, as a mark of our renewed and strengthened friendship," Georgina purred, studiously avoiding her husband's glance.

"I would love it, but I know how much it means to you and Hendrik."

"Take it as a mark of our friendship," smirked Georgie.

Brunelda, rose unsteadily and moved around the table to embrace first Georgina and then her brother who was clearly overcome with the emotion of the moment, holding his napkin to his eyes.

As Brunelda returned to her seat, Georgie leaned across to her husband and whispered "That's the cost of me helping you."

The others looked on in surprise as the couple dissolved into a fit of giggling.

The evening continued in this successful vein until the last ports and brandies were finished. Hendrik requested the waiter to call two taxis as he settled the bill.

As they left the restaurant the second of the two cabs drew up and they were soon on their way back to Paul Kruger Street. Pulling up outside the van Wyk offices just after eleven, the vigilant security guard already had the front doors open for them and they were soon safely ensconced in the comfortable living room of the first floor apartment.

"Anyone for a nightcap?" asked Hendrik, holding a bottle of cognac in his hand.

"Not for me," replied Brunelda, "I'm off to bed, good night everyone."

Angie took Brunelda's lead and also wished everyone a good night and thanked Hendrik for the dinner. Hendrik, Georgina and William sat quietly with their brandies. Will confessed to having probably drunk too much and Hendrik and Georgie readily agreed although both knew that each other was perfectly sober. With little further conversation they bade each other good night and made their ways to bed.

Closing the bedroom door, Hendrik sat next to his wife on the edge of the bed.

"Well done, you," said Hennie quietly kissing his wife on the cheek.

"Well done you, too," replied Georgie, looking at her husband. "I think we carried that through as well as we could have expected."

Georgie wanted to make some humorous remarks about the evening, especially the gift of the painting of the Battle of Blood River to her sister-in-law but somehow it all seemed so trivial. After all, they had only one more night together.

"Before we go to bed, darling, I must ask you to sign a few

documents," sighed Hendrik. "I have made arrangements for your personal bank account to be transferred to London, that's your money and I don't want you to lose it by sequestration."

Georgina looked on passively as Hendrik fetched his attache case and removed the relevant documents which Georgina signed without comment.

"I have also arranged for considerable amounts of money to be placed in various private bank accounts in England for your use. Access to this money will be made apparent to you when you reach London," he continued, without enthusiasm.

"Who else will know where I am?" asked Georgie, quietly, staring at the floor.

"Only my PA, Janet Steyn, trust her if you cannot get through to me. I have arranged suitable financial packages for her and Brunelda should the company go down." His voice trailing off to a whisper.

"I'm just so worried about all this cryptic stuff. Can't you just give me the information I will need now?

Hendrik became agitated, "I've explained all this, it really is safer for you to know nothing until you get to London. Anyway, I hope to join you in a couple of days, but should that not be possible, you will need to make your own decision whether to seek out this information, the possession of it may compromise your own safety. Trust in Janet's advice but the decision can only be yours."

"I can't say I understand but I'll do as you ask, darling," smiled Georgina, squeezing Hendrik's hand. "But what about Angie and your sister if you fly out to London?"

"Janet Steyn will have to take care of them. We must look after ourselves."

Still fully clothed Hendrik and Georgina stretched out on top of the bed, side by side and hand in hand. Georgie had intended to use all her considerable feminine allure to make this last night together something memorable. Something most men could only fantasize about. However, with the time still a few minutes before midnight, the strain of the last few days, culminating in the shattering news her husband had imparted to her not six hours previously was finally taking it's toll. The intolerable burden of maintaining a facade of careless good nature, of always having a witty remark, of always looking stunning, of keeping the group together and amused, now finally overcame her. The enormity of the potential disaster that confronted them, that she had managed to force to the back of her mind and made worse by the need to keep it from the others, now rushed forward and overwhelmed her.

Within minutes and still fully dressed, they were both fast asleep.

CHAPTER EIGHT

Wednesday 12th February 1969
Pretoria, SA
★
Salisbury, Rhodesia
★
Nairobi, Kenya

By 7.30 the next morning Hendrik, Angie and William were in the kitchen drinking their first coffees of the day. Suitcases were packed and standing in the corner. The earliness of the hour was the last subterfuge that Hendrik needed to make. Clearly it would not have been necessary to start this early had they only been flying up to Salisbury, especially as they had the use of a chartered aircraft. Fortunately, no comments were made and Angie and William seemed keen to get started. Only Brunelda was still in bed.

A few minutes later Georgina stepped into the kitchen dropping her suitcase in the doorway.

"Goeie môre, everyone," she smiled.

Hendrik stepped forward and kissed her. Nobody was surprised that Georgie was looking striking in tight black trousers that hugged her figure, high heeled black boots, white silk top and a black zipped motor cycle style leather jacket with the deep collar turned up level with the top of her ears. She had a small Louis Vuitton cabin bag over one shoulder. Georgie took a few sips of coffee but now that the time to depart had arrived she was keen to be gone.

Anticipating his wife's mood, Hendrik picked up the telephone and requested a taxi.

Meanwhile, as Brunelda was still in bed, Georgina quickly put on the van Wyk diamonds as she had agreed with Hendrik the previous night.

"If everyone is ready, I think we should make our way downstairs." said Hendrik, trying to sound upbeat and cheerful but failing miserably. Only his wife noticed the change in manner as she glanced in his direction.

Arriving in the street, the taxi was already waiting. The driver loaded the cases in the boot as Will and Angie took the rear seats. Hendrik stepped forward and took his wife in his arms, kissing her passionately. Before he could kiss her again Georgie had ducked out from his embrace and was getting into the front passenger seat of the cab.

Hendrik crouched on the pavement by the taxi door as Georgina wound down the window. He stared at his wife through grief stricken eyes.

"Georgie, I…," commenced Hendrik.

"…Bye Darling," said Georgina, smiling as she reached out with her left hand to stroke his face. Before he had a chance to reply Georgina had withdrawn her hand and turned to face the driver, "Wonderboom Airfield please driver."

As the taxi began to pull away from the kerb, Georgie looked back towards her husband and smiled again. The cab gathered speed as Will and Angie waved through the back window. Georgina, in the front seat looked resolutely forward. They were gone.

No one spoke as the taxi made it's way north through the early morning streets of the city centre. After five minutes, and perhaps sensing Georgina's subdued mood, William broke the silence.

"Rhodesia here we come," said William and the two girls laughed for no apparent reason.

"Miekles Hotel is supposed to be the best in Africa." said Angela brightly.

"Not much competition up there I'd have thought," replied Georgie, trying hard to be cheerful, "I wouldn't be surprised if it had a thatched roof." The remark was greeted by genuine laughter this time, even from the driver. The irrepressible Georgina van Wyk was back in control.

Any more conversation was suddenly drowned out by the discordant wail of a siren. A plain blue four door saloon drew level with them very closely on the offside. A small revolving blue lamp on the vehicle's roof filled the inside of the taxi with an unearthly blue pulsating light. The front seat passenger of the other vehicle was waving the taxi to pull over.

Stopping by the nearside kerb they waited while the other car pulled up in front and the passenger, a white man about thirty five years of age wearing a grey suit walked back and stood by the passenger door.

Georgina wound down the window, looked at the man on the pavement but said nothing.

The man in the grey suit lowered his head to the window.

"Please get out of the car, mevrou," he said calmly.

"No." responded Georgina, equally calmly as she pressed down the door lock button and commenced winding up the window.

Visibly rattled, he quickly placed his hand on the window, "Mevrou, I am a police officer, please get out of the car."

"No." replied Georgina again, leaving the window only a few inches open.

Fumbling in an inside pocket the man produced an identity card and held it to the window.

"Now we're getting somewhere. Why have you stopped me, Sergeant Wessells?"

"I would like to ask you a few questions."

"What about?"

"Where are you going?"

"That's my business." continued Georgina remaining calm, "And now I'll ask you a question, if you are a police officer why are you not in uniform and why is your car not marked?"

"I am a detective,"

"Congratulations, now if you don't mind we have a plane waiting."

"Don't try and get clever with me Mrs van Wyk." said the detective, his suave manner beginning to crack.

"I'm not trying to get clever, officer, I am clever and if you know who I am I suggest you contact your superior, Captain Marius Adendorff at your Cape Town office and he will tell you exactly where I am going. It's no secret, except apparently from you."

"Mrs. van Wyk, Rhodesia isn't far away and the arm of the South African Government is very long."

"Ah, so you knew where I was going all the time."

"Where is your husband, madam?" asked Wessells, trying another line of questioning.

"You know I'm not going to answer that, so if you don't mind, I really need to get on." With that she wound up the window indicating that the interview was terminated.

Wessells hesitated for a few moments before walking back to his car and getting in. It slowly pulled away.

Georgina turned to the alarmed looking cabbie.

"Please drive on, I think we may be a little late now."

"Crikey! said William, "What was that all about?"

"I've no idea," smiled Georgie sweetly, "My fame seems to have spread."

Driving on in silence, Georgina was secretly furious with herself as she went over the events of the last few minutes. Her towering arrogance in allowing herself to humiliate Sergeant Wessells in that way had very nearly blown the whole plan in the first few minutes. Why, oh why, could she not have adopted her usual strategy when stopped for speeding in her Jaguar, namely, smile sweetly at the officer, offer up her driver's licence, show a bit of leg and keep quiet. It was a plan that had served her well on numerous occasions in the past, but now, when the stakes were infinitely higher she had to open her big mouth and let her enormous ego run riot. Idiot, she thought. If, by chance, she had got away with it this time and there was no guarantee, then she promised herself that she would be much more careful in any future dealings with the security services.

Eventually the entrance to Wonderboom airfield came into view and the taxi slowed to a halt adjacent to the red and white chevroned security kiosk. A similarly painted barrier blocked the road.

A little glass door slid open in the side of the kiosk and a security guard peered out. The taxi driver sat back in his seat allowing Georgie to lean awkwardly across him.

"Georgina van Wyk and two companions flying to Salisbury by chartered flight this morning." she said in a raised voice, hoping the man in the box could hear.

Apparently, he had heard and without further comment the barrier was raised electrically and the taxi moved forward towards the airport buildings.

Arriving at the front entrance William was first out of the taxi and had soon obtained a porter and trolley to unload the baggage from the vehicle boot. Georgina paid the cab driver including a generous tip, after all, she would not need all these Rands for much longer.

Following the porter into the building the trio looked around the small departure lounge. As they approached the only departure desk that appeared to be staffed, Georgie was suddenly aware of three men hurrying in her direction. One was tall, slim, about fifty years of age with short well trimmed grey hair and an enormous, outlandish handlebar moustache of the sort once worn by British fighter pilots in the Second World War. He was immaculately dressed in a three piece navy blue pin striped suit and his waistcoat sported a heavy gold watch chain. His ensemble was completed by a white shirt, a rather loudly striped tie and black shoes polished to a mirror finish. The other two were in the uniforms of the South African Immigration Service.

Georgina felt the panic rise in her throat, her stomach churned. Urging herself to keep calm she stopped as they stepped into her path.

"Mrs. van Wyk?" he enquired in a cultured South African accent.

Georgie fought to control her rising panic, resolving to answer all reasonable questions politely and succinctly.

"Yes, I am Georgina van Wyk."

"Let me introduce myself, I am Orlando Meyer and I'm the Chief Immigration Officer for the Pretoria and Johannesburg region." He held out his hand.

Polite, but dangerous she thought, taking the proffered hand and saying nothing. Be very careful.

"I was told by security that you had arrived, so I've hurried down to greet you and invite you along to our special facility for VIP's.

Alarm bells continued to ring in Georgie's head. Special facility? She didn't like the sound of that.

"So, if you would like to point out your luggage, one of my

colleagues will bring it along with us, while my other colleague will look after your companions."

"Very well. Will this take long?"

"Oh, I shouldn't think so. A few questions, a little look in your bags and you will be back with you friends. If you would like to come this way."

Georgina smiled across at Will and Angie, "I'll see you shortly then."

Orlando Meyer led the way into a small room leading off from the administrative offices of the airport. On entering, Georgina's nose immediately wrinkled at the smell of stale sweat hanging in the stuffy atmosphere. There was no pretence of comfort, the walls were painted brick, the floor grey, unforgiving concrete. A grey metal desk stood in the centre of the room, with two wooden chairs and a large metal table at one side. The only other furnishing was a telephone attached to the wall. Apart from the door they had entered by there was a second in the opposite wall leading who knows where. One small barred window admitted a weak light through it's dirty obscured glass. Georgina noticed that both doors were now closed and secured by press button combination locks. So much for a VIP suite, this was a detention room she thought with alarm.

The uniformed Immigration Officer placed Georgina's large suitcase on the metal table and stood in front of it.

"Please take a seat," said Meyer, offering her the chair in front of the desk while he sat opposite her, the desk between.

Georgina sat, her nerves still on edge.

"First, may I get you a coffee, tea perhaps?" commenced Meyer.

"Thank you, no."

"Okay, then if you're quite comfortable, let's start. Why, may I ask, are you travelling up to Salisbury?"

"My cousin, William Robinson, whom you've just met has enrolled in the British South Africa Police. He's due to start his training at Morris Barracks in a few days so my husband thought it would be nice if we accompanied him and his fiancé and made a bit of a holiday of it."

"Quite so and may I enquire where your husband is this morning?"

"He has to remain at our Pretoria Office for a short while longer, he intends to join us later today or tomorrow."

"You see, that wasn't too difficult was it? My problem is trying to understand why you were so obstructive when the police spoke to you earlier."

So that was it, she feared the incident that morning would come back to haunt her and it had. Just keep calm, subdue the ego and think before you speak.

"Quite simply, the police officer frightened me. I was tired and I wasn't expecting to be stopped. I thought we were going to be robbed. Added to that the officer was rude and aggressive."

Damn, that was a mistake, don't start making personal attacks.

"I'm very sorry to hear that, I do hope that you haven't considered me rude madam, I cannot abide rudeness, for any reason."

"Of course not."

"Good, then that little problem is resolved, Let us get on. I have to say I was just admiring those rather splendid diamonds you are wearing."

"Oh, they're nothing, just costume jewellery, fakes."

Meyer leaned forward, steepling his thin, manicured, almost feminine fingers as he stared closely at Georgie's throat.

"Mrs van Wyk, I know very little about jewellery, but it occurs to me that wearing fake diamonds that size would be rather vulgar and as I do not believe you have a vulgar atom in your body, I can only conclude that I am looking at a cool quarter of a million dollars. They're real, aren't they?

Gripped by panic she forced herself back into her chair in a subconscious attempt to preserve her body space, stiletto heels scraping noisily on the hard floor. This man was clever, maybe her intellectual equal, what should she say? She needed to answer quickly.

"Yes, they are real, you have good taste Mr Meyer. They are the van Wyk diamonds and have been in the family since 1880. My husband asked me to take them to Salisbury as we hope to establish a Rhodesian associate. He is keen for me to create an impression. It was his suggestion that I wear them and claim they were fakes, for security you understand."

"Good advice, but if I may say so, you do not need diamonds to make an impression."

"Thank you,"

All this time Georgina had been aware that her suitcase had been opened and searched by the uniformed officer. Out of the corner of her eye, Georgina saw him close the case and shake his head in the direction of Mr Meyer.

"I notice you have rather a lot of luggage for just a few days."

"Mr Meyer, without being immodest, I have noticed that the South African press take an inordinate interest in my activities, you may perhaps have seen my photograph in the newspapers. As a representative of my husband's company, I try to look my best on all occasions, however casual. I suppose I am a bit like you, always on duty."

"Bravo, Mrs van Wyk, like me, always on duty," laughed Meyer, clapping his hands. "And what a success you make of it. You look stunning this morning."

"Thank you, I try my best."

"Just a quick look in your shoulder bag and I think we can get you on your way," smiled Meyer, rubbing his hands together enthusiastically.

Georgina, for all her intelligence was still unsure how this interview was going. She picked up the Louis Vuitton bag and passed it across the table.

Meyer had a quick check inside producing her wallet. Flicking through the various sets of bank notes he looked across the table.

"Rather a lot of money for a short holiday?"

Try as she may, Georgie's arrogance broke loose.

"That's a rather subjective question, I would think two or three thousand dollars just about right for a few days away, it all depends on one's standards." Georgina instantly regretted her remark.

"Touché, laughed Meyer, jumping to his feet and clapping his hands. "What a superb answer,"

"Thank you," was her guarded and bemused reply.

"Well, I think that's all, Mrs. van Wyk. Thank you for answering my questions so patiently and I'm sorry to have detained you. It's been a pleasure meeting you and I hope you enjoy your stay in Rhodesia."

Turning to his assistant he continued. "Please reunite Mrs van Wyk with her friends."

Punching the exit code into the door, Meyer held it open for Georgina to pass. "Good bye again and please remember that we are always vigilant in the protection of South Africa, whatever the threat."

"Yes, I know Mr Meyer, that is why I choose to live here," she replied with a smile.

Out in the public area she soon saw that Will and Angie had already passed through the departure desk and were waiting on the other side. They waved and Georgie waved back in acknowledgement. With the assistance of the uniformed Immigration Officer, Georgina was through the departure gate in as much time as it took to stamp in her passport 'VERTREK / LEFT and the date.

"God, what was all that about, what did Biggles have to say?" asked Will and Angie excitedly.

"I'm really not quite sure," pondered Georgie. "But I think I've just been gently reminded not to be rude to policemen."

"Really," said Will, looking puzzled. "Just so long as you know what's going on then."

"Forget about that now," interrupted Angie, excitedly pointing across towards the exit door. "Here come our two pilots if I'm not mistaken…Hey!… Hello boys…over here!"

Georgina slapped Angie's arm, "Angie, people are looking!"

"Sorry, but they are good looking, aren't they?"

Looking in the direction that Angie was pointing Georgina recognised the two pilots, both dressed in smartly pressed navy blue uniforms and hurrying quickly towards them.

"Mrs van Wyk," said the first of the pilots, "I'm Captain Jan Kruger and this is First Officer Cameron Munro, we've been your crew since Cape Town. Is everything okay? As we'd just heard that you'd been dragged off for questioning."

"Thanks for your concern, but it's fine. I was taken off to a grotty little room they called their VIP suite, but was more like a cell to have my bags searched and a little chat with the Chief Immigration Officer. Anyway, he seemed satisfied with my answers, so here we are."

"Mmmm," said Kruger, rubbing his chin thoughtfully and looking at his companion. "Was that the smart chap with the handlebar moustache?"

Georgina nodded.

"Yes, we'd seen him earlier," continued Kruger, First Officer

Munro nodding in agreement. "Whoever, he is I can assure you he's not the Chief or any other Immigration Officer. You must understand, we know all those boys and girls, what with flying around SA for a living."

Georgina nodded, she was now all attention to what the airman was saying.

"You see, we'd just completed our pre flight checks," said Cameron Munro, taking up the story. "We were coming in for a coffee and to look out for you, when we saw this chap, couldn't miss him really with that 'tache, getting out from the back seat of a police car. The way the police driver was jumping around we guessed he was pretty important."

"So, we thought no more of it," said Kruger. "Until we heard one of the maintenance chaps saying that a fantastic looking girl had been dragged off by some smart old boy with a moustache and two Immigration Officers."

"We guessed the girl was you," concluded Munro, turning a little red as he looked at Georgie.

Georgina smiled in acknowledgement of the complement and Angie let out a little giggle as she looked across at her friend.

The story concluded, everyone looked at Georgie. She remained silent for a few moments. She couldn't help thinking that Hendrik may have been right to take the extreme precautions he had arranged for her. These shadowy, higher authorities her husband was dealing with, whoever they may be, were clearly following her movements. She was suddenly doubtful of Hendrik's chances of calling them off without serious implications for himself.

This morning's events were a clear indication that her movement's were being observed but what alarmed Georgina most was her fear that, like a cat with a mouse, she was being allowed just so much rope before being dragged back. Her only course of action now was to press on and trust to luck.

"Thanks for your concern boys," said Georgie, snapping back to life. "Whoever he was, I'm okay now and ready to get on, so next stop Salisbury."

As the group walked across the short distance of tarmac towards the waiting LearJet, followed by a porter, pushing a trolly with their cases, Georgina took the opportunity of observing her two pilots. After all, according to Hendrik, they had apparently been eager to accept the responsibility of seeing her onto the flight from Nairobi to London.

Captain Jan Kruger was probably in his late thirties, short fair hair, slim, fit and around 5'10" tall. Georgina, thought that from the width of his shoulders he probably had a good muscular physique under the uniform jacket that sported four gold rings on each sleeve. Quite a hunk really, she smiled to herself.

As a contrast, First Officer Munro, with three gold rings on his sleeve to denote his subordinate rank, was a couple of years younger, perhaps an inch shorter and dark haired. Munro, although clearly fit, was perhaps a little more stocky in build than his colleague.

All in all, Georgie considered herself well satisfied with her chaperones, only praying that she would not have to call upon their services beyond their responsibility as aircrew.

Arriving at the LearJet, the baggage was soon stowed away and the three companions seated in the small, luxurious, eight seat cabin.

Georgina was amused that on this leg of their journey, the door to the flight deck remained open.

Almost before they had got their seat belts buckled the small jet aircraft started to taxi gently forward. Georgina was interested to see forward onto the flight deck where the two pilots were both busily engaged in the procedure of take off. Turning onto the main runway the Learjet rolled to a halt and waited like a sprinter at the start of a race. Through the open cabin door, Georgina heard Captain Kruger speak to Air Traffic Control, she saw practiced hands moving quickly and confidently across the myriad of controls in front of and between the pilots. The muted roar of the two rear mounted jet engines suddenly increased to drown out any conversation. Through her feet she felt the whole airframe vibrating as if straining against a huge, restraining hand. Then, with the engines screaming, the aircraft lurched forward. Rapidly gathering speed, Georgie felt herself forced back into her seat by the tremendous acceleration, much more than her 'E' type could ever manage, even with William driving.

In parallel with the noise and high pitched vibration from the engines she was now aware of the much lower and more intrusive bumping and vibration from the undercarriage as it charged across the irregularities of the runway. Then came that moment when the aircraft was suddenly free of the ground and soaring joyously upward into it's element, the open sky.

Georgina looked at her new Cartier wristwatch, it was 9.45.

After a few minutes the sound of the engines dropped back to a more muted roar as the LearJet levelled out into it's flightpath, north and a little east towards Salisbury in neighbouring Rhodesia, the other side of the Limpopo.

Captain Kruger squeezed through the narrow doorway into the passenger compartment, leaving his colleague, Cameron Munro with control of the plane.

"Good take off, Captain," said Will, enthusiastically.

"Thank you," smiled Kruger. "These are great little planes you know, but they need careful handling, there's quite a lot of power in a small airframe so they can be a bit unforgiving."

"Would you like to come up onto the flight deck and see what's going on?" continued Kruger to William and Angie.

"Yes, please," beamed Will. "I'd love that."

"I'll take you first then, Mr Robinson, then you, Miss Arnold as there's not much space up front. We've got nearly two hours before we arrive at Salisbury so there's plenty of time."

Kruger looked back inquiringly at Georgina who smiled and waved her hand.

"You all enjoy yourselves, I'm going to have a sleep." With that she reclined her comfortable seat and in a few moments the stress and tiredness of the last couple of days together with the relief of being free of Pretoria, once again overtook her and she fell deeply asleep.

Georgie awoke with a start as Cameron Munro handed her a cup of coffee.

"Better sit up now Mrs Van Wyk, we'll be starting our approach to Salisbury in about ten minutes."

"Good heavens," exclaimed Georgie, taking the cup and looking at her watch. "It's 11.15, I feel I've been asleep for hours."

"Yes, and you've missed all the fun," said an exuberant William. "Both Angie and I have had a turn at flying the plane."

"God," frowned Georgie. "No wonder I had nightmares, does this 'plane have parachutes?"

"It was all fine," assured Cameron. "You can have a turn on the flight up to Nairobi, Mrs van Wyk."

Georgina flashed an angry glance at Munro, before realising that Will and Angie would have to know the truth within the next half hour whatever was said.

"Who's going to Nairobi?" asked Angie, with a questioning look at Will.

"There's really no drama, Angie, I meant to tell you earlier but with all the excitement I forgot, then when we took off I fell asleep. Hendrik has asked me to go up to Nairobi and sign some papers for a client. It's all connected with the business that has delayed him in Pretoria. I know it's a nuisance and I'm sorry but Hendrik and I should both be back with you late tonight or tomorrow at the latest."

"Georgie," pouted Angie.

"Come on Angie, don't tell me you wouldn't like a night out alone in Salisbury with Will," smiled Georgie. "And on a 'Capital Law' expense account."

"Oh, we couldn't do that, I mean, charge it to your firm," insisted Will, shaking his head.

"Why not? I do it all the time and meanwhile, I will be making lots of money in Kenya."

Georgina was relieved as once again, a change of plan had not appeared to unduly alarm her companions.

Cameron Munro returned to the flight deck and seat belts were fastened. Georgina could hear the Salisbury air traffic control on the radio as the LearJet banked to line up with the approach to Salisbury airport. The touchdown was almost imperceptible and Georgina could feel herself being thrust into the safety belt by the rapid deceleration of the aircraft.

After five minutes taxiing, the LearJet drew up near to the arrivals building. Angie and Will were soon disembarked with much kissing and hugging and promises to see each other soon. Georgina felt guilty in wishing them gone, she felt she was slowly breaking under the strain of being cheerful and upbeat. She felt grubby, tired and hungry.

As soon as Will and Angie had departed and the aircraft was secured, Jan and Cameron joined Georgie in the passenger compartment.

"I hope you don't mind me saying so," said Jan Kruger, looking concerned. "But you look all in Mrs van Wyk,"

"I'm exhausted," she replied with a weak smile. "And the biggest part of my journey is still ahead."

"I'm sorry to let the cat out of the bag by mentioning Nairobi," apologised Cameron.

"Don't be. They had to know anyway, at least you didn't mention I was going on to London. That would have caused some problems."

"We have to refuel before we can take off," continued Jan. "Nairobi is over 1900 clicks and our range is only 2500 so we need to be full up. This would normally be a good opportunity for you to have a wash and a meal but we cannot really let you off the plane unless you want to go all through the business of customs and immigration."

"God, no," frowned Georgie. "All I want is to be safely on that London flight. Is there a chance one of you could get me something to eat and I'll make use of your little WC on the plane."

"Yes, of course Mrs van Wyk," said Cameron. "Anything special to eat."

"No, just surprise me," Georgina replied, handing Cameron some money. "And get yourselves whatever you want."

'One other thing, it would make me really happy if you boys would call me Georgina or Georgie."

Both men were clearly delighted to comply with Georgina's request.

The Learjet was taxied forward to the refuelling bays and while Jan supervised the replenishment, Cameron disappeared in search of food. Within an hour and a half of landing, the aircraft was climbing into the skies bound for Nairobi. It was still only 1.00pm.

As the 'plane levelled out and flew on in the direction of Kenya, Jan Kruger released his seat belt. Easing himself out of the pilot's seat he stepped back into the passenger compartment.

"Would you like to eat now, Georgina," he enquired, "I'm afraid it's only cold, but there's some very fresh croissants, butter, jam and some fresh orange juice, what else? yes, assorted sandwiches and chocolate bars."

"Thank you, Jan, that sounds great, will you join me?"

"I'd love to, just let me take some food forward to Cameron, you know that we mustn't eat the same, in case one of us is ill?"

"Heavens, yes, I don't want to end up flying the thing myself!"

Jan Kruger took a selection of food forward to Cameron Munro on the flight deck. Cameron had been careful to make his purchases from a selection of food outlets in the airport and the choices the two men made for their meals reflected the need to avoid any chance of them both suffering from food poisoning or stomach upsets.

Returning to the passenger compartment, Georgina was surprised as Jan rearranged the seat configuration into what he called 'Conference Mode' by reversing the backrest of the seat opposite Georgina so that they faced each other across a small tabletop that let out from the wall.

Guessing that Captain Kruger had pulled rank on his colleague for the privilege of sharing a meal with her, she was amused how her flagging spirits rose with the presence of an attentive and good looking man.

She was surprised how good the croissants were, or was she just particularly hungry? Having done the food justice she settled back with a glass of fresh orange juice and watched as Jan cleared the paper plates and other debris of the meal into a large waste bag.

"Well, I feel better for that," said Jan, rubbing his hands and smiling."

"Yes, it was great, just what I needed. How long to Nairobi?"

"It's about three hours, I've tried to plan our arrival so that you have as little waiting time as possible. Your husband did explain to me that you needed to get away to England with as little fuss and attention as possible, so Cameron and I will stay with you and try to smooth your way through Kenyan Customs."

"You really are very kind, both of you, and I do appreciate it," said Georgie giving Jan one of her most disarming smiles.

"It's a great pleasure, I assure you."

The conversation continued for some time, Jan Kruger was clearly interested in the purpose of his delightful passenger's clandestine departure from Africa. Enquiries that Georgina was able to brush aside with charm and consummate ease.

"Come on, Georgie," said Jan, emboldened by their conversation together. "Have a go at flying the 'plane."

Georgie smiled her agreement and the two made their way into the cockpit. Jan offered her his seat and she sat next to First Officer Munro.

Even with all her troubles she found the view breathtaking as both men vied with her in explaining the complexities of flying a twin engined jet.

"My mother can fly you know. She's a partner in a small aerial photography business in west London."

"Really, what 'planes do they operate?" enquired Cameron, with interest.

"Not 'planes in the plural, plane in the singular," laughed Georgie. "I think it's a Beagle Airedale."

"Nice little jobs those," said Cameron with obvious insincerity.

"To be honest," continued Georgie. "She's not a natural pilot, like you two. I think she hates it. She's happier flying a desk, but when her business partner had to give up his pilot's licence through ill health, it was a case of learn or lose the business.

Both men agreed that Georgie's mother had done remarkably well.

Reaching into the top pocket of her jacket, she handed each pilot one of her mother's business cards.

"In fact, boys," said Georgie, warming to her subject. "If either of you are ever in London, then please look us up. We may be able to offer you a days flying for pay, but even if we cannot do that I think I can assure you of a good night out in London at least."

Clearly delighted with the possibility of a further meeting with this delightful and glamorous young woman, both men carefully pocketed the contact details.

Georgina was enjoying the company of these two airman and the conversation on the flight deck continued for an hour or more. When Cameron Munro eventually vacated control of the aircraft to his colleague, Georgie felt it only fair that she should accompany him back into the passenger lounge where they continued to talk. He was clearly delighted as she chatted with him about her early life in England. It had always been a policy of Georgina's to make friends wherever possible, on the principle that they might one day come in useful.

About 3.30pm Cameron returned to his seat on the flight deck as they made their first contact with Nairobi air traffic control and by 4.00pm they were on the final approach to Nairobi airport.

After another near perfect landing, the LearJet was slowly taxied to it's allocated bay near the arrivals building. With the engines eventually cut, Cameron opened the passenger compartment door and as if by magic, a motorised staircase drove into place to allow them to disembark.

"That's perfect timing," said Jan, looking at his watch. "It's

4.30 now and your flight is at 5.45, so come on we haven't any time to lose."

Georgina was amazed at the speed with which the two airman piloted her through the customs procedures. A judiciously proffered fifty dollars to the Kenyan Immigration and Customs officer also ensured that the time consuming procedure of searching her luggage would be considered unnecessary. In another five minutes she could be the first passenger to board the BOAC Vickers VC10.

"Don't forget, look me up if either of you are in London," smiled Georgie, kissing both men in turn. "And will you please ring my mother as soon as I've taken off, let her know what time I'm arriving, believe it or not, she's no idea what's going on."

It couldn't possibly be this easy – could it? Georgie thought. Before the public address system had even announced the first call for passengers for her flight she found herself being ushered towards the awaiting airliner. Looking back, she waved at the two pilots.

As she walked along the corridor leading to the tarmac Georgina was suddenly aware of a man raising a camera to his eye. There was no need to panic she thought, he could simply be a press hack, she was used to them but it would probably be wise not to be photographed at present, so she raised a magazine to the side of her face as she passed.

"That photo won't be worth much," she smiled to herself as she continued towards the doors to the waiting 'plane.

A few minutes later she was seated in the first class accommodation at the front of the aircraft, gratefully unzipping and removing her high heeled boots and luxuriously massaging her aching feet.

She would not be able to truly relax until the big VC10 was

in the air but it began to seem she might just have got away with it.

Idly looking out of the window she watched a trail of fellow passengers making their way from the departure building towards the waiting plane. However, only two other passengers joined her in the first class compartment and they looked harmless enough, an elderly English couple.

So, at 5.45pm precisely, right on time, Georgina was experiencing her third take off of the day. She felt safe at last. Now she could finally relax and enjoy a few large gin and tonics, a good hot meal and a proper sleep. Next stop London, her mum and a hot bath.

CHAPTER NINE

Heathrow Airport, London, England.

It was nearly eleven in the evening as Georgina collected her suitcase and trundled it behind her on it's little wheels as she made her way across to arrivals lounge. Thank heaven she was not detained for more than a few minutes in the customs area and then her British Passport was stamped as a formality.

At last she was free of the airport and aircraft. Allowing for the three hour time difference between Nairobi and London, she had been travelling for eighteen hours, that included three take offs and three landings, being interviewed by the police twice and three lots of sad farewells. Even though Georgina had enjoyed a hot meal and a decent sleep on the VC10, she was now feeling dirty, tired and near the end of her endurance. Perhaps it was the fatigue, but she felt a new and unexpected anger towards her husband for putting her into this situation. Through his stupidity and greed she found herself in London on a cold, damp winter's night instead of relaxing in her beautiful Cape Town house enjoying the hot South African summer.

All she could think of now was to find a taxi and get home to Chiswick where hopefully her mum, a hot bath and bed would be waiting.

Ahead, Georgie could see an illuminated 'TAXI" sign with a depressingly long queue of people waiting beneath it when suddenly, she heard a familiar voice calling out, "Georgina, Georgina,"

Looking round Georgie was overjoyed to see her mother running towards her. They threw their arms around each other.

"Oh Mum," cried Georgie, unexpected tears running down her cheeks. "I didn't expect you to come and meet me, I was going to get a cab."

"Nonsense," replied Joyce Browne, holding her daughter's face in her hand's and kissing her again. "As soon as I received the call from your pilot, Mr Kruger, I called BOAC, checked your arrival time and now I'm here. It's so lovely to see you, but why didn't you give me some notice?"

"Mum, you're fantastic. Can I save the explanations until tomorrow. I'm so tired I feel sick, all I really want is a bath and bed."

"Of course, Georgina, let's get you to the car."

It seemed to take an age for the two women to trudge through the massive short stay car park to where Joyce had parked her car. Eventually they arrived at a new Volvo Estate parked in the far corner. Joyce unlocked the cavernous rear luggage compartment and they heaved in Georgie's suitcase and shoulder bag.

"Wow, Mum. This is a step up from the old Minivan I remember, business must be good."

"It's something else we cannot really afford, but with all the cameras we have to carry, not to mention VIP guests, how can we afford not to have it. Anyway it wasn't a Minivan, it was a Mini Countryman, it had windows and wooden bits."

"Of course, Mum, sorry," laughed Georgina as she thankfully sank back into the large black leather passenger seat of the Volvo's luxury interior. Her mother started the engine, engaged 'drive' and confidently steered the large estate car out of the car park towards home.

They were soon heading east along the new M4 motorway

into London. This was the first time Georgie had been in England since she left for South Africa as a thirteen year old child, nearly eight years ago. She looked across at her mother as she chattered away and realised, with some surprise, that her mum had transformed from a suburban housewife into a successful business woman. The little minivan that Georgie remembered as a child had now been replaced by a top of the range Volvo Estate. Georgie also noticed, with approval, that her mother was well dressed, not perhaps Georgina's choice but nevertheless smart and clearly not cheap. After all, she was now a managing director. Georgina had to say those two words to herself again, managing director of a small, but increasingly successful photographic company. But the most amazing fact about this transformation was her mother's pilot's licence.

"You're really doing well, Mum, I can see that. Nice car, pilot's licence, new aircraft and now you're MD, I'm so proud of you."

"Trouble is, dear, it's all on borrowed money. We have to have the 'plane otherwise we can't operate, the same with the car, we have to carry lots of equipment and clients expect us to look successful but it's all show, just a facade really. Sometimes I lay awake at night wondering how we will pay for it all."

"But Mum, every small company is like that the world over and you've done this all yourself, you're the boss."

"Yes, and I didn't want that either but poor Richard had his heart in the flying. True, he started the business but he wasn't a business man. I didn't want to take control but Richard insisted I became MD. To be honest it broke his heart when he had to give up flying and now he is really just a high paid filing clerk and receptionist. Anyway, you're the real success story, any progress I may have made is nothing compared to the illustrious Georgina van Wyk and her millions!"

"Well, that's the whole point isn't it Mum, I just married into the money, you are actually making it."

"Not so much as you'd notice, but thanks for the complement anyway, I'm in so deep now the only way is forward."

Georgina smiled to herself, it was great to see her mother again and what a successful mother too.

The traffic at nearly midnight was very light and it was not long before they turned off the Great West Road and in a few more minutes turned left from Sutton Court Road into Staveley Road and home.

As Georgie's mother carefully edged the big Volvo between the two brick gate posts and up to the garage doors, Georgina was pleased and surprised to experience the old comfortable feeling of coming home, the same feeling she remembered on arriving home from school when she was a child. During the long flight from Nairobi, she had wondered to herself what this moment of homecoming would be like. She had feared that the old house would seem small and inadequate after her grand and ostentatious life in Cape Town, but as they unloaded the cases from the back of the car and her mother opened the front door, she gratefully realised she was home.

To be fair, Georgina's childhood memories of this pre war semi detached house were accurate. By London standards it was large, with four comfortable bedrooms, lounge, dining room, garage and pleasant front and rear gardens. Conveniently located in the fashionable west London suburb of Chiswick, it was an increasingly desirable property, very suitable for the managing director of Wilding Photography.

"Can you remember where your room is, Georgina," smiled her mother. "I've made up the bed, take your case up and I'll put the kettle on, or would you like a bath first, the water's hot?"

"Oooh, let me have a quick bath, Mum. I've been dreaming of a bath all the way from Nairobi, then I'd love a cup of tea, give me fifteen minutes."

Georgina opened the door of her old bedroom, heaved her case onto the single bed and looked around approvingly at the smallest of the four bedrooms. At the back of the house, she had to admit that it did seem small by her standards, in fact the entire first floor would only just match the size of her bedroom suite in Cape Town. But is was cosy, comfortable and familiar.

Georgie removed the van Wyk diamonds with a sigh of relief, placing them on her dressing table. Hendrik had been right, she thought, with the exception of the policeman at Pretoria, nobody had noticed them. Taking the few steps along the first floor landing towards the bathroom, Georgina heard her mother shout from the kitchen, "There's one of my dressing gowns in the bathroom, save you getting dressed, don't be long."

"Okay Mum, thanks," replied Georgina as she entered the small bathroom. Turning on the taps in the bath the room soon started to fill with steam. As Georgina undressed she noticed that the bathroom suite was new and very smart, another confirmation that her mother, despite her protests to the contrary, was doing very well, thank you very much!

Sinking down thankfully into the hot water, a thought entered unbidden into her head. I wonder if there is a significant other in Mum's life?

Resisting the temptation to lay in the bath for an age, Georgie allowed herself just fifteen minutes before climbing out and into her mother's terry towelling dressing gown. Of course she was in England now and was amused that even the bathroom was thickly carpeted, no shiny marble floor tiles here, whatever next. Tying the gown tightly around her and with a towel around her hair, she made her way down the Wilton covered stairs to the kitchen where her mother was pouring two cups of tea.

Georgina took the offered cup and saucer and sat at the kitchen table, her mother sitting opposite.

"This was delivered for you this afternoon at the office by hand," said Joyce, indicating a white envelope at the end of the table.

Without speaking, Georgina pulled the letter towards her. Glancing across at her mother she noticed the typed address was care of 'Wilding Photography.'

By now curiosity had got the better of Georgie's mother as she left her chair and was peering over her daughter's shoulder.

"Who delivered it Mum?" questioned Georgie continuing to examine the envelope.

"Some young girl, her face was familiar and she knew who I was, but I can't remember where I've seen her before."

"Mmmmm, curiouser and curiouser," murmured Georgie, continuing to examine the letter from all angles.

"I wonder what's in it?" breathed her mother.

"Only one way to find out," declared Georgina with sudden resolution, tearing the envelope open and removing the single page contents.

Castle and Castle Solicitors
Hogarth Parade
Chiswick High Road
London
W4
Tel. 01 994 1019
Mrs. G. van Wyk
c/o Wilding Photography
By Han

Dear Madam

This office has been pleased to receive instructions from your husband, Mr. Hendrik van Wyk to make certain arrangements for your forthcoming stay in London.

I would also advise you that we have facilities for the safe storage of any items you may wish to place in our care.

If you would telephone, or call at our offices at your earliest convenience these matters may be explained to you.

Yours faithfully

Harry Castle LLB

"That's short and sweet," said Georgina, handing the letter to her mother.

"That's where I knew that girl from. She's the receptionist in the solicitor's, nice girl, lives in Devonshi..."

"...that's the firm just along from you isn't it?" interrupted Georgie.

"Yes, we use them quite often, they've been there for years."

"Good old Hennie," said Georgie, smiling to herself. "I bet he's organised everything."

"Darling, it's a wonderful surprise to see you, of course, but could you give me just some idea of what's going on? I know we mere mortals don't live the exciting lives of you society high fliers, but it would be nice to have a clue, at least."

Georgina smiled at her mother and took her hand. At that moment she would have loved to unburden all her problems but Hendrik had been so insistent on the utmost secrecy and to be honest, Georgina was not at all certain of what was going to happen herself.

"Mum, it's complicated," said Georgie quietly, trying to think what to say to her mother. "The business, Capital Law, I mean, have been doing some work for the South African

Government lately and Hendrik has seen fit to question some of their er…practices…mmmm…Hendrik thinks that it may lead to some expensive legal action against us and he has asked me to come to London and errr…set up an office here, out of the reach, as it were of the South African authorities.

Georgina hoped that would satisfy her mother, for the time being at least.

"What are these items they are offering to take care of," questioned Joyce, suspiciously.

"Err…the van Wyk diamonds, Mum."

"You have them here, Georgie?" said an incredulous Joyce.

"I was wearing them when you met me at the airport, they're on my dressing table upstairs."

"Are you mad, what are they worth, for heavens sake?"

"Last time they were valued, about half a million dollars, who knows now."

"Sounds to me like you're asset stripping," replied her mother, sharply, looking at her steadily over the top of her tea cup. "Be very careful my girl."

"Yes, Mum, I will," said Georgie, avoiding her mother's stare.

Joyce Browne was no fool.

"Georgina, has all this got anything to do with the killing of your brother-in-law, Johannes?"

Georgina was shocked that her mother knew about the murder.

"Mum, how did you know, we purposely didn't tell you so as not to worry you?" replied a startled Georgina.

Joyce Browne got up from the kitchen table without speaking and left the room, returning a moment later and dropping yesterday's edition of 'The Cape Times' on the table.

Georgie glanced with surprise at the newspaper.

"I've taken the Cape Times everyday since you went to South Africa all those years ago. At the beginning, I just wanted to learn about life in SA, the life that you were living and I was no longer part of, but later, when you began to make a name for yourself, I opened an account with a press research company to collect any photographs or items about you. Silly really."

Joyce passed a green photograph album to Georgina.

Opening the album, Georgina gasped to see, on the first page an article about a prodigious new tennis star, Georgina Browne from Cape Town and a picture of a happy looking girl holding a silver cup. Flicking through the pages were further clippings of her sporting successes, her marriage, appearances at Cape Town Society functions and, on the last page the 'Murder of Capital Law's Chief Accountant' with all the graphic details, including a photograph, to Georgina's amazement, of her coming out of Wynberg Hospital with Brunelda in a wheel chair.

Georgina closed the book and looked up at her mother.

"Mum, I'm so sorry, I had no idea you knew. Why didn't you say? We just thought there was no point worrying you as you were so far away and we didn't really know what was going on ourselves. I will explain more as soon as I can, I promise," pleaded Georgina as she got up from her chair and hugged her mother.

"I know," replied Joyce, kissing her daughter and smiling. "It's okay, really, I guessed you had your reasons, but I must admit I was worried. So I was not completely surprised to receive the 'phone call from your pilot, Mr Kruger that you were on your way. But you must be shattered and you really need to go to bed. After all, you have to ring Mr Castle in the morning."

Joyce Browne took the empty cups and put them in the sink, "You go up, and I'll see you in the morning…I'll lock up and set the alarm. Remember not to come down in the night or you'll set the thing off and we'll have the police round."

"I promise," said Georgie as she kissed her mum and went up the stairs to bed.

She was asleep within minutes.

CHAPTER TEN

Thursday 13th February 1969
Chiswick, west London.

Georgina awoke as her mother gently kissed her cheek. The sun was shining through the already opened curtains.

"It's ten o'clock, Georgina, here's your tea, don't let it get cold and don't forget you have to ring the solicitor this morning."

"Yes, Mum," it was just like being a child again and she liked it. She was surprised not to be missing her home in Cape Town. She was just revelling in being brought her tea by her mum. "You're late for work?"

'I'm having the morning off."

Taking a couple of sips of tea, she got up, put on her gown and ran downstairs. Picking up the letter from the kitchen table, Georgina glanced at it before reaching for the kitchen telephone extension. She dialled the solicitor's number.

"May I speak to Mr Harry Castle please?"

"Georgina van Wyk."

"Thank you."

"Mr. Castle? Georgina van Wyk."

"Eleven, well…yes…I'd better get a move on then, thank you, I'll see you at eleven."

"Good bye."

Georgina replaced the receiver, turning to her mother.

"They don't mess about, do they. I've got an appointment in less than an hour."

"I'll drive you," said her mother. "You've got half an hour."

Georgie took another sip of tea and disappeared upstairs again, descending twenty five minutes later looking every inch a business woman in a blue chalk stripe suit that showed just the slightest evidence of spending several days packed in a suit case. Putting on a pair of black high heels, she looked at herself in the hall mirror. Not bad, must try harder she thought, making a mental note to buy at least the fundamentals of a new wardrobe at the first opportunity.

"Ready?" asked her mother, as she picked up the car keys from the hall table.

"As I'll ever be," frowned Georgie, looking in the mirror again, smoothing down her skirt and picking up her travelling bag.

"I wish I looked half as good," said Joyce. "Come on, then."

Ten minutes later they parked the Volvo in a side street and walked the few yards to the entrance of the photographers in Chiswick High Road.

"Look, it's only four doors down," said Joyce, standing in the street at the front of the shop and pointing along the row of Victorian shop fronts. "Let me know how you get on."

They kissed as Georgina stepped off to walk the few more yards to the premises of Castle and Castle Solicitors.

The door opened with a 'ding' as she entered the small reception area. A young girl sat typing at a desk facing the door. She looked up at Georgina.

"Can I help you, madam?" she enquired politely.

"Yes I hope so, I have an eleven o'clock appointment with Mr. Harry Castle, my name is Georgina van Wyk."

"One moment, please," said the girl picking up the 'phone.

Before Georgina could take stock of her surroundings, an internal door opened and a smartly dressed, slim, good looking man around thirty years of age entered the reception.

Holding out his hand he smiled at Georgina.

"Harry Castle, It's a pleasure to meet you, Mrs van Wyk, please come through."

Georgina smiled and shook the offered hand before preceding Mr Castle into a short corridor.

"Please ensure we're not disturbed, Linda," said the solicitor as he followed Georgina, indicating an open office door on the right.

Harry Castle's office was very small, furnished only with a desk, three chairs, two wooden filing cabinets and a large bookcase stuffed with law books and modern paper files. One window looked out to the rear of the property.

"Please take a seat Mrs van Wyk," said Harry Castle affably but pronouncing 'Wyk' as 'Wick'.

"Thank you, by the way, my name is pronounced 'Vake', fan 'Vake'."

"Oh, I am sorry, Mrs fan 'Vake'," apologised the solicitor, as he attempted to pronounce the name properly. "I shall remember that in future."

"Please don't apologise," said Georgie, "It's an old Afrikaner name."

"Well, thank you for coming in, have you been in London long?" enquired Mr. Castle.

"Exactly twelve hours," laughed Georgie. "My plane arrived at eleven last night and as soon as I got home, I read your letter and here I am, thank you for seeing me so promptly."

"It's a pleasure, it's quite an honour, you know, for a small High Street firm like ours to receive instructions from your husband. I hope we have arranged matters to your satisfaction."

'To be absolutely honest with you, Mr Castle," said Georgie guardedly. "I'm not sure what my husband has requested you to do on my behalf, all I know is that I am in London in my capacity as a partner in the business with a view to opening a London office."

Georgina had no idea how much this solicitor knew, but she doubted that Hendrik would have said more than was absolutely essential.

"Okay, let's get down to business," said Mr. Castle, opening a brown manilla file that was already on his desk. "We have purchased on your behalf a two bedroomed second floor flat in Apollo Court, in Barrowgate Road, not far from here."

"Good heavens!" said an astonished Georgina.

"Yes, I hope it will meet all your needs, I have to say, as solicitors we have never received instructions like these. I can only hope that all is to your satisfaction. As soon as we have finished here I will be pleased to show you the apartment."

"Thank you, Mr Castle," said Georgie smiling and wondering what else her husband had arranged for her. "Please go on."

"We were also asked to decorate and furnish the apartment to the highest standards and in the shortest possible time," continued the solicitor, with some discomfort. "Here we decided to place the work with an interior designer, I can only hope that it also meets with your approval."

"We shall see," said Georgie, smiling. She was beginning to enjoy this.

"Now I come on to financial matters," said Mr Castle, turning the pages in the file. "I will only give you a brief resumé of the arrangements your husband has made on your behalf. Various bank accounts have been opened in your name with Lloyds Bank Ltd, further down the High Road. I think it best if you make a further appointment to see the manager there and he will be able to explain matters in greater detail. However, I am able to advise you that a current account cheque book awaits you at the bank and you may immediately draw on a balance of £25,000. I can also give you this £2,000 in cash now, against your signature.

Good old Hennie, thought Georgie as she signed for the thick wad of notes.

Harry Castle turned another page in the file and looked at Georgina across the desk.

"You will be pleased to know that in various accounts and investments, including gold, you have at your disposal, assets amounting to over three million pounds."

"Well, that should do for the time being," smiled Georgina, showing no sign of surprise.

Throughout the interview she was aware that her solicitor had a habit of playing with a silver ball point pen, he continually span the writing implement absent mindedly between his fingers in a similar manner to which a conjuror will juggle a silver coin between his digits as part of his act. Georgina became fascinated with this casual exhibition of manual dexterity, until Harry Castle caught her stare.

"Oh, I'm sorry, Mrs. van Wyk," he smiled, putting the pen down on the desk. "It's a habit I've had since I was a child, my parents tell me I was continually playing with pens, even as a baby."

Curious, thought Georgie.

"Now, madam, I believe you may have some items to deposit with us."

Georgina took a velvet bag from her case and emptied the van Wyk diamonds on to the solicitor's desk.

"Good God," said a startled Harry Castle, staring at the pile of gold set diamonds glistening on his desk, "Are they real?"

"Mr. Castle, please," scolded Georgie, lifting an eyebrow.

"I beg your pardon, Madam, of course they are real, I will give you a receipt and they will be kept in the safe in our strong room, they are magnificent."

"Perhaps," mused Georgie, taking pleasure in the solicitor's discomfort. "Personally, I find them a little … ostentatious?"

The high street solicitor took the opportunity to scurry off and lock the jewels away. Feeling slightly hot under the collar and conscious of being captivated by his stunningly beautiful client with her seductive South African accent he was finding this the strangest interview he had ever conducted.

Returning to the office, he sat down again behind his desk. Georgina remained silent as she looked around the room.

"May I ask, have you come by car Mrs van Wyk?" said Castle as he removed a large manilla envelope from the file.

"Yes, my mother's car, her office is just a few doors along the road."

"Then may I suggest we take my car and have a look at your newly acquired property."

"Yes, let's." replied Georgina, rising from her chair and smoothing down her skirt.

Within ten minutes Georgina was standing outside a small and very ordinary three storey block of apartments, close to the main road leading to and from the M4 motorway. She was aware that Harry Castle was watching her closely.

"Mr. van Wyk was most insistent," commenced Mr. Castle. "That the apartment should not attract…er… attention, that it should be typical of the area and…"

"…be very boring," interrupted Georgie, looking at the nervous solicitor and raising her eyebrow. "Well you've succeeded, Mr. Castle, let's look inside."

Georgina walked towards the communal front door of the block and pulled it open. Harry Castle, hurrying behind her held the door as she entered the stairwell. Looking with disdain at a small collection of potted plants that stood forlornly outside the door of a ground floor apartment, Georgina started to climb the stairs, acknowledging to herself that the standard of decoration was good and the place was clean.

"The second floor you say?" enquired Georgie, without smiling. "I don't dare to suppose that there is a lift?"

"Err…no…Mrs van Vake," replied Mr Castle, brightly, "It's not far."

"Yes, I know where the second floor is, thank you," said Georgie with heavy sarcasm. "It's been my experience that it invariably comes after the first floor, even in South Africa."

Actually, Georgina thoroughly approved of this location. It was clean, bright and above all ordinary. She felt that she might be able to slip in and out of this well located property unobserved and with very little fuss, should the need ever arise.

Arriving at the second, or top floor landing Mr Castle bustled forward with several keys attached to a large paper label. There were two doors on opposite sides of the landing. He opened the one marked six and stood back with some pride for Georgina to enter.

A short entrance hall led into a large square living room that narrowed to form a dining area with a separate kitchen beyond. Off the entrance hall were four doors, two leading to double bedrooms and the other two being the bathroom and a utility cupboard containing the central heating boiler.

The whole flat was newly decorated in brilliant white with a deeply piled plain dark green carpet throughout. The living room was conventionally but expensively furnished as was the comfortably large, well equipped kitchen.

Without making any comment, Georgie, walked from room to room, opening cupboards, looking out of windows, feeling curtains and running her fingers along surfaces. She paused for several minutes in the bathroom and was pleased to notice the white marble floor. Well, at least someone in England has some taste, she thought.

When Georgina returned to the living room, Mr Castle was standing by the window with an expectant expression.

"It will do," said Georgina, languidly but then thought better of it, Castle and Castle had done a superb job of providing her with a splendid little bolt hole. Although, Hendrik had not discussed any of this with her, he must have been planning it for weeks, she thought.

One serious thought occurred to Georgie as she stood in her new London apartment. For Hendrik to go to all these lengths to protect and provide for her, he must be very fearful of the outcome of his forthcoming meeting with the South African government.

"No, I'm being unfair, Mr Castle," said Georgina, bestowing upon him one of her most disarming smiles, "It's excellent and I congratulate you on a superb job in such difficult circumstances."

Harry Castle positively glowed with pleasure on the receipt of such praise.

"There's one other thing that I need to show you, Mrs van Wyk," said Mr. Castle enthusiastically. "And it's downstairs."

She waited on the second floor landing as Harry Castle carefully locked the apartment door. They then made their way back down to the ground floor and out into the quiet suburban street.

Georgina glanced up at the second floor windows, yes it was nothing if not discreet, she thought. All smiles now, the solicitor led her around the side of the block to a row of six identical garages, one, she presumed for each apartment in the block. He approached the door of the end garage, marked six.

Unlocking the metal 'up and over' door he waited until he had Georgina's full attention.

In a manner reminiscent of a circus compere, Harry Castle turned the handle and lifted the door a few inches. Georgina was astonished as he gave her a swooping bow and flung the door upwards.

"Taa Raa," he shouted, laughing.

There, looking out at her from the darkness of the garage interior was the unmistakable form of a red Jaguar E.Type.

Georgina clapped her hands and laughed.

"It's exactly the same model I left back home in Cape Town, my husband's little joke." she smiled.

"Yes, Mr van Wyk, insisted on the exact model and colour," said Mr Castle, pleased that car had been well received. "It isn't quite new, just a few months old. We couldn't get delivery of a new one in time, but this is in perfect condition, I drove it back from the dealers myself."

I bet you did, thought Georgie. "Thank you, it's perfect."

"Do you want me to drive it out for you?" he enquired, hopefully. "It's taxed, insured and full of petrol."

"No, No, leave it there please," said Georgie, amused to see Harry Castle's face drop, just like a little boy who had had his favourite toy taken away from him.

Reluctantly, Mr. Castle closed and locked the garage door and placed the house keys into the large envelope he was carrying.

"Well, Mrs van Wyk, that's about it," he said, holding out the envelope. "Here are all the keys, that's the flat, garage and car. I'll give you the document folder from the car and I'd be grateful if you would sign everything where marked and return it to me as soon as possible. Any problems, please don't hesitate to call me, I just hope that everything has met with your approval."

"Thank you, Mr Castle, you have done a splendid job," smiled Georgie, and she meant it. "My husband certainly chose the right firm for this commission. By the way, has my husband settled your account?"

"Oh, yes madam, it was settled immediately by his personal assistant, Mrs Steyn, I think it was."

Good old Janet, thought Georgie.

As they walked back towards the car, Georgina noticed that her solicitor appeared a little agitated. Something was coming she thought.

Harry Castle coughed, stopped walking, coughed again and looked at Georgie.

"Mrs. van Wyk," he said, looking at his wristwatch. "I was just wondering, if you have no other arrangements, of course, if I might take you out to lunch?"

"Mr Castle," replied Georgie, with mock formality. "The last thing I ate was a BOAC in flight meal more than twelve hours ago, so I gratefully accept, but I warn you I could eat a horse and most probably will."

"Excellent, Mrs. van Wyk, excellent," beamed the solicitor, holding open the passenger door of his blue Rover 2000. "May I suggest the 'Steam Packet', down on the river just by Kew Bridge?"

"Sounds great."

"It's only, a public house I'm afraid, but we use it often from the office and the food is very good."

Harry Castle started the engine and they made their way towards Kew Bridge.

"Mr Castle, there really is no need to apologise, your invitation is most opportune and I'm very happy to eat anywhere you recommend, I'm sure it will be excellent,"

"Is this your first visit to England, Mrs van Wyk?"

Georgina laughed.

"No, no, my South African accent is a fraud, I'm English. I was born in Titchfield in Hampshire and my parents moved to London when I was small. I lived in Chiswick until I was thirteen."

"So,...South Africa...I mean, it's none of my business, but..."

"...It's no secret, Mr Castle, My father died when I was thirteen and my mother invested all her money in 'Wilding Photography', but it wasn't just financial, Mum had to work very long hours to get the business back on it's feet."

"She is making a great success of it."

"She certainly is, but back in the beginning she worried that my childhood was suffering, so it was agreed that I should go and live with my aunt and uncle in SA. The rest is history."

"How interesting," enthused Mr Castle, "But here we are, 'The Steam Packet'."

'The Steam Packet' public house was an attractive building looking out over the River Thames, a few hundred yards downstream from Kew Bridge. Harry Castle parked the car on the opposite side of the road and they crossed back over towards the pub.

"Mr. Castle," commenced Georgie, looking at her companion. "As our business has been completed to my entire satisfaction and I'm looking forward to my first meal in England for nearly eight years, why don't you call me Georgina?"

"Oh, yes, I'd like that very much and please call me Harry."

"Come on, then, Harry," Georgina laughed."Let's eat."

★

One and a half hours and a very acceptable lunch later Georgina took her leave of Harry Castle outside her mother's office in Chiswick High Road.

"Thank you, Harry, for an excellent lunch and all your hard work," smiled Georgina as she closed the car door.

"It really has been a pleasure," enthused Harry, through the open passenger door window.

"I'll drop those papers in tomorrow, thank you again. 'Bye." Georgina turned away as the Rover drove off to park in the next street.

Georgie smiled to herself with satisfaction, another successful conquest, she thought, he may be useful in the future.

Stepping across the pavement, she pushed open the door of 'Wilding Photography.' The reception area was unoccupied and she looked around for a few moments at the carefully lit specimen photographs that adorned the room. Weddings, babies, graduations, anniversaries, all the usual bread and butter work of a high street photographer. What was more interesting however was the large photograph of the company Beagle Airdale, surrounded by the resulting aerial photographs produced. That's where the money is to be made, thought Georgie but she still couldn't quite believe that her own mother was a pilot, not until she had seen it with her own eyes.

"Hello, can I help you?" said a voice from behind her.

As Georgie turned to face the young man who had entered through the inner doorway, she noticed his expression change from confident interest to one of alarm.

"Oh, I'm ever so sorry," he replied with hesitation. "You

must be her, I mean Georgina, err, Miss Browne, Mrs Browne, no Mrs von errr, something, The boss told me to expect you before lunch."

"Mmm, yes," replied Georgie, raising an eyebrow with amusement. "I am Georgina van Wyk, Mrs Browne's daughter and you are?"

"I'm Bob Simmons, I'm a photographer here," he replied with obvious pride, wiping his hand on his trousers and holding it out for Georgina to shake. "If you would like to wait here a moment, I'll let the boss, I mean your mother know you're here."

"I'll tell you what, Bob, you just show me where she is," said Georgie, amused at the young man's discomfort.

"Okay then, follow me, please," said Bob, then remembering his manners. "Perhaps, you'd like to go first?"

"Just lead the way," smiled Georgina.

In a moment Georgina was standing in her mother's office, it was very similar room to Harry Castle's office a few doors along. Joyce Browne sat behind an ordinary wooden desk, but instead of the solicitor's shelves of law books, Joyce had four large filing cabinets, a coffee table and three easy chairs. The walls were decorated with photographs.

"Well, hello Georgina, I'd rather thought we might have had lunch together," said her mother with heavy sarcasm.

Georgina gave a little giggle, glancing at Bob Simmons who was still hovering in the doorway, staring at Georgie as if she was another species.

"That's what I intended too, Mum, but Mr Castle invited me to lunch and I thought it rude to refuse."

"I suppose I should have anticipated that," said her mother with resignation. She was about to continue the conversation but was aware of Bob's continued presence in the doorway.

"Robert, would you get us a couple of coffees, please," requested Joyce.

Bob Simmons was proving to be an ideal employee, smart, keen, intelligent and eager to learn. Both Joyce and her partner, Richard Wilding liked him. However, she noticed a frown pass across his face on receiving the request.

Joyce was surprised and continued to watch Bob with interest, a case of bruised male ego if I'm not mistaken, she thought.

"Do you take milk and sugar, miss?" Robert enquired with little enthusiasm.

'Black, no sugar," replied Georgie, without giving the boy the satisfaction of a glance not to mention a thank you.

As Bob Simmons left the office, closing the door behind him, Joyce looked sharply at her daughter. She loved her dearly but had noticed an arrogance since she had married into wealth that did not always become her. She felt protective, not of her daughter, but of her employee, Bob Simmons. Georgie was the same age as Bob but her mother was acutely aware that he was no match for her daughter when it came to experience of life and relationships.

"Leave the boy alone, Georgina," said Joyce, sharply.

"I haven't said anything," smiled her daughter with wide eyes and raising her hands as if in surrender.

"No, and you don't need to," continued Joyce, wagging her finger, "He's already staring at you as if you are some goddess, he's a nice lad, your age, but he couldn't cope with you, remember you are a married woman."

"Yes mother, however have I managed without your advice?" said Georgie, petulantly. "Don't you want to know how I got on?"

"Yes, of course I do, Georgina," replied her mother, a little ashamed of her outburst.

"Well, you may be interested to know that I am now the owner of 6 Apollo Court in Barrowgate Road with a red Jaguar in the garage and pots of money in the bank."

Joyce did not reply for a few minutes, she was wondering what all this secrecy and urgency was all about.

"What's going on, Georgie?" asked her mother with a worried expression.

Before her daughter could reply, there was a knock on the door and Bob Simmons entered carrying a tray with two coffee cups, milk and sugar.

Holding the tray in one hand, he picked up a cup and saucer, handing it to Georgie who took it with a smile.

"Thank you, Bob," said Georgie, smiling at the boy.

"Pleasure, miss."

"I think, as we are going to get to know each better, you had best call me Georgina."

"Great, thanks, err, Georgina," smiled Bob, as he collided with the door on the way out.

Joyce Browne frowned at her daughter, but said nothing.

Both women watched as the door closed, then turned to face each other.

"Mum, please, I've got far too much on my mind to be interested in your precious office boy. I know I owe you an explanation as to what's going on and yes, I do know more than I've told you, but I don't know it all and until I speak to Hendrik, it's still best I don't say anything, I'm sorry."

"When do you think Hendrik will ring?"

Georgina raised her eyes to heaven.

"Tonight, I hope. He knows I only arrived yesterday and he also knows I would be with the solicitor today, so I guess he will figure I will be with you this evening."

"Let's hope so, dear, you are worrying me. You realise that

however much money you have, the purchase of a flat takes time, even without having to arrange a mortgage, Hendrik must have instructed Castle and Castle two months ago at the very latest."

"Yes, mum, that had occurred to me as well, Hendrik has obviously been making plans long before I became aware of any problems," replied Georgina thoughtfully.

"Come on, Georgie, let's go home," said Joyce clapping her hands together, then, as an afterthought. "Or are you going back to your new place?"

"No, good heavens, no," replied Georgie with some alarm. "I need my mum, Hendrik will know that and he'll ring your place, I know he will."

Joyce had come round her desk by now and put both her arms around her daughter and hugged her.

"Tell me what you can, when you can, darling," whispered Joyce in Georgina's ear. "But whatever happens we're in this together."

Georgina returned the hug and started to cry, she had tried to hold her panic and dismay in check for days but now she could no longer control herself and the tears became body convulsing sobs. In the privacy of this small office, Georgina's arrogance, sarcasm, confidence and condescension melted away as she cried on her mother's shoulder.

★

When they eventually arrived home at Staveley Road, both mother and daughter remained engrossed in their private thoughts.

Joyce turned on the television, but neither woman paid attention to the programme. Georgina went upstairs and changed out of her business suit and into a pair of jeans. She would have liked a bath, but could not risk being far from the telephone in case it should be Hendrik.

As Georgina came back downstairs the telephone rang, her mother was at the hall table in an instant.

"1459," said Joyce, Georgina hanging expectantly over the white painted bannisters.

"Yes, Richard, he rang at lunchtime," said Joyce calmly, glancing up at Georgina. "They want a meeting, looks as if they will go ahead, yes. Look Richard, I can't chat now, I'm expecting a call from South Africa, yes she's fine, she's sorry she missed you too, yes, but I must go now, bye Richard, bye."

Joyce replace the receiver.

"It was Richard Wilding, dear, sorry," apologised Joyce, as if it was her fault that he'd telephoned.

Georgina sighed and continued down the stairs, she looked in the kitchen where her mother was standing at the work surface reading the local paper that had just been delivered.

Without speaking, she crossed the kitchen and looked out of the window into the back garden. It didn't seem as big now as she remembered it as a child.

"The garden looks smaller, somehow."

"Well, it would, Georgie, but it's big for London," replied her mother, looking up from the paper and glad of some conversation. "Too big sometimes when I have to cut the grass. Don't forget, you're used to that great garden in Cape Town, that would hold a small English village."

Georgina laughed.

The house returned to silence except for the unheeded voices from the television. Joyce went back to her newspaper and Georgina wandered from room to room unable to settle. A casual observer would have noticed a tension similar to the scenes in those old black and white movies where fighter pilots in front line squadrons languidly lounged about during the hot summer of 1940 listening and waiting for the dispersal telephone to ring and send them racing to their Spitfires.

Then it happened.

The loud ring of the telephone shattered the silence. Again, Georgina's mother was first to the receiver in the hall, only a few feet from the kitchen.

"1459", she answered, breathlessly, "Yes, I'll, hold on."

Joyce excitedly handed the receiver to her daughter, "South Africa, they're connecting you."

Taking the receiver from her mother, Georgina sat on the floor with her back to the wall, next to the telephone table. She noticed, with satisfaction that there was a pad and pencil next to the 'phone.

Joyce pointed towards the living room indicating that she would leave her daughter to take the call in private but Georgie shook her head as she caught her mother's arm. So Joyce settled herself on the bottom stair, looking through the bannisters at her daughter.

"Hendrik, darling, how are you?"

"Yes, yes, I'm fine."

"Mum met me at the airport in her smart new Volvo,"

"Yes, I saw him this morning,"

"Look darling, this is a trunk call, we could be cut of at any moment, I'm fine, I own a nice flat, with a Jaguar in the garage and I've oodles of cash in the bank, but what's far more important is you. Have you been to see them yet?"

"You have, how did it go?"

Georgina listened in silence for several minutes, interspersed with the occasional, yes and no.

"Then come here, Hennie, please, do the same as I did, get the charter company, or whatever they call themselves to take you to Nairobi and jump a BOAC direct flight. I've got the money, flat, everything, Please say you'll come, I'm frightened."

"I'm sorry, I'm sorry, I forgot. Well if they're listening, I HOPE YOU ALL DIE, YOU BASTARDS." Georgie shouted down the 'phone, wiping tears from her eyes.

"No, let Janet take care of Brunelda, don't go back to Cape Town, I want you here."

Georgina began to cry quietly as she listened in silence.

"Yes, Yes, I can do that but where is it, just tell me, for God's sake."

"But what does that mean, you're talking in riddles."

"Yes, I heard you, but let me write it down."

"If ... you ... have ... the ... time ... you'll ... find ... it."

Georgina read back the sentence she had written on the pad.

"I might be good at crosswords but what the fuck is all that about," said Georgie giving her mother a guilty glance.

"But you can get it yourself, when you arrive at Heathrow."

"Hendrik, darling you can't fight the government, they're too powerful."

"I am calm, I'm listening."

Another long silence.

"The bastards."

"Don't go, no, Hendrik."

"Promise me you'll come straight to London, promise."

"I love...you."

"The lines dead mum, he's gone."

Georgina dropped the telephone receiver on the floor and buried her head in her arms and began to cry uncontrollably.

Her mother gently took the receiver and placed it back on the 'phone and sat on the floor next to her daughter, putting an arm around her shoulder.

Joyce said nothing, her daughter would tell her in her own time.

The two women continued to sit in silence side by side on the floor in the hall with their backs against the wall. Eventually, Georgina's crying subsided to an occasional sniff.

After a full ten minutes had passed in this way, Joyce Brown slowly removed her arm from around her daughter's shoulders and got up from the carpet. Standing, looking down at Georgina, she bent and took one of her hands.

"Come on, Georgie, let's have a cup of tea," said Joyce, pulling gently on her daughter's hand.

Georgina, eyes red and puffy from crying, looked up at her mum. She sniffed.

"I don't suppose the managing director of Wilding Photography has such a thing as a very large gin and tonic about her, does she?" replied Georgina with a sniff and a brave attempt at a smile.

"I might have," said Joyce, in mock reproach, pulling her daughter to her feet. "I think I'll join you and then we can have a little chat about your language, you certainly didn't learn it in this house."

"Sorry, mum," she said with an embarrassed giggle. "Was I swearing? I tell you what, you should hear me swear in Afrikaans, I'm bloody brilliant! Come on, where's that fu… bloody gin?"

"Georgina, your language," said her mother as both women continued with alternating bouts of giggling, nose blowing and eye wiping. Joyce, was relieved and proud to see her daughter recovering so quickly from the despair that the telephone call had plainly induced.

Back in the living room and seated in a large comfortable armchair, Georgina raised the glass appreciatively to her lips and took a long slow sip. Her mother, seated opposite, watched as her daughter continued to hold the glass in both hands in front of her face, deep in thought.

A few moments later, and clearly having made a decision, Georgina took another sip of her gin and tonic before replacing the now half empty glass on the coffee table.

Georgie looked across at her mother.

"Do you want to hear a long sad story, mum?"

"When you're ready, I'm listening,"

"You already know about Johannes, don't you?" commenced Georgie, taking a quick sip of her G and T. "What you don't know is that our African gardener, Amos was also murdered shortly afterwards and in similar circumstances. I found his body, mum, in our tennis store, impaled on the wall with a Zulu assegai."

"Oh, my God," gasped Joyce, her hand over her mouth.

What made it even worse, was his little grandson, David saw the body. The boy was in a terrible state. Janet Steyn got him into a mission school after we left for Pretoria and I've made up my mind that I'll do all I can to help the little chap. It's funny, I don't take much notice of the servants, so long as they do their work, but David was different, he was willing and happy, I liked him and I think he liked me."

Joyce smiled, leaning forward to squeeze Georgie's hand.

"But I digress. For you to understand, I must start again and go back to the beginning. Hendrik has always had a great interest in politics and was, is, a prospective candidate for the National Party in next year's general election. To cut a long story short, I gather that it was suggested to him by some party officials that if he errr… how shall I put it? Used his extensive business and legal connections to assist the government …"

"I don't understand, darling, how can you assist a government?" questioned Joyce, frowning.

"South Africa hasn't got many friends abroad, Mum, what with apartheid and other things. The government, apparently, is very aware that there are growing calls in the UN and other places for a trade embargo. So far, the big players, the UK and America have resisted these calls as they have big investments in South Africa, you know, British and American Tobacco, firms like that. Well, these are the very sort of companies that Capital Law deals with."

Georgie drained her glass and looked expectantly at her mother who dutifully refilled it.

"Hendrik, agreed to pass on any useful information he obtained to the government, he saw it as his patriotic duty."

"Oh dear," frowned Joyce. "I'm always very wary of patriotism. For what return, money?"

"God no, Mum," gasped Georgie. "That's the last thing we need, I don't mean to boast, but we're rolling in it. No, power, that was the bait, they promised Hendrik, power. Once in parliament, he would be a member of the government in two years and probably Minister of Justice in a couple more. The way Hendrik saw it, he had a great power base, as he represented the Afrikaner voter and I would attract the English speaking whites. You'll laugh mum, but he even spoke of your daughter being a future First Lady of South Africa!"

"I'm not laughing, Georgie."

"If that wasn't bad enough, the worst was yet to come. Hendrik seems to have got involved with a very shady department of the police. I still don't understand exactly, but they seem to operate a team of terrorist informants they recruit from the illegal African National Congress, the ANC. Well, Hendrik used the company to pay these 'Askaris' they call them, to save a direct accountable, financial link to the government. He would pay them as messengers, porters, that sort of thing and recover the money by invoicing the government for legal services the company had not performed. Yes, mum, madness, I know but I think Hendrik had sniffed the promise of power."

Joyce covered her face with her hands as Georgie took another sip of gin.

"The inevitable happened and Johannes, who, as you know is the company chief accountant discovered the irregularities in the accounts. I don't think anyone else would have found them as Hendrik knew the business well, but find them he did. He confronted Hendrik, I knew nothing of all this at the time. Hendrik, then came to his senses I think and went to these people and said he wanted out. Apparently, they were sympathetic and told Hendrik not to worry, they would sort it out. The rest, I think you can guess."

"Georgie, are you really suggesting the government killed Johannes?" exclaimed Joyce.

"We think so," said Georgie, calmly staring at her mother. "Although they admit nothing. The murder of our gardener was just another warning."

"When did you first discover all this, did Hendrik confide in you?"

"No, My first inkling that something was wrong was when I answered the front door one morning," said Georgie with resignation. "There on the step of our house, as large as life, was a black man in a cheap suit asking to see Hendrik. Mum, you must realise that in South Africa that is a bit unusual in a big house. He said his name was Sibanyoni and he made some impertinent remarks that I found very unpleasant, but I was surprised when Hendrik agreed to see him and even more surprised when I could hear them arguing in Hendrik's office. Now that really is unusual in South Africa."

"Go on."

"Well, I think he was one of these 'Askaris.' What's more, I think he murdered Johannes and Amos on the instructions of the government and I know the police think so too as they have issued a warrant for his arrest."

"But you thought the police were in on it?"

"Not at the level of the murder squad, mum, I think the chief investigator of Johannes's and Amos's murders, a Captain Adendorff and his team are honest coppers. The dodgy people are far higher up the ladder."

Joyce nodded.

"That brings me pretty well to the end of the story," said Georgie in conclusion, "As a last resort Hendrik arranged to see someone in Pretoria really high in the Ministry of Justice, I'm not sure who. He was going to demand an end to his involvement. Well he's seen him. I asked him just now how the interview went and Hendrik said he simply didn't know. He said he was listened to with sympathy and told not to worry. You have probably guessed mum that's why I'm here with a power base to try and protect Hendrik should he be arrested."

"But how?"

Georgina laughed and looked at the ceiling. She took another sip of gin.

"Hendrik, really frightened now has arranged all this business in London for me through our friends 'Castle and Castle'," said Georgie, "However, it seems he has assembled a dossier of evidence that I can use to bargain, negotiate, with the government for his release should he be arrested, but he was not prepared to trust this to Castle and Castle. It sounds ridiculous, like out of a spy novel but he's hidden it somewhere, heaven knows where, for me to find. What's more, the government probably know the evidence exists so Hendrik thinks it may be better for me not to recover it if I don't need it. That's what worries me most, it's a real 'Catch 22' situation, Hendrik says not to recover it if I don't need it but how do I know if I need it if I don't know what it is! "

"Well, where is it Georgie?" asked an amazed Joyce. "He must have told you."

"No, he said the telephone line was probably bugged," said an exasperated Georgie. "The only clue he would give me was what you saw me write down, 'If you have the time you'll find it' or something like that. He said with my cryptic brain I would solve the conundrum with ease. God, mum I know I'm brilliant but I haven't got a clue."

Joyce went into the hall and fetched the writing pad and returned to her armchair.

"If you have the time you'll find it," said Joyce quietly, looking at the pad. "What on earth can it mean?"

"How should I know?" snapped Georgie, crossly.

"Well, I'm sure I don't," frowned Joyce, looking at her daughter.

The two women then sat in silence. Joyce doodled on the writing pad trying to make some sense of what was going on. Georgie, however, sat motionless, staring at the coffee table, a deep frown of concentration on her beautiful face.

After what seemed an age, Joyce tossed the writing pad and pencil on the coffee table.

"Look at the time. I'm going to start dinner, I've got some nice salmon, fish is good for the brain, you know."

"What did you say?" said Georgina, darting a quizzical look at her mother.

"I said fish is good for the brain, dear," replied Joyce, making her way towards the kitchen.

"No, that's it," shouted Georgina, "You said, 'look at the time,' that's it, time, don't you see?"

Joyce returned to her chair as her daughter hurriedly unfastened the clasp of her wristwatch.

"With all that has been going on, Mum, I completely forgot," commenced Georgie with enthusiasm. "But on our last night in the flat above our offices in Pretoria, Hendrik gave me this watch."

"Yes, I'd noticed it on your wrist, is it gold?" asked Joyce, examining the elegant timepiece.

"Of course, it's gold, Mum," said Georgie, with some irritation. "The thing is, I thought it odd at the time. Granted it's a lovely watch but I have a draw full of lovely, expensive watches, in fact I've got another Cartier watch almost the same as this one. But Hendrik was so insistent I should have this gift. I even remember him telling me that I would need it in London. The clue has got to be somewhere here."

Georgina examined the face of the watch as her mother leaned over her shoulder.

"It's just a normal Cartier gold face," said Georgie, turning the watch over to look at the back. "Here, there's something on the back though, something engraved."

"What does it say?" said Joyce straining over her daughter's shoulder.

"It's too small, have you got a magnifying glass?"

"I've got better than that, I've got a jeweller's eye glass, we use them for examining aerial photographs.

Joyce Browne rummaged for a few moments in a sideboard drawer before returning triumphantly with the small black plastic encased eyeglass.

Georgina held it to her eye and examined the back of the wristwatch.

"There's the usual Cartier marks and stamps and things but something else, it's all brightly cut so I can see it is newly engraved. Write this down Mum."

Joyce grabbed the pad and pencil and looked expectantly at her daughter.

"APVZ on one line and under it KX, got it?" dictated Georgie, fiddling with the eyeglass, "How do you use these bloody things?"

Joyce carefully wrote the letters down and put the pad on the table. Both women stared at the writing in silence.

APVZ
KX

"Mean anything?" asked Joyce.

"Nothing, I shall have to think about this."

"Well, I shall get on with some dinner," decided Joyce. "There are no servants here you know, if one wants to eat one has to cook it oneself."

The sarcasm was lost on her daughter who was still deep in thought.

"I'm sorry, Mum, I'll come and help you," apologised Georgie getting up from the chair.

"No, I'm only joking, your job is to crack that code, you are the crossword wizard after all."

"I don't think it's like a crossword though Mum," said Georgie, thoughtfully, "You see, with a crossword there is always the chance, however clever one is, that the solution may be impossible to find."

"I don't follow," said Joyce, busily slicing carrots.

"What I mean is," continued Georgina. "The answer to a crossword clue may be impossible to find because it is a word or expression that is unknown to the solver. But in this case the clue is specially written for me by someone who wants me and no one else to solve the riddle. So I must know the answer, however arcane it at first appears. Do you understand what I'm saying, Mum?"

"Yes, I think so dear," replied her mother with little confidence.

"So this APVZ KX means something very apparent to both myself and Hendrik, I know I have the answer, I'll probably kick myself it will be so obvious." said Georgina, almost to herself.

She thought on in silence for a few moments as she helped her mother in the kitchen.

"What I think we need to do is forget about the clue for a while and just wait for something to pop up."

"I can't see anything popping up for me any time soon," responded Joyce, opening the oven door and putting in the foil wrapped salmon steaks.

"That's the whole point though, isn't it Mum, the solution is for me to find and no one else. So I think that what we should do is both take a day off and go shopping tomorrow."

"I cannot take a day off, just like that," protested Joyce. "I have a business to run."

"Of course you can, you're not indispensable and you know you want to. As for me I have to get some new clothes. Georgina van Wyk cannot possibly live out of a suitcase containing two pairs of jeans, a suit, a pair of boots and half a dozen pairs of knickers."

Both women burst out laughing.

"Come on, Mum, it would be fun and there hasn't been much fun around lately. We can take the District Line from

Turnham Green to Sloane Square and then we can get a taxi up to Bond Street, spend lots of money, have lunch and a cab home with all our goodies. Please say yes."

"Okay, yes, but I must go into the office first. We can leave the car there and walk round to the station," laughed Joyce. "It will be fun, I haven't been shopping for clothes in months."

"I can see that, Mum, then the key to the riddle will suddenly pop up when we least expect it, trust me."

The rest of the evening passed in much more convivial terms than either of the women could possibly have anticipated earlier that afternoon. They agreed that it must have been the result of good home cooking, the indomitable female spirit, the thought of a shopping expedition and gin although not necessary in that order. Nevertheless, Joyce Browne and Georgina van Wyk retired to bed a little unsteadily and with high hopes of a successful day in the morning.

CHAPTER ELEVEN

Friday 14th February 1969
Valentine's Day
The West End

The next morning at about 9.15am Joyce and Georgina set off in the Volvo for the short journey across Chiswick to the offices of Wilding Photography in the High Road. Georgina was introduced to Richard Wilding, her mother's business partner and did her best to make a good impression.

Also in the office that morning were a couple of freelance photographers who were using the darkroom facilities and Bob Simmons, who was hurrying about with an air of self importance. It was no surprise to Joyce that her daughter was immediately the centre of male interest and all four men appeared to be competing for her attention, what man wouldn't she supposed with some dismay.

By ten o'clock the two women finally escaped from the clutches of Wilding Photography and the offers of tea, coffee and lifts to the station. In all honesty, it was only a short walk back along Chiswick High Road and down Turnham Green Terrace to the Underground station on the District Line. Georgie had entrusted Bob with the folder of now signed documents for return to Harry Castle at the nearby solicitor's office.

Georgina put all her worries to the back of her mind

and concentrated on the serious business of shopping. She thoroughly enjoyed her first trip on a tube train in years, particularly as that part of the District Line was in the open air. As they emerged onto the pavement outside Sloane Square station, Georgina linked arms with her mother and directed their steps with determination towards the opposite side of the square.

"Come on, Mum," enthused Georgina, smiling in anticipation. "We'll start with Peter Jones, then a cab up to Harrods, then on to Bond Street, let's spend, spend, spend."

She was true to her word and the day was spent in a blissful whirl of shops, sales assistants, fitting rooms, taxis, more shops, more sales assistants, more fitting rooms and even more shops. Joyce was apprehensive at first of the money that Georgina was spending but after watching her daughter casually dispose of more and more money she resigned herself to the joy of shopping. They bought shoes, boots, hand bags, perfume, make up, clothes, more clothes and presents. For every item they purchased, many others were tried on and discarded. The two women carried as many carrier bags as they could manage from cab to cab and shop to shop but a Harrods van would deliver other items to be received at Wilding Photography, together with loaded taxis accompanied by porters from expensive Bond Street shops. Somehow, during the day they even managed to fit in some lunch.

They arrived home at Staveley Road tired and happy. Even the cavernous luggage compartment of the Volvo estate had met it's match with more bags and parcels piled in the back seat. After several trips backwards and forwards from the car to the house they sat in the living room, massaging their feet and surrounded with parcels and bags.

"Tea?" asked Joyce.

"Please," said Georgie. "And I must ring Hendrik later, it's Valentine's Day."

Salisbury, Rhodesia.
The same day

William Robinson and his fiancé Angie Arnold strolled arm in arm along Fourth Avenue back towards Meikles Hotel.

"I'm getting a bit concerned, Angie," said Will, casually kicking a stone into the kerb as they walked along. "I mean to say, we've been here since Wednesday. Georgie promised to be back from Nairobi yesterday at the latest and here we are, Friday, another twenty-four hours and there's no sign of anyone, not even a telephone call. I'm worried."

"It does seem a bit odd," agreed Angie, "And where are Hendrik and Brunelda? They were supposed to join us yesterday too."

"Something has happened, I'm sure," continued Will. "Don't you think it a bit odd, Georgina rushing off to Nairobi like that?"

Angie nodded.

"Well, there's only two nights left for any fun. Tonight, which is Valentine's night after all and Saturday night and then you have to be in the barracks at Morris Depot Sunday afternoon ready to start your training on Monday morning."

William nodded his agreement.

"Another thing, Angie, we're running up a terrific bill at Meikles, you know?" said William with a worried expression. "We've only got Georgie's word that it's all being paid for and dinner here is a weeks wages you know. Stupidly I haven't got Hendrik's Pretoria number, so I'll ring that Janet Steyn as soon as we get back and see what's going on."

"It is Friday afternoon, do you think Janet will still be in the office?"

"I've got her home number. Hendrik gave it to me, he says that as his PA she is permanently available, she likes to be indispensable."

"I wonder what Mr. Steyn says about that?"

"I don't think there is a Mr Steyn. Least I've never heard mention of one, married to her work, I suppose."

The couple strolled on in silence until they turned a corner and Meikles Hotel came into view. They passed the old two storey, balconied colonial style building, built in 1915 that had been the site of the first Parliament of Southern Rhodesia in 1924 but as they approached the modern high rise wing where they were staying, William stopped suddenly.

"What on earth is going on, Angie?" he exclaimed as they both peered through the trees at the distant sight of half a dozen police cars and two ambulances parked at random angles in front of the hotel reception.

"Come on," urged William. "This looks exciting."

As the couple hurried towards the hotel they became aware of khaki uniformed British South Africa Police officers busily trying to hold back the large numbers of people who had been attracted by the commotion. Other officers were examining what looked like a body laying in the roadway covered in a blanket.

"It looks like someone has been injured," said Will as he pushed forward in the crowd for a better view.

"Do keep back sir," shouted a white woman Patrol Officer in her airforce blue shirt and skirt. "There's nothing to see." She turned to give instructions to three African constables trying to establish a cordon, a silver bar on each shoulder indicating her officer rank.

"Has there been an accident, officer?" persisted William, straining forward for a better view.

"Yes, something like that, but please keep back, sir," replied the young woman with rising annoyance. "You really aren't helping, you know."

William desperately wanted to tell the officer that he was a colleague, well almost, but thought better of it. Meanwhile Angie had moved a short distance away to try and get a glimpse in the back of the ambulance that stood with it's back doors open.

Suddenly, she turned back towards William, a shocked look on her face.

"Will, Will," she shouted. " I can't believe it, it's Brunelda."

"What, it can't be," replied Will, pushing his way towards the ambulance.

But there could be no doubt, Angie was right, there, sitting in the back of the vehicle, being spoken to by the uniformed crew was Brunelda du Plessis.

"Hey, Brunelda," shouted Will. "Brunelda, it's us, Angie and Will, where's Hendrik?"

"Brunelda, over here, it's us." echoed Angie.

However, Brunelda either didn't hear or took no notice, continuing to stare blankly at the side wall of the ambulance.

Will tried to push forward but was firmly held back by an African constable manning the cordon. Looking around in desperation, William and Angie were suddenly aware of the woman officer they had originally spoken to hurrying towards them.

"Sir, do you know this woman?" she questioned, pointing into the back of the ambulance.

"Yes, ma'am, we were expecting them yesterday, we're all from Cape Town" shouted William, excitedly, "She is Brunelda du

Plessis, she and her brother, Hendrik van Wyk have rooms booked in Meikles, we were worried they hadn't arrived yet. What's happened?"

"Sir, madam, please come with me," said the officer, ushering them past the cordon. "The senior investigating officer will need to speak to you."

The woman Patrol Officer led the way to an unmarked Peugeot saloon car that was standing within the cordon, some fifty feet from the ambulance. She approached a young man in a grey suit who was leaning against the car and speaking on a radio microphone.

"Sir, I think this gentleman knows the lady in the ambulance."

"Really," said the plain clothes officer with sudden interest, making his way towards William and holding out his hand. "How do you do, I'm Detective Inspector Harris and you are?"

"Oh, my name is William Robinson, I'm South African, from Cape Town and this is Angie, sorry, Angela Arnold my fiancé," explained Will, shaking the detective's hand, "My cousin is Georgina van Wyk and she is married to Hendrik van Wyk and that is his sister, Brunelda du Plessis sitting in the back of that ambulance over there."

"And what are you doing up here in Rhodesia, Mr Robinson?" asked Inspector Harris.

"Well, we've all come up for a bit of a holiday really. I should explain Inspector, you are probably unaware but Brunelda's husband Johannes du Plessis was murdered a couple of weeks ago back in Cape Town. He was the chief accountant of Capital Law, it was a terrible shock to us of course and the police haven't caught the murderer yet. Then last Sunday, Hendrik, I mean Mr van Wyk's gardener was murdered in similar circumstances. You must realise that by then we were all in a panic, so Mr and Mrs van Wyk arranged a bit of a holiday for us all."

"Why, Salisbury?"

"Sorry, I should have explained," continued Will. "I'm due to start my training with the BSAP at Morris Depot on Monday morning so Angie and I were coming up anyway. The plan was for us all to stop over in Pretoria where Mr van Wyk had some business to attend to and then we'd travel on up to Salisbury."

"So why didn't you travel together?" asked Harris.

"That was the plan, Inspector. But Hendrik, Mr van Wyk, I mean, had to stay on in Pretoria a bit longer than expected so it was agreed that his sister would stay with him and the rest of us continue on to Salisbury. Hendrik promised to join us that night or yesterday at the latest."

"You say the rest of you came up to Salisbury, does that include Mrs van Wyk?

"That's the odd thing, when we landed at Salisbury, we were using a chartered jet, Inspector," explained Will with some embarrassment. "Georgie, sorry, Mrs van Wyk, suddenly announces that she has to continue on up to Nairobi, again on urgent company business, she's a partner in the firm, Inspector. We were a bit stunned, but thinking back the pilots seemed to know all about it."

"Where is Mrs van Wyk now, sir?"

"Another mystery, Inspector. We were expecting Georgie back yesterday, but we've had no message and I've no idea. I should explain, sir, that we are staying here at Meikles as guests of the van Wyks, we couldn't possibly afford these prices ourselves. I was saying to my fiancé just a few minutes ago that I would have to ring the company and find out what was going on, and then we see all this."

Inspector Harris rubbed his chin while looking carefully at William.

"If Miss Arnold would wait here with my colleague for a moment, I would like you to come with me."

Detective Inspector Harris led William away from the car towards the body laying in the road. It was now surrounded with forensic officers and photographers in white overalls. Harris knelt down next to the corpse and took a corner of the blanket in one hand.

"Sir, you must have some idea by now of the identity of this body," said Harris quietly as the other officers stood back.

"Yes, Inspector."

Detective Inspector Harris, pulled back the blanket to reveal the the face of Hendrik van Wyk. Harris looked up at William questioningly.

William nodded.

"Shot through the chest twice, sir," advised the detective quietly. "And his case was stolen."

Harris immediately replaced the blanket, stood up and took William's arm, hurrying him away and back towards the car.

"The body, it's Hendrik." said William, visibly shocked as he took Angie in his arms.

"Mr Robinson, I appreciate this has been a terrible shock for yourself and Miss Arnold," said Harris, sympathetically. "May I suggest you return straight to your room, one of my officers will go with you. We can deal with statements tomorrow, that's no problem but it is most important that we speak to Mrs van Wyk as soon as possible so can I request that you contact Cape Town immediately."

"Yes, of course officer, it may take some time to place the call though."

"Don't worry sir," smiled Harris. "My officer will make sure you are connected without any delay. Meanwhile, I'm advised that Mrs du Plessis is in deep shock and will need to be admitted to hospital. I promise I will keep you informed of any developments as soon as they happen"

"Thank you, Inspector," replied William, clutching Angie's arm. "Anything I can do, of course."

Detective Inspector Harris returned to his investigations while a shocked William and Angie made their way up to their hotel room accompanied by the Woman Patrol Officer.

Will unlocked the door of the fourth floor room and Angie went straight to the bathroom closing the door.

"Have you the Cape Town number you want to call, sir?"

Hendrik handed the officer a card from his wallet.

"That's the number, and I need to speak to Janet Steyn, please officer, she's Mr van Wyk's PA."

"Please, Mr Robinson, I'm Patrol Officer Jenny Scott, just call me Jenny, I'm here to help."

Lifting the receiver of the telephone next to the bed she spoke to the operator, meanwhile William walked to the window and stared down at the organised chaos in front of the hotel fifty feet below.

After a few moments Angie emerged from the bathroom and rested her head on her fiancé's shoulder.

"Thank you, operator, this is Patrol Officer Jennifer Scott, BSAP and I need to speak urgently to a Janet Steyn on the following Cape Town number."

She read the number into the 'phone.

"Yes, I can confirm that I am ringing from Meikles Hotel on room extension 435 and this call is on the authority of Detective Inspector Harris, BSAP. As quickly as you can please, this is urgent…Yes, I'm waiting by the 'phone, thank you."

She replaced the receiver and looked across at William and Angie.

"It should only take a moment, sir, they are connecting us now."

"Thank you," replied Will, as the couple turned from the

window and sat in the armchairs next to the bed, "Please, can I get you a coffee, drink?"

"No, I'm fine, but let me..." She replied taking the small electric kettle from the dressing table.

Jenny was stopped in mid sentence by the urgent ring of the telephone, she snatched it up before the first pulse had ended.

"Patrol Officer Scott, BSAP," she snapped, looking across at the expectant Will and Angie.

"Hello, this is the British South Africa Police in Salisbury, Rhodesia. Am I speaking to Janet Steyn?...Thank you madam, I have Mr William Robinson to speak to you,...hold on please."

William, who was standing at her shoulder, took the 'phone.

"Janet,... thank God we've got through to you. It's terrible, Janet, Hendrik has been killed,...murdered,...Angie and I were walking back to the hotel and saw all this commotion, police and ambulances...and Brunelda was in the back of the ambulance,...no we didn't even know they were in Rhodesia, we haven't heard from anyone."

Will ran his free hand through his hair.

"They should have been here Thursday at the latest and now it's Friday...and Georgie is in Nairobi and we haven't seen her since...LONDON, Georgina is in London, that's impossible..." gasped Will, staring wildly at Angie. "How can Georgie be in London, she said she was just going up to Nairobi to sign some papers and would be straight back...God, Janet what's going on?...If only you could...I really don't know what to do,...I don't know, she's alive but in shock, the police say...yes gone to hospital,...we're okay, but we still have three rooms here and I have no idea how to pay the bill...thank you...thanks Janet...yes, Angie is okay, just shocked like me...yes, of course, hang on,"

"Mrs Steyn want's to speak to you," said Will handing the receiver to Jenny.

"Patrol Officer Scott, Yes Madam, Mrs du Plessis has been taken to hospital, she is not injured but appears to be in deep shock,...Detective Inspector Harris, ma'am...yes. They seem to be fine, but I shall stay here as long as I'm needed...Mrs van Wyk will need to be informed...thank you...Will you let us know as soon as you arrive...oh, I see...yes, of course."

"She would like to speak to you again, sir."

"Hello, Janet. Oh wonderful, but what is Georgie doing in London, why didn't she tell us?...okay, but when do you think you will be here...okay, yes, good bye, see you tomorrow."

"She should be here by twelve o'clock, if she can get hold of the charter LearJet, otherwise the first commercial flight," explained Will. Then, turning to the police officer.

"Mrs Steyn has asked us not to make any statements until she arrives, That's a bit embarrassing really, especially as I'm joining you on Monday morning to start my training but I must take her advice, you see, as well as being Mr. van Wyk's PA she is also legally qualified."

"Sir, we quite understand," smiled Jenny. "Statements can be taken tomorrow, it's not a problem, now how about some coffee, you both look like you need it, you have had a terrible shock."

Jenny Scott busied herself making coffee and after nearly an hour of small talk the police officer took her leave, wishing William success in his training and after receiving assurances from Will and Angie that they were okay. They could contact a special police number should they need any further help. William gave the officer assurances that they would dine in the hotel and remain in their room that evening. A uniformed police officer would be present in the hotel throughout the night.

Saturday 15th February 1969

At 11.45am the next morning a taxi pulled up outside Meikles Hotel in Salisbury. The liveried commissionaire opened the rear door of the cab and from the back seat emerged a slim middle aged woman with dark collar length hair and wearing spectacles with heavy black frames that gave her a studious appearance. She was carrying an old and battered, brown leather brief case. Leaving the driving seat, the cab driver opened the boot and lifted out a red travel bag and handed it to the doorman.

Carrying the brief case in her right hand and with the commissionaire preceding her with the travel bag, the woman, dressed in a smart grey trouser suit, black sweater and wearing grey high heeled shoes, walked quickly and confidently through the large entrance door, into the hotel and up to the reception desk.

"Good morning, madam," asked the female receptionist, politely. "May I help you?"

"Yes, my name is Janet Steyn," said the woman impatiently in a heavy South African accent. "And I am here to see two of your guests, Mr William Robinson and Miss Angela Arnold."

"Of course, Madam," replied the receptionist. "We were expecting you, it's room 435 on the fourth floor. If you would wait a moment I will get a porter to carry your luggage."

"That, will not be necessary," said Janet Steyn, picking up the travel bag from the floor and slinging the strap over her left shoulder before turning towards the lifts. "435 on the fourth floor?"

"Yes, madam," said the receptionist, picking up the 'phone. "I'll let them know you are on you way up."

Will Robinson was waiting on the fourth floor as the lift doors opened.

"God, I'm glad to see you Janet," greeted Will, with honest relief, kissing Janet on the cheek, as he took her shoulder bag, "We're over here."

Quickly greeting Angie, Janet Steyn assumed complete control of the situation. She decided upon a plan of action that Will and Angie accepted totally with consummate relief that the responsibility was being lifted from their shoulders.

Sitting at the small desk, Janet telephoned, first the hospital, ascertaining that Brunelda was stable and comfortable, but still in shock, leaving Will a little ashamed that he had not thought to make the same enquiry earlier in the day. Next she spoke to the police and arranged for an officer to call at the hotel at 3.00pm to take statements in her presence.

With that done, in what seemed only a few minutes of intense activity, Janet sat back and took the cup of coffee Angie offered her, listening to the couples account of the events of the previous day.

After pausing for a few moments to consider William and Angie's incredulous demands for an explanation of Georgina's presence in London, Janet simply explained that Georgina's absence had become essential in a rapidly developing law suite in which the company was involved. Why had they not been informed? Well, until Georgina arrived in Nairobi it had been far from certain that her departure for London would be necessary so there was no need to worry them.

Janet Steyn was aware that this was a wholly unsatisfactory explanation, however, in the present circumstances it was as far as she was prepared to go. She was here to protect the interests of the company and the only remaining partner, now her employer, Georgina van Wyk. William Robinson and Angela Arnold were not directly involved and provided she protected their interests, which would not, as far as she could see, be difficult, then there was no need for them to be further involved. Janet knew more, but that information would be reserved for Georgina and only Georgina.

So it was further decided, much to Angie and Will's relief, that Janet would occupy one of the two vacant rooms for that night. Then, while Angie could go off with Will to see him checked into Morris Depot on Sunday afternoon, Janet would collect Brunelda with a private nurse and meet Angie at Salisbury airport where the LearJet would be waiting to fly them all back to Cape Town. That just left her with the onerous duty of informing Georgina of her loss. The body would not be released for burial while the police enquiries continued.

CHAPTER TWELVE

The same day
Chiswick

The offices of Wilding Photography were a scene of organised chaos. Cameras being loaded into camera bags by photographers about to leave for weddings and others being unloaded by staff who had just returned. New rolls of film being signed for and a continual traffic up and down the steep staircase to the basement dark rooms. Joyce Browne was sitting at the reception desk where a freelance photographer, returning from an early wedding was counting out six rolls of exposed film together with his job sheet. After a few moments conversation Joyce was about to descend the stairs to the dark room when she was distracted by the front door crashing open.

Into the already busy front office struggled her business partner Richard Wilding. Placing a large and heavy camera bag on the floor he held the door open as Georgina swept in behind him.

"And how did your assistant shape up on her first wedding for Wilding Photography?" asked Joyce with a smile.

Richard, smartly dressed in a grey suit, smiled and shook his head as he stood with his hands on his hips, trying to catch his breath.

"Well, it's the first time I've ever been asked by the client if my assistant can be in one of the photos," he laughed, looking at Georgie and back to Joyce.

Mrs Browne was filled with a mixture of pride and resignation as the hive of activity of a moment before was reduced to silence as the male photographers stopped work and stared at her daughter.

From the expression on her face Georgina van Wyk was enjoying her day. Dressed expensively in a figure hugging and very short, mustard coloured skirt, matching military style jacket fastened to her neck with brass buttons and brown leather boots, she looked stunning as she closed the door, pretending not to notice the admiring glances of the men.

"I was paying attention to Richard and helping him to arrange the guests for each picture, when the brides father and the best man I think he was, asked if I would pose in a photograph with them, well I thought it rude to refuse."

Everyone laughed.

"In that case, you can go to the reception with the proofs and take some orders," smiled Joyce, glancing archly at the others. "You'll probably take double the normal money"

"Unless, of course the bride decides to strangle you," laughed Richard. "Anyway, tell your mother what you thought of your first wedding as a photographer's assistant."

"It was good, the bride was quite pretty – I suppose, but the brides mother, what a fright," explained Georgie raising her hands in mock horror. "What was she thinking of, blue hair, a dress that looked as if it was made from a pair of curtains for a woman half her size and a potted geranium on her head."

"Don't laugh at the clients, Georgina," frowned her mother. "They pay our wages."

"Oh, I wasn't laughing," replied Georgie, with wide eyes and raised eyebrows. "I was just amazed that anyone would want to go out in daylight looking like that."

"My daughter is a snob," laughed Joyce, looking around at

the others who had by now, smilingly resumed work. "Right, if you want to come down with me, Georgina, you can have a look how the film is developed."

With that, Joyce picked up the six rolls of film and associated docket from the desk, making her way towards the staircase through the internal door. One of the freelances left the shop with his camera bag and his colleague disappeared along the passage to one of the back rooms.

Georgina was about to follow her mother when the telephone rang. She looked around at the now empty office.

"I'll get it Mum. Wilding Photography, how can I help you?"

*

Ten minutes later Joyce Browne climbed the stairs from the basement having entrusted the unexposed film to Bob Simmons in the dark room. Where was Georgie? she wondered, certain in the knowledge that her clever daughter would be more that capable of dealing with any enquiry.

As she entered the front office, Georgina was seated at the reception desk, staring fixedly ahead, the telephone receiver still held in her right hand.

"What's the matter, darling?" asked her mother, hurrying across the room to her daughter's side.

Georgina didn't respond, didn't move her head, all that her mother noticed was a single tear trickle down her cheek.

"Darling, please tell me."

Slowly, Georgina turned her head to face her mother, tears now running freely down her cheeks.

"Hendrik is dead, murdered," replied her daughter, quietly and almost calmly, only the tears giving way to her grief.

"Oh, darling," whispered Joyce, putting both arms around Georgina and hugging her to her body.

Georgina did not resist the embrace, neither did she return it.

"That was Janet Steyn," resumed Georgina in a quiet and calm monotone. "Hendrik, was getting out of a taxi at Meikles Hotel in Salisbury, William identified the body, he was shot twice in the chest."

Joyce continued to hold her daughter.

"Mum, take me home please," whispered Georgina, almost inaudibly, still holding her emotions in check.

★

The two women drove the short distance to Staveley Road in silence. Joyce felt wretchedly inadequate as she watched her daughter from the corner of her eye or took the occasional glance when traffic conditions permitted. She was Georgina's mother but she could think of nothing to say that wouldn't appear trite and banal in these sudden and dreadful circumstances.

Pulling onto the drive, Joyce quickly made her way to the front door and opened it before turning back towards the car to help her daughter, but Georgie was just behind her.

Entering the hall, Joyce closed the door and threw her arms around her daughter, relieved to have the opportunity to offer some comfort, however slight, at a time when words seemed pointless.

After a few minutes Joyce felt her daughter gently pushing her away and extricating herself from her mother's embrace.

"Mum, just let me go upstairs and lie down for an hour," whispered Georgina, between noisy sniffs.

"Let me at least call the doctor, darling," pleaded her mother, taking her daughter's hand.

"Doctor?" snapped Georgina, her blue eyes flashing behind the tears. "My husband has been murdered five thousand miles from here and you want to call a doctor."

"Well, darling, he might be able to give you something."

"What, make me sleep, mum?" her voice rising above a whisper. "And end up like Brunelda, not knowing what day of the week it is."

Georgina pulled her hand free of her mother and started up the stairs towards her room, "I don't need to sleep," she called down as she opened her bedroom door. "I need to think."

"Shall I bring you up a cup of tea?" said Joyce, instantly regretting such an inadequate remark.

"Later, Mum," came the reply as she closed her bedroom door.

Still wearing her coat and with her handbag and car keys on the hall floor, Joyce walked into the living room and sat in an easy chair. The tears that she had been valiantly trying to hold back for her daughter's sake burst through her defences and she cried deep silent sobs.

After nearly half an hour, a red eyed Joyce went to the hall and retrieved her handbag. Delving inside for a handkerchief she blew her nose noisily. This won't do, she thought to herself, as if anything would do at such a time.

Hanging her coat in the hall she went to kitchen, filled the kettle and lit the gas. How long should she leave Georgina upstairs, she wondered? Joyce wanted so much to offer comfort to her little girl, but realised that for the time being there was really nothing she could do. One thing was for certain, she would not leave her daughter alone, there was plenty of food in the house and she could send out for more if required. As for the business, Richard would have to take care of things. Her place was here, her daughter wanted to be on her own at present, well okay, she would respect that wish, but her mother would be near when she was needed.

Taking her cup of tea to the kitchen table, Joyce switched on the small, wall mounted, TV and sat down. Although looking at the picture, she was taking no notice of the programme as she sipped her tea, deep in her own thoughts.

The noise of the upstairs lavatory flushing shook Joyce from her trance. Looking at her watch, she realised she had been sitting at the kitchen table for nearly two hours.

Aware that her attentions might still be unwelcome, Joyce felt that she could sit around no longer, she must try again to talk to her daughter, there had to be something she could do.

Making some more tea she poured two cups and carried the tray upstairs. Placing it on a side table she knocked gently on Georgina's bedroom door.

"Come in, Mum."

As Joyce entered the room, Georgina was sitting up on the bed, with her back against the headboard, her beautiful blue eyes were still red and puffy but she had stopped crying.

"I thought you might like some tea, darling," said Joyce, apologetically, offering the tray.

"Thanks, Mum," replied Georgie, attempting a smile. "Put it on the table and sit down."

Joyce sat at the dressing table by the window. Pleased to be with her daughter, she was nevertheless uncertain what to say.

"How do you feel, darling?" asked Joyce, acutely aware of the banality of the remark.

"Mum, from the first time I was confronted by that dreadful black man, back at the house in Cape Town I had a bad feeling about all this. Then poor Johannes, then Amos the gardener, things got slowly worse and worse. But hope springs eternal, all the time I tried to make light of it, tried to bounce back. After all, Hendrik was a clever man, we were rich, anything could be sorted, surely, however bad it seemed."

Georgina picked up her cup and saucer from the bedside table and took a sip.

"Even when we were in Pretoria, I tried to treat the trip as a holiday. It was great having Will and Angie with us, I was even getting along with Brunelda, my arch enemy, so I tried to put it all to the back of my mind. But when Hendrik told me of his plans, and the secret arrangements he had made for me, well then I knew it was desperate. As the taxi pulled away from outside the Pretoria office, I had a feeling I would never see him again. Although we never mentioned it, I think Hendrik thought so too."

Joyce crossed over to the bed and put her arm around her daughter.

"Then, when I saw Harry Castle the other day, he explained to me all the arrangements that Hendrik had made for me and the more than three million pounds he had put at my disposal, well then I knew he was preparing for the worst."

"Three million pounds," Joyce shook her head in disbelief, her daughter truly did exist in a different world.

"But you seemed so happy when we were shopping," challenged Joyce. "And this afternoon, making everyone laugh at the office."

Georgina raised her eyebrows and stared at her mother in contemplation.

"I must admit that I did feel a tremendous relief to be in England, to see you and to feel safe in my old bedroom, it was magical. There was always a chance, Hendrik may have got away, I was still hopeful…"

Georgina turned her head to stare at the far wall.

"Life has to go on. It will go on," said Georgina with great determination. "Let me sleep now Mum and I promise we will talk tomorrow."

Joyce wanted to say lots but this wasn't the time. She got up quietly and left the room. Closing the door behind her, she made her way to her own bedroom. Joyce looked around the room, lost for what to do. It was too early for bed and no possibility of sleep. The tumultuous events since Georgina's unexpected arrival a few days earlier began to spin through her mind as she tried to make sense of the nightmare that was enveloping her daughter.

Her thoughts turned to the code engraved on the back of Georgina's new Cartier wristwatch, the last minute gift from Hendrik on which he placed so much importance. She accepted Georgina's opinion that the solution to the conundrum might only be discovered by her but nevertheless it was an interesting problem and she really had little else to do.

Removing several carefully arranged shoeboxes from the bottom of her fitted wardrobe a small safe was revealed. Dialling in the combination she took out the pretty timepiece and the jotter covered with Georgie's doodles. Returning downstairs, Joyce sat herself at the kitchen table where the light was best and examined the watch, turning it over carefully in her hands. The first thing she would do was check the transcription her daughter had made on the telephone message pad, however, even with her reading glasses, she was unable to decipher the tiny engravings.

Retrieving the jewellers' eye glass from the sideboard in the lounge, Joyce carefully examined the cryptic cartouche. Removing the glass from her eye, she replaced her glasses and checked the pencilled copy her daughter had made on the pad.

That was interesting she thought to herself as she re examined the watch with her eyeglass.

"Georgie's got the letters right," she whispered to nobody but herself. "But there's more."

Joyce recalled her daughter complaining that the eye glass was difficult to use, she had clearly missed some small markings that might be crucial. Intrigued now, she picked up the pencil and began to carefully copy exactly what she was seeing through the glass.

A.P. v Z
KX

Excited now, Joyce compared what she had so carefully written, with her daughter's more casual transcription.

APVZ
KX

"Silly girl," said Joyce, still talking to herself as she compared the two versions.

It was clear that Georgina had missed the two minute full stops after the 'A' and 'P'. After some more thought it occurred to Joyce that capital letters with full stops might be a persons initials: 'A. P.' After all, there were no full stops following the other letters.

"I'm sure that's significant," she mused to herself. "But who is A.P.?

Clearly, Joyce realised, there was no point her wracking her brains trying to put a name to the initials, if initials they were. Her daughter was correct in her assumption the solution would probably be apparent only to her.

"And why is the 'v' a small letter and the Z a capital but without a full stop?" she muttered.

Joyce continued to puzzle over her new discoveries deep into the night. She was no nearer a solution, why should she be, the clue was not intended for her, but she was certain this would mean something to her daughter.

Resting her chin on her arms Joyce continued to study the cryptic markings on the pad in front of her as her brain raced back and forth through the events of the day.

"Perhaps it's all pointless now, anyway," she muttered as her eyes closed. In a few moments Joyce was fast asleep.

CHAPTER THIRTEEN

Sunday 16th February 1969

Joyce Browne awoke with a start and it took her a few seconds to realise where she was and why. It was still dark outside and a glance at the kitchen clock confirmed it was twenty minutes past four in the morning. She had an excruciating pain in the back of her neck and her arms had lost all feeling.

She sat up and stretched, slowly flexing her neck from side to side and feeling with alarm the almost audible creaks from her vertebrae. Rising unsteadily to her feet she hobbled the couple of steps to the kettle and, supporting herself on the work surface, lit the gas.

A few minutes later Joyce was sitting in an easy chair in her living room and enjoying the reviving properties of the day's first cup of tea. What to do? Early though it was, she didn't want to go to bed, so having finished her tea she went upstairs and ran a hot bath. After which, feeling much better and barefoot in blue jeans and an old cowl necked sweater she made her way quietly back down the stairs.

To Joyce's surprise, Georgina was sitting at the kitchen table clad in a white dressing gown.

"Hello, Mum," said Georgina, with an attempt at a smile. "I heard you running the bath, couldn't you sleep either?"

"No dear," she replied, kissing Georgie on the cheek. "I've been sitting at the table puzzling over your wristwatch all night."

"And?"

Joyce hesitated.

"Well, I did find something we missed," said Joyce, almost as an apology. "But it doesn't matter now, does it? Not now Hendrik…" her voice tailed away to nothing.

"Not now Hendrik is dead, you mean. It's okay, you can say it. You can rest assured, Mum, that I shall most definitely pursue this mystery that Hendrik went to such great lengths to hide for me. How can I do otherwise, how can I continue with my life, knowing that this stuff exists and I have no idea what it is. So tell me what you've found."

Joyce explained to her daughter the discovery she had made during the night and the two women stared at the new cryptic markings pencilled so carefully on the pad.

A.P. v Z
KX

"Well done, Mum. Yes, I missed that and I think you may be right, A.P. might be initials. It's just a matter of thinking whose they are."

"Darling," frowned Joyce, taking Georgina's hand in hers. "Should we be doing this? I mean to say, you have had a terrible shock…"

"Mum, listen to me. Although we were only married a few months, I did love Hendrik but as I said last night I had an idea things might end this way. Not like the terrible, unexpected shock when Dad died. You could say I was subconsciously preparing for it."

Joyce nodded.

"And I think I have no choice but to solve this mystery. I haven't had a lot of time to think about it but I am determined to save the company, my company. True, I don't need money but I want my property back, my house in Constantia, everything in it. You run your own business, Capital Law is now my business and I intend to have it back. I also want Hendrik's and Johannes's murders solved and the best way to do that is to find this hidden evidence. I have no funeral to attend, that will not be for weeks, no death certificate to obtain, no grieving relatives to receive, in fact nothing to do. So let's get on with the job in hand, shall we?"

"Oh, Georgie, be careful," whispered Joyce, frowning. "You can't fight a government."

"But I have to," she continued, clenching her fists. "Don't think for a moment that whoever is behind all this won't expect me to recover this stuff whether I do or not, so I might as well have the protection this evidence may offer me. The thing is, I may have to bargain for my safety as well. Had you thought of that, Mum?"

"Have you any ideas who AP might be?"

"Not yet," replied Georgie, staring at the message pad. "Why, I wonder, is the 'v' small and the 'Z' big."

With Georgina deep in thought, the minutes ticked by in silence. Joyce stifled a yawn as she got up from the table, opened the door of the refrigerator and looked in.

"Is it too early for breakfast, do you think?" enquired Joyce, doubtfully.

"The small 'v' could be 'van' or even 'von'," muttered Georgina, resting her chin in her hands and ignoring her mother's question. "They are common names in South Africa, my name for instance, or van de Merwe, or van Rensberg or van Vuuren and in most cases people write the 'van' in lower case, so that makes sense."

Abandoning for the time being her proposition of an early

breakfast, Joyce returned to the table. She was pleased and surprised to note that a sparkle had returned to Georgina's blue eyes. Three times in as many days Joyce had seen her daughter rebound from news that would crush most people, whatever emotions drove Georgina, they were formidable indeed. At that moment Joyce felt a fierce pride that the woman sitting at the table in front of her was her daughter.

"Can you think of any van Z's then, Georgie?" asked Joyce, brightly, finally abandoning any further attempts to maintain a decorous atmosphere of sympathetic grief.

"The only van 'Z' that I can think of would be van Zyl," said Georgina, looking at her mother whom she was glad to sense was now fully back on the case. "The trouble is, I don't know any van Zyl's"

"Perhaps, they were friends of Hendrik."

"Well, what would be the point of that, Mum?" exploded Georgina, throwing her hands in the air in desperation. "It's got to be obvious to me, hasn't it? If you haven't got any better suggestions than that I think you would best be employed getting on with some breakfast, don't you?"

Incredible though it was, both women burst out laughing.

"Sorry, mum," apologised Georgie, still smiling but looking a little shamefaced at her mother. "But, I'm starving."

Joyce put her arms around her daughter.

"I'm so proud of you," she whispered, tears welling up in her eyes. "You really are amazing."

"I'm surprised you've only just noticed my brilliance. Anyway, I haven't done anything yet."

Glad to be smiling, Joyce busied herself preparing an early meal as Georgina continued to puzzle over the conundrum.

Twenty minutes later the two women were sitting together enjoying a full English fried breakfast.

"We haven't given any thought yet to what KX means," mused Georgina, noisily slurping tea, with a forkful of sausage and egg poised to follow.

"KX, Kilo X-Ray," repeated Joyce, thoughtfully, as she continued to tackle her food. "That sounds like an aircraft call sign."

"Don't understand?" said Georgina, looking up from her plate with interest.

"It's the phonetic alphabet. The air traffic control people use it, all pilots are tested to make sure they know it. Sometimes the radio messages in the 'plane get broken up by atmospherics. That can be dangerous if there are misunderstandings, so each letter becomes an easily recognised word, for example, alpha, bravo, charlie, delta and so on. So if my call sign was KX, I would say Kilo X-Ray. You must have seen it used on the TV detectives."

"We still haven't got TV in South Africa, but now you mention it I remember the pilots on my charter 'plane saying things like that," said Georgina, interested now in this chance revelation. "So what would be APVZ?"

"Alpha, papa, victor, zulu," chanted Joyce, with satisfaction at teaching her daughter something.

"Zulu, that's interesting," repeated Georgina, laying her knife and fork on her plate. "Zulu, yes very interesting."

Breakfast over, the next couple of hours were spent in showers and baths and hair washing, followed by coffee and newspaper reading until at around 11.00am, mother and daughter agreed on a Sunday stroll to nearby Chiswick House and it's peaceful grounds.

Georgina and her mother walked slowly through the gardens. They were, for the most part, deep in their own thoughts, stopping to watch the ducks paddling across the pond in pursuit of the scraps of bread thrown by a group of children standing on the bank.

Continuing their stroll they approached the Palladian magnificence of Chiswick House.

"I remember playing here when I was little," said Georgina, gazing at the elegant building.

"We used to come here every Sunday," smiled, Joyce, slipping her hand though her daughter's arm. "And your Dad used to play cricket here for Turnham Green in the afternoon."

They were suddenly disturbed by a football whistling past them, a little too close for comfort.

"You're in goal, Andy," shouted one mud encrusted boy to his pal as he threw his coat down as a goal post.

"Come on, Mum, once more round the lake, then home," smiled Georgie as they walked away, keeping a weather eye open for the muddy football as the boys' game got under way.

They had only taken a few steps when Georgina suddenly stopped, turned and watched the two boys at their game.

"What is it, Georgie?"

"That boy, he called his pal Andy," replied Georgina, still watching the lads playing, "That rings a bell but I can't think why."

"The puzzle you mean?"

Georgina nodded, holding her hand up for silence as she stared at her feet, deep in thought. Turning, she continued very slowly along the path, before stopping again.

"Andries Pretorius," shouted Georgina, turning excitedly towards her mother, "A.P. is Andries Pretorius."

Georgina's yell, as well as startling her mother, had caused other promenaders to turn their heads and stare.

"I've got it, Mum," continued Georgina, triumphantly, "I've got the whole top line, "Andries Pretorius versus the Zulus, A.P. v Z"

"You've lost me."

Georgina continued to explain

"Do you remember the dreadful old painting that hangs in my dining room in Cape Town?" asked Georgina, as they quickened their pace towards home. "The one with the man and the old girl loading the rifle in the middle of a battle?"

"Vaguely."

"Well, I hated that picture from the moment I saw it. It's huge and gloomy in a great gilt frame with a brass plate at the bottom with the inscription, 'Andries Pretorius at the Battle of Blood River. 18th December 1838.' The trouble was, Hendrik treated the thing as an heirloom, saying that the old lady in the picture was a van Wyk ancestor."

"I'm still lost, Georgie."

"Hendrik tried to teach me the history of the thing. About the Voortrekkers or pioneers and their search for new farmland, free of British rule. It's called 'The Great Trek' Mum and is famous in South African history. There were different groups, each perhaps five hundred strong, men women and children, travelling in ox waggons with all their belongings. One of the groups was led by a man called Piet Retief who tried to negotiate with the Zulus and was murdered and all his followers killed. The Zulus then attacked another group, again about five hundred strong with a huge army, or impi I think they're called. Well, this time the Voortrekker leader, Andries Pretorius, formed the waggons into a circle or laager and the Zulus were defeated with huge losses and not a single pioneer killed."

"That's interesting but how does it help us in London in 1969?"

"The painting became a standing joke between the two of us. Hendrik knew I hated it so that's why I think he has used it for the clue as it would mean nothing to anyone else.
Now, think Mum, where is this evidence likely to be?"

"I don't know Georgie, it could be anywhere." replied Joyce, shaking her head in despair.

"I think it will be in a left luggage office or safe deposit, somewhere in London," explained Georgina, looking at he mother triumphantly. "And what's more, I think that the box number will be 1838."

"Oh, now I see," said Joyce, making a show of patting her daughter on the back. "The penny has finally dropped, you are clever, Georgie."

"All I need to know is where?" continued Georgina, pushing her hands deep in her pockets."That must be the KX, Mum, any ideas."

"Well, now you've explained that it's a location, the answer is easy. It has to be Kings Cross Station."

Georgina stopped walking and turned to face her mother.

"That's brilliant, Mum," enthused Georgie, wide eyed and mouth open in a pretend scream. "You're a genius."

Joyce, smiling, blew on her finger nails and rubbed them on her lapels.

"Box 1838 at Kings Cross. It's worth a try."

"You bet it is. I'm on a mission tomorrow, Mum."

Arriving home, Joyce immediately went to her safe and recovered the wristwatch and notepad, as they reviewed the clues at the kitchen table over more coffee.

"If Hendrik had any doubts about the clue," explained Georgina, her eyes sparkling. "They would have been settled when we arrived in Pretoria, last week. While he was working, the rest of us, at Brunelda's insistence, spent the day visiting the Voortrekkers Memorial. History isn't my cup of tea but it was impressive and there are wall carvings depicting The Great Trek. That's when I think he decided on the code, as late as that. I believe he had the engraving done that day, when we were all at the memorial. He must have been satisfied with his decision as the painting and the memorial came up in conversation at dinner the same day. So, he would have known that it was in my thoughts."

While Georgina was speaking, her mother sat examining the watch.

"You know, dear, with all our attention on the engraving," said Joyce, holding the watch against her wrist. "I never noticed what a beautiful thing it is, it must have been very expensive."

Georgina glanced casually at the timepiece on her mother's wrist.

"I suppose so. If you like it, then keep it, Mum. As I said, I've got several like it."

Joyce pulled the Cartier from her wrist and pushed it across the table as if it was red hot and burning her.

"I didn't say it for that, Georgie, I wouldn't dream of taking it. It's yours, it's the last thing Hendrik ever gave…" Joyce's voice faltered as she realised the enormity of her remark.

"Yes, I know Mum," replied Georgina, pushing the watch back across the table and smiling at her mother. "But I have lots of presents from Hendrik and to be honest I don't really fancy wearing this one, so I can't think of anyone better than my Mum to have it. So put it back on, please."

After more coaxing, Joyce was persuaded to wear the watch but only after promising that first thing tomorrow she would get Bob Simmons to photograph the inscription with a macro lens.

In the afternoon Joyce divided her time between the newspaper and taking surreptitious glances at her new Cartier wristwatch while Georgina switched on the television. This was a new fascination for her, there being no television service in South Africa. Georgie would watch anything, from westerns to comedies, from the news to kids' programmes it was all the same to her.

While Georgina was engrossed in the television, her mother watched her surreptitiously and with great concern over the top of her 'Sunday Express'. It was just twenty four hours since she had received the news of her husband's murder but now her daughter was planning an expedition to London in the morning in search of some nebulous evidence that was surely irrelevant now anyway. And she was excited about it, animated, eyes sparkling. Joyce worried. When would the real shock set in, as it must? After hearing of Hendrik's death, by telephone of all things, Georgina had succumbed to grief for a matter of hours. Joyce had difficulty reconciling herself to the two of them puzzling over the inscription on the back of a watch at five in the morning. Georgina was only human, some sort of breakdown must come eventually, but when? Joyce was determined to be there when the time came. She had been absent for much of her daughter's upbringing but she was here now and she wouldn't let her down.

CHAPTER FOURTEEN

Monday 17th February 1969
Kings Cross, London

Eight – thirty the next morning, Monday, found the house in Staveley Road a hive of activity. If Joyce Browne was totally honest with herself she would have preferred to see her daughter observing even a short period of decorous mourning, but it was clearly not to be. On entering the kitchen she was confronted with the sight of her newly widowed daughter sitting at the table, loading a piece of toast with a mountain of marmalade. Joyce envied Georgina her happy ability of being able to eat whatever she liked, in whatever quantities she liked, whenever she liked, without putting on an ounce of weight.

"Tea?" enquired Georgie, holding aloft the tea pot, her speech almost incoherent through a mouthful of food.

In answer to Joyce's nod, Georgina filled a cup with tea, leaving her mother to add the milk.

"Are you sure this is right?" frowned Joyce, sitting opposite her daughter. "I mean, rushing up to London on this wild goose chase."

"Absolutely," replied Georgie, brightly, reaching for another slice of toast, "Who else am I going to trust to do it, hey?"

"Georgina, at least take Bob Simmons with you. You don't know London and I would feel much better if there were two of you. After all, you don't have any idea what might happen."

"Bob Simmons, your office boy? Don't be ridiculous, none of this has anything to do with him. Anyway, he's just a kid, what use would he be?"

"You'd do well to get off your high horse, miss. I've told you before, he's not an office boy, in fact he's six weeks older than you, he's lived in London all his life and maybe he's not as clever as the high and mighty Georgina van Wyk, but he's sharp and quick witted. I'm worried sick about your safety, so I'll thank you not to be so bloody patronising, this is England not South Africa."

Accustomed to being obeyed without question, Georgina was more shocked by her mother's outburst than she would have liked to admit. The challenge had hit home and Georgina felt uncomfortable, in fact she'd never before heard her mother use even the mildest expletive.

"Who's to say he would want to come, Mum?" said a chastened Georgie, avoiding her mother's gaze.

"Don't pretend to be naive, Georgina," continued Joyce, eyes still flashing with anger. "You know as well as I do that he cannot take his eyes off you whenever you're in the office. You would only have to whistle for him to follow you anywhere."

Without speaking, Georgina followed her mother into the living room.

"Okay, Mum, I'm sorry, I'll take him along if you like, he may be useful."

"It's not if I like," replied Joyce, sharply, rejecting the proffered olive branch, "I just think it's common sense not to go alone. At the very least Bob could run for help, heaven forbid."

Georgina put her arms around her mother in final capitulation.

"You are quite right, Mum, I wasn't thinking, was I?"

Arriving at Wilding Photographic's offices at 9.35am Joyce protested her need to get on with some work, but was inwardly still irritated at her daughter's lack of propriety and her condescension, as well as regretting her own outburst. She swept through the reception area and into her office at the rear of the premises, closing the door. She was uncertain who, in the office was aware of Hendrik's death. Certainly Richard knew but who else had he informed? With her daughter still bouncing along as if nothing had happened, this was all very upsetting.

Meanwhile, Georgina's bad start to the day was exacerbated by the slightly unsettling fact that Bob Simmons appeared to be taking no notice of her presence in the office. Instead of his usual fawning attention, to which Georgina had become accustomed, he was seated in the wheeled typist chair with his face pressed to a very thin gap between the sliding partitions separating the window display from the rest of the reception area.

Puzzled, Georgina, dressed in her zipped black leather motorcycle style jacket, roll neck sweater and tight blue jeans, crossed the room and looked down at Bob's head.

Bob removed his eye from the gap in the partition and looked up at Georgina.

"Have you noticed that you are being followed?" said Bob, replacing his eye to the partition.

"Followed, who by?" snapped Georgie, suddenly all attention.

"Well, I've noticed that whenever you come into the shop,

a man, goes into the café opposite and sits in the window watching our door. Then, when you leave, he leaves. There's usually two of them and they have a car parked in Mayfield Avenue and take it in turn to watch the mews leading to our back entrance as well. I've been checking them out"

"Is he there now?" asked Georgie, rushing to the glazed entrance door.

"Don't look out the door, he'll see you. Look through this gap."

Bob, eye to the partition, was about to vacate his chair so that Georgie could look through the one inch by six inch gap in the wooden screens when, to his surprise, she sat on his right knee, pressing her face close to his as they both looked through the same gap.

"I can see him," she said excitedly. "He's looking over at the shop."

"Don't worry," whispered Bob. "He can't see us."

To be honest, Bob Simmons was having great difficulty concentrating on his restricted view of Chiswick High Road. His senses were completely overwhelmed by the close proximity of the object of all his recent dreams. Georgina, in looking through the aperture, had her face so close to Bob's that her hair tickled his cheek, her perfume completely swamped his senses and when she turned her face to speak, he felt a frisson of excitement course through his body as her lips brushed his ear. In addition to her perfume he delighted in the peppermint smell of her breath.

Bob was experiencing an almost irresistible urge to kiss this beautiful young woman, similar to the urge to jump when standing on the edge of a high cliff or building. Such action would obviously lead to disaster but nevertheless the impulse was hard to resist. He was aware that succumbing to his desires would, at the very least, earn him a slapped face and the loss of the best job he had ever had. Still it was almost too much for a young man. Bob's dilemma was suddenly resolved to his complete and utter surprise as Georgina slid her left hand around his neck and, pulling his face even closer to her's, kissed him full on the lips.

"You're a genius Bob. I wondered if I was being followed, but I hadn't noticed anything. I expect they're watching the house too."

"Who are they, Georgie?" asked Bob, still savouring the taste of her kiss.

"Fancy coming up to London with me, Bob?" smiled Georgina, ignoring his question.

"Of course, when?" replied Robert Simmons with mounting excitement.

"Now."

"Fantastic," exclaimed Bob, wide eyed, his brain in a whirl. "But what about Mrs Browne?"

"That's okay, it's sorted. The trouble is we've got to get to Kings Cross Station, but we can't risk being followed by these monkeys." Nodding her head in the direction of the café opposite. "I was going to walk round to Turnham Green, so thank heavens you spotted them or I wouldn't have stood a chance of not being followed."

Georgina glanced at Bob's perplexed face. Of course, he had no idea what she was talking about. She would have to tell him something.

"Bob, my husband has hidden important documents for me somewhere in London and I have to find them. I think they may be in the Left Luggage Office at Kings Cross. The trouble is, our friend opposite wants them as well but he doesn't know where they are. Sorry, I can't tell you any more than that."

There was silence for a few moments as Bob and Georgina surveyed the traffic congestion outside.

"We'll never lose them in a cab." said Georgie, half to herself, half to Bob. "Not in this traffic and if I tried to get out in Mum's car from the back they'd just follow in theirs. It would be the same if I went back to my new flat and got the Jag, they'd just follow."

"We would lose them on a motorbike," Bob grinned at Georgie.

"What your bike, is it here?"

"It's out the back, you could have my crash helmet. They will take no notice of me going off on my bike, I can then ride round to the front, up the pavement and right to the shop door, as soon as you see me you jump on the back and we're away, before they know what's going on. Then I can weave through the traffic up to Hammersmith and on to Kings Cross. They would never catch us."

Bob hurried out to the back of the building and returned a few seconds later handing a rather tatty, silver painted crash helmet with a pair of goggles to Georgina. She inspected the greasy interior with obvious disdain.

"I think I'll take my chances without one, thanks." said Georgina, screwing up her pretty nose in disgust and handing back the headgear.

"Well, it's not a legal requirement yet, just recommended for safety," explained Bob, a little crestfallen.

"Best you don't have an accident then," replied Georgina, with a wink. "Are you prepared to give it a go, I mean, get us through this traffic so we're not followed?"

"Of course I am," said Bob, grinning like a Cheshire cat, his eyes sparkling with excitement. "You stand by the door and watch out for me."

It was decided as quickly as that. Putting on his hemet, Bob disappeared through the back of the building and a few seconds later Georgina heard a thunderous roar as the Gold Star burst into life. Turning back towards the front door she just had time to zip up her jacket and turn up the collar when she heard the bike's approach. Georgina pulled the door a few inches open, at the same time keeping her face turned away from the glass to delay recognition until the last possible moment. True to his word, Bob pulled the machine up within three feet of the door and, keeping the engine revving noisily, looked excitedly towards Georgina. She threw open the shop door and was on the back of the bike in two strides.

"Hold me tightly round the waist." he shouted over his shoulder as he let in the clutch.

"In your dreams," Georgie shouted back, trying to find the pillion footrests as the big old BSA lurched forward.

Forcing several startled pedestrians to leap out of his way, Bob accelerated back across the pavement towards the road. Laughing aloud as he felt Georgina's arms tighten around his waist, he bounced the bike down the kerb and accelerated hard across the front of a red London Transport double decker bus that was just pulling away in the traffic. The strident sound of the bus hooter was drowned by the roar from the 500cc single as they gained the outside lane, taking a Keep Left bollard on the wrong side.

Georgina's only backward glance afforded her the satisfaction of seeing a man run from the café and stand, hands on hips staring in their direction. Looking forward again a lorry, headlights flashing appeared to be on a certain collision course with the bike, when Bob suddenly cut back in to the left hand side, avoiding disaster by an inch at the most.

'This is going to be exciting,' thought Georgie, as the Goldie hurtled on towards Hammersmith.

For his part, Bob was in heaven, adrenalin pumping, the girl of his dreams on the pillion, he could feel her arms around his waist, her body pressing into his back and her thighs tight against his.

He weaved in and out of the slow moving traffic, one moment racing up the outside, the next moment squeezing through a claustrophobic gap between two lorries, so tight, Georgie's knees were brushing the sides of the trucks.

Onwards they raced, leaning so far over as they came into the roundabout at Hammersmith that the footrests were scraping the road surface and then, straightening up, accelerating madly onwards, engine thundering, towards Kensington.

Certain there could be no possibility of being followed, Bob slowed the bike to a more reasonable pace in acknowledgement of the increased numbers of police officers in the West End. He continued to weave through the slow moving traffic, passing Hyde Park on the left, across Hyde Park Corner and on down Piccadilly. Leaning over again at a perilous angle, to negotiate Piccadilly Circus, up Shaftesbury Avenue until he turned north and made his way to the Euston Road, then right towards Kings Cross.

Passing the entrance to the station on their left hand side, Bob turned left into York Way and stopped by a row of solo motorcycles parked by the kerb. Georgina got off the bike and fussed with her hair as she waited on the pavement. Meanwhile, Bob backed the big old Beeza onto the end of the line of bikes. Dismounting, he hauled the machine back onto it's centre stand. Turning off the petrol, he secured the back wheel with the chain and padlock he had been wearing as a necklace.

Robert Simmons couldn't resist running his hand with pride over the petrol tank, the big engine clicking and ticking away to itself as the hot metal and oil began to cool. Stepping onto the kerb, his pride surged even further at the sight of Georgina studying her appearance in the rear view mirror of a nearby motor scooter, flicking up her hair with her fingertips. She seemed always to look stunning, whatever she was doing or wearing. A passing van driver blew a wolf whistle as he drove past.

"That was a brilliant ride, Bob," said Georgie, smiling and squeezing Bob's arm. "Surely nobody could have followed us."

"Only another bike and nothing did, I kept an eye on my mirror all the way."

"Right, let's get on," continued Georgina, as she turned towards the station, swinging her bag across her shoulder.

"Where are we going?" asked Bob, hurrying to keep pace. "You want the left luggage office don't you?"

"No, I want the nearest ladies at the moment," smiled Georgina, stopping to look around as they entered the station concourse. "I'm not going anywhere 'till I've done something about my hair, I look an absolute sight."

Bob smiled to himself as they set off across the busy station towards the distant overhead sign, Georgina's stiletto's clicking on the paving stones.

"Get a couple of coffees," ordered Georgie, indicating a nearby snack bar as she disappeared into the ladies. "I shan't be a minute."

Bob walked the few yards to the small cafeteria, ordered two coffees and found a table where he could see the entrance to the conveniences. A full ten minutes passed while he sipped his coffee before he saw Georgina striding with elegant confidence towards him. As he watched her he couldn't help but notice the glances she attracted from the men she passed. Was she aware of this attention? Of course she was. His ego knew no bounds as Georgina sat next to him and picked up her coffee.

"Georgie," Bob frowned as he lifted his cup to his lips. "I don't quite know how to say this, but…"

She studied his face, waiting for him to continue.

"…Mr Wilding told me about your husband," he muttered in embarrassment. "He said I was not to mention it, but I just wanted to say how sorry I am…I can't think of any way I can help, but if there's anything…just say, I really like you Georgie and I think you're very brave…"

Replacing her cup in the saucer, she smiled at Bob. He darted a glance at her as she reached over and touched his fingers.

"Thanks Bob, you're a nice guy. Even my mother cannot understand why I didn't take to my bed in tears. She even wanted to call the doctor. But I'm not like that…I'm upset, of course I am…and the time will come for me to sit down and cry…I loved Hendrik. But at the moment I have to see this through, as I've said I cannot tell you much, but my husband upset some really big people back home. They've murdered three already and there's a chance I could be next…"

Bob's eyes nearly popped out of his head at this revelation.

"In fact…perhaps I'm being selfish involving you in my problems at all…"

"No, I want to help, I'll protect you, you'll see."

Georgina could not resist a laugh as she squeezed Bob's hand. He could have no idea how out of his depth he was, but she was surprised how much she liked having him around.

"You're a real help already. Now, if you've finished your coffee, let's go and find this left luggage office."

Bob paid the bill and they walked out onto the concourse. An enquiry with a passing porter directed them to the far side of the station.

Standing at a long wooden counter, a bell rang as Georgina

pressed a button marked 'Enquiries'. After a couple of minutes an elderly man in a British Railways uniform appeared from behind a row of black metal lockers.

"Yes, miss, can I help you?"

"I hope so," commenced Georgina in a very business like manner. "My name is Georgina van Wyk and I have come to collect the contents of your locker number 1838."

The railwayman stared at her for a moment before scratching his head with a pencil.

"It doesn't work like that, miss," he explained, as if talking to an imbecile. "When you deposit luggage to collect later, you get given a key with a number on it."

"I haven't got a key," frowned Georgina, suddenly doubting her solution to the riddle on the Cartier watch Hendrik had given her.

"No, and we haven't got a box 1838, either."

For once in her life Georgina was lost for words. What seemed yesterday such a certain solution, was now in doubt.

"I didn't leave the luggage, it was my husband," was the only explanation she could come up with on the spur of the moment.

"You're Australian aren't you Miss, I can tell by your accent," said the official sagely, tapping his nose and winking. "My sister went to live in Brisbane just after the war, loves it there. I've often thought of emigrating myself."

"You've got a good ear for an accent, I'm from Sydney, myself," turning her head and winking at Bob. "I only arrived in London yesterday and it seems I've got my husbands instructions all wrong and I can't contact him because he's at the North Pole. What am I going to do?"

Georgie gave the railwayman her most forlorn wide eyed expression as Bob turned and faced the windows.

"Now don't you worry Miss," said the man, falling hook,

line and sinker for Georgie's damsel in distress routine. "I'm a Londoner, born and bred and I've been on the railway for thirty years, so there's not much I don't know, see."

"I'm sure there isn't."

All the big London Stations use the same left luggage system as we do, so there's no use looking elsewhere. What were your husbands exact instructions, Miss?"

Georgina put her hand to her brow in a very theatrical impression of being deep in thought. "I'm sure he said, Box 1838 at Kings Cross."

The left luggage man thought for a few minutes before his face suddenly lit up.

"I'm just thinking that Box 1838 sounds a bit like a safe deposit number, not left luggage at all."

Georgina's mocking sarcasm melted away in an instant as she listened attentively to what the man was saying.

"The railway hasn't had safe deposits for years, people have to use the banks nowadays, but as I recall, there's a security company somewhere down the Kings Cross Road that has safe deposits. That might be your best bet."

"Perhaps it was 1838 at Kings Cross ROAD not station," she said excitedly, turning to Bob, who was now at her shoulder and all attention.

"What's the name of this firm, have you an address, a 'phone number?"

"That's the trouble, miss, I can't remember exactly. It's a funny name though, I remember that."

"Come on, man. This is important," demanded Georgina, beginning to lose her temper.

"I'm doing my best, I'm trying to remember," he replied indignantly.

Georgina took a deep breath, glancing at Bob. Producing a

five pound note from her jacket pocket, she pushed it across the counter towards the railwayman who pocketed it in an instant.

"It's on the tip of my tongue, miss. Summer and Winter, Light and Dark, something like that,"

"Look, let's just walk down the Kings Cross Road and see if we can find it," suggested Bob, trying to help.

"Don't be ridiculous," snapped Georgie, angrily, "That could take days…"

"That's it,' shouted the clerk, in triumph, "Days and Weeks, Days and Weeks Security. I said it was a funny name."

"'Phone number, 'phone number, look it up man," gasped Georgina, followed quickly by, "please." and a plaintive smile.

Grumbling to himself, the elderly clerk bent down and retrieved a very dirty and tatty 'A to D' London telephone directory from under the counter.

"Let's see now, now where did I put my glasses?"

Georgina snatched the directory from his hand and spun it round on the counter to face her. Opening it towards the rear and flicking through the pages with lightening speed she ran her finger down the columns. After a few minutes Georgina looked up in frustration.

"There's no Days and Weeks listed."

"It sounds like Days but I think it's spelt different, Miss, I'm sure."

Georgina returned to the directory with doubled intensity, flicking the pages violently back and forth in her mounting frustration.

"Here it is," she shouted in triumph. "Daize and Weekes, Daize and Weekes, 3 Dickens Place, Kings Cross Road,"

Bob Simmons already had the office door open and Georgina was about to hurry past him back onto the station concourse when she stopped suddenly, returning to the counter.

"Thank you very much for all your help," she cooed at the bemused railway official, thrusting another five pound note into his hand. "If anyone should ask, this says you couldn't help me."

Back on the station Bob turned in the direction of the York Way entrance.

"No Bob, we'll take a cab, your bike draws too much attention."

"But nobody followed us, you agreed they couldn't have, so what does it matter?" Anyway, Kings Cross Road is only across the way, we could walk."

Georgina looked at Bob with rising anger.

"Maybe we weren't followed, but we don't know who might happen to be on the station by chance, do we?"

Without waiting for an answer, Georgina hurried away towards the station's main entrance, leaving Bob to follow in her wake.

Back in the street the couple waited in silence at the empty cab rank, Georgina deep in thought. After a few moments a black taxi, orange 'For Hire' light illuminated, pulled up next to them.

As Bob opened the back door for Georgina to get in, he lowered his head to speak to the driver.

"Dickens Pl…"

"…Shut up," hissed Georgie, elbowing Bob aside and speaking to the driver herself.

"The Cab Office, Penton Street."

Climbing into the back of cab, she glared at her companion.

"Listen, you moron, If anyone was watching us they could follow, couldn't they? Or take the cab number and trace the driver later. This isn't a fucking game."

Smarting from Georgina's sudden and aggressive outburst,

Bob sat in silence. This was the first time he had seen the explosive side of her character. Feeling surprised and hurt, he sat in silence, nursing his damaged pride.

For her part, instantly dismissing her companion from mind, she considered her next move.

Driving the short distance up Pentonville Road the taxi turned left into Penton Street and was immediately engulfed by a mass of near identical black cabs. Bob stared, cabs in front, cabs behind, cabs turning left, turning right, parked. In fact every vehicle in sight was a black taxi.

Without speaking, Georgina paid the driver and got out of the cab. Hurrying around the corner, she hailed a taxi that was pulling out from the Cab Office yard. Bob remained silent as she gave the driver the Kings Cross Road address and got in.

Driving back down Pentonville Road, Georgina glanced across at her companion.

"That's where they test all the cabs, I knew there would be dozens, all identical. I had a school friend who's Dad was a cabbie. Nobody following could have seen what cab we changed to, could they?"

"I'm sorry, Georgie, I..."

"...You were just trying to help, Ja, Ja, I know," replied Georgina, nudging Bob in the ribs, her temper having subsided as quickly as it had been roused.

A few minutes later they were standing on the pavement in Dickens Place, just off the Kings Cross Road, surveying a terrace of old and rather down at heel shop fronts. First and second floors extended above each premises.

Number 3 was distinguished by a small, plain black number on a plain green front door. Unlike the adjacent shop fronts, there was no name or advertisement over the window, which was blocked out with translucent sheets. The only other identification appeared to be an unpolished brass plate fixed to the brickwork by the door.

"Yes, this is it, Daize and Weekes Security," said Georgie, reading the brass plate. "I doubt we would have found it without the full address."

"Not very welcoming," said Bob over his shoulder as the door resisted his push. "Shall I ring the bell?

"Well, I'm not standing out here all day."

Bob Simmons pressed the brass push button and was rewarded by the sound of an electric bell ringing somewhere within the house. After a few moments they were both surprised to be addressed by a voice from the ether.

"Can I help you?"

Bob, cautious of provoking the displeasure of his companion a second time, stepped back respectfully allowing Georgina to approach the door.

Unable to locate any trace of a recognisable microphone or speaker, Georgina felt a little foolish as she introduced herself to the green front door.

"My name is Georgina van Wyk and I wish to recover the contents of a safe deposit box."

"Please come in," responded the disembodied voice, as, with a loud click, the door yielded to her push.

As the door swung shut behind them Bob and Georgina found themselves standing in a small, dark passage, perhaps as little as three feet wide and no more than six feet long, lit by a single, naked, low wattage bulb hanging from a grey plastered ceiling. The feeling of gloom and decay was further enhanced by brown painted wainscotting and peeling wallpaper. Underfoot were worn floorboards.

On the left was a closed green painted door that Georgina

imagined would lead into the shop. There was a similar closed door at the end of the passage.

Bob glanced through the gloom at his companion as she surveyed her surroundings with dismay.

"This can't be the right place, can it?" he whispered, frowning.

Raising her eyebrows and shrugging her shoulders, Georgina was about to reply when the sound of footsteps preceded the opening of the left hand door.

Without speaking, a small and rather fat little man stood to one side and gestured for them to enter the room.

Stepping through the doorway, Georgina confirmed her belief that this room was the original shop behind the translucent window. However, she was surprised that the street from this side of the glass was clearly visible. They had obviously been carefully observed before being admitted. The rest of the room was entirely in keeping with the standard of decoration they had discovered in the entrance passage. Worn, bare boards on the floor, acres of brown paint and dull peeling wallpaper. She noticed another closed door in the centre of the wall opposite the shop window. The ceiling was ornamented with a large brown stain indicating a plumbing disaster of long ago.

Claiming Georgina's attention with a polite cough, the little man began to speak with a surprisingly bright, cheerful and friendly voice.

"Good morning, my name is Daize, I understand, Miss, that you wish to inspect one of our deposit boxes?"

"…Err, yes," fascinated by the man's appearance, this was the only reply Georgie could muster. "My husband, Hendrik van…"

"…No, No, Miss," said the man, sternly holding up his hand for silence. "It is a specific rule of this house that we do not require or solicit any personal information concerning our clients, except a box number and a signature. Total and utter privacy and security are our watchwords."

"Yes, of course."

Crossing to the far side of the room, the man stood behind a large and incongruously elegant antique desk, gesturing Georgina to the chair opposite. He politely waited for her to sit before occupying his own chair. There being no other furniture in the room save a metal filing cabinet, Bob was forced to stand. Not wishing to interfere he selected a position near the window where Georgina could, nevertheless, see him.

"Charming, charming, he muttered with a smile as he beamed at Georgina from across the desk. "Now, a few formalities," he continued, unlocking one of the desk drawers and reaching inside to produce a leather bound ledger.

Georgina took this opportunity to study the figure sitting opposite. He was probably fifty-five to sixty years of age with a round cheerful face and totally bald head. Kind, bright grey eyes peered through round glasses with thick, black frames giving him the appearance of a large and benevolent owl. Interesting though his features were, what fascinated Georgina most was his mode of dress. Mr Daize wore a plain black jacket, black waistcoat sporting a huge gold watch chain and striped grey trousers with shiny black Oxford shoes.

Old fashioned but smart conceded Georgina to herself with a private smile. However, the real eccentricity in Mr. Daize's appearance was a stiff, white, stand up collar and black tie reminiscent of Neville Chamberlain. The tie was secured with large diamond pin. His whole ensemble was completed by a red carnation in his button hole.

"And now, Mrs van Wyk, can I trouble you for that all important number?" he beamed expectantly, then glancing across at Bob Simmons who remained by the window. "Please do not speak it aloud but write it down on this pad."

"Yes, of course."

Georgina jotted the number 1838 on the proffered pad and pushed it back across the desk.

Glancing at the pad, Mr Daize frowned.

"My dear young lady, this is only a four figure number and I was anticipating rather more."

Georgina held her breath as her clever brain raced through the possibilities of a mistake in her deductions. Within seconds a solution presented itself. The date of the Battle of Blood River as described on the painting in her Cape Town dining room was 18th December 1838.

"I do apologise," replied Georgina with more confidence that she actually felt. "I only gave you the last four."

Taking back the pad she wrote down the number 18 12 18 38, arranging the numbers in pairs to disguise the fact that the sequence was derived from a date.

"Quite so, miss," beamed Mr Daize as he looked at the pad, " Excellent, just a signature here, and then I can take you to your box."

Georgina took the offered ledger and was surprised to see her own photograph at the top of the page. Adding her signature, she acknowledged to herself this further proof that Mr Daize was well aware of the identity of his visitor before he answered the door bell.

"One last formality, Mrs van Wyk. If I might ask you to leave your shoulder bag with your companion?"

"Oh, yes, if you wish."

The request having surprised her, she handed her bag to Bob who, glad to be of some use, stepped across the room to receive it.

"Thank you, sir," said Mr Daize, making his first acknowledgement of Bob's presence. "I will have to ask you to remain here sir, when we go into the next room."

With that, Mr Daize rose from the desk, unlocked and opened the second door, beckoning Georgina to precede him into the next room locking it behind them.

Georgina was not surprised to find the room was in a similar state of disrepair to the rest of the building, but was distinguished by being totally devoid of any furniture. Just a naked bulb hung from the ceiling and a Victorian fireplace in one wall, the hearth blocked long ago with a sheet of painted hardboard. At the opposite end of the room a single, gaunt, curtain less window admitted a dim light through whitewashed glass.

"Please stand quite still," requested Mr Daize, rubbing his hands together and beaming at Georgina, who returned his smile with a look of perplexed amusement. Nothing, however, could prepare her for what happened next.

Feeling a slight vibration, Georgina looked down and to her utter amazement, watched as the old worn floor began to slide away towards the other side of the room, leaving her and Mr Daize marooned on the first six floorboards that had remained stationary. Totally disorientated by the moving floor Georgie staggered slightly, grasping the little man's arm for support.

"Please don't be alarmed, Mrs van Wyk," giggled Mr Daize, patting her hand. "Our safe deposit is in the basement and so a trap door in the floor would have been difficult to disguise, perhaps a rug? Totally unsatisfactory, so my partner and I decided on a completely moving floor. Security is paramount, paramount, but I must admit I do enjoy seeing the amazement on our clients' faces as they watch the mechanism for the first time.

Georgina tightened the grip on her companion's arm as a pair of brushed aluminium hand rails rose slowly from the chasm between two of the steel beams that replaced the joists in supporting the sliding floor.

"Please, it's quite safe," smiled Daize, inviting her to precede him down the staircase, now clearly lit by a blue light emitting from the walls.

Stepping forward, she hesitatingly placed a stiletto booted foot on the first step. Then, taking a deep breath and tightly grasping the handrails she began to descend, glancing back to ensure Mr. Daize was following.

Arriving at the lower level, Georgina stepped past a hugely thick open door and was stunned to find herself standing in an ultra modern room, totally at variance with the Victorian decay of the ground floor. The walls and floor were formed from a shiny blue glasslike material, the ceiling similar but in white. The atmosphere, far from being musty and dank as could be expected in such an old house, was fresh and comfortably warm. Georgina was further intrigued by the pleasant, ambient light, the source of which she was unable to identify. There were no discernible light fittings, no brightness or shadow, just light exuding from the room.

"Good heavens, this is unbelievable," muttered Georgina, turning to stare at Mr Daize.

"I'm glad you like it, fun isn't it? Now you see why we keep the upstairs in the condition you find it. Camouflage for what is below."

Mr. Daize was understandably proud of his establishment and clearly delighted in surprising new clients.

Before Georgie could ask any further questions, a section of the shiny, blue wall slid open and the near double of Mr. Daize stepped into the room, the door sliding closed behind him, leaving only the faintest outline in the wall to identify it's location.

Bewildered though she was, Georgina could not resist a sudden giggle as the new arrival held out his hand.

With perfect manners, Mr Daize stepped between the two.

Mrs van Wyk, may I introduce my business partner, Mr Weekes. Mr. Weekes, Mrs van Wyk"

"How do you do?" said Georgina, shaking his hand with as much formality as she could muster.

"How do you do?" replied a delighted Mr. Weekes.

Mr. Weekes's apparel was identical to his colleague, Mr. Daize. He was of a similar height and build, he wore similar spectacles. The only difference Georgina could discern was a fringe of fluffy white hair framing his otherwise bald head.

"If I show the young lady into the reading room," said Daize to his colleague. "Perhaps you will fetch her box from the storeroom, Mr Weekes."

"Certainly, Mr Daize, you see that our client is quite comfortable while I collect the box, yes, yes, quite so."

However seriously Georgina viewed her current situation, she couldn't help but be amused by her two hosts. As the men conversed and nodded together she hid her smile with a hand, looking from one to the other, her sparkling wide open eyes and raised eyebrows betraying her amusement.

As his colleague departed along the shiny blue glass corridor, Mr Daize ushered Georgina through another electric sliding door into what he called the reading room.

This room was approximately twelve feet square and lit in the same enigmatic manner as outside. However, it was the two items of furniture that attracted Georgina's attention. The desk was a single sheet of clear moulded plexiglass sheet, the chair was similarly formed.

Georgie gasped as she ran her hand across the completely transparent desk.

"I've never seen anything like it. It's stunning."

"You're not the first person to admire it, miss," replied Mr. Daize, beaming with pride. "But I have to confess we had the design made for security reasons rather than style. What we needed was something where nothing could be hidden. No microphone, no miniature camera, no weapon. This room can be searched in a glance.

"Yes, I can see that," said Georgina, admiringly. "But the design is fantastic."

"The manufacturers doubted at first, whether it could be made," replied Mr Daize, enthusiastically, "It was truly ground breaking…"

"…And very, very expensive," interrupted Mr Weekes, as he entered the room carrying a large steel box and placing it on the plastic desk. "Now, Mr Daize, sit our young lady down and she can get to work."

Georgina was ushered around the desk to the chair.

"Please make yourself comfortable," smiled Mr Daize, pulling out the chair.

Sitting down she felt the chair being pushed in behind her legs, then Mr Daize rejoined his colleague as they both stood facing her across the table.

"We'll leave you on your own now," smiled Mr Weekes, Mr Daize nodding vigourously.

"Call if you need us,"

"Take as long as you like," they said in turn.

Georgina watched with amusement as the two little men, still smiling, backed out of the room, the door sliding shut behind them. Now alone, she spent a few moments looking around this space age room and running her hands over the contemporary desk. Becoming accustomed to the near silence she detected the slightest humming noise, that she guessed was probably an air conditioning unit somewhere in the basement. Eventually her attention was drawn to the grey steel box on the desk in front of her.

Feeling unexpectedly apprehensive, she pulled it closer to her. Taking a deep breath and suddenly aware of her own heart beat, she lifted the lid and looked inside.

Giving a little gasp, she removed a large, sealed, manilla envelope bearing her name written in her husband's familiar hand. Turning it over and over in her fingers she set it aside on the desk, unopened.

The next item she recovered was a stout brown cardboard box about twelve inches by eight by four inches deep. Placing it on the desk in front of her she slowly opened the carton to find it contained something wrapped in white cloth. Carefully unwrapping the heavy object she was taken aback to discover a large, black, automatic pistol, two boxes of ammunition and a cleaning kit.

Georgina whistled under her breath. Taking care not to touch the firearm she carefully re wrapped it and placed it in the box with the ammunition and accessories and set it aside. Trust Hendrik to include the cleaning kit, she smiled to herself.

Next, her eyes alighted on a smaller box that proved to contain three audio tapes numbered A1, 2 and 3 and two 'Super 8' cine films marked C1 and C2.

Now Georgina lifted out three cardboard files, each entitled 'OPERATION SLAPELOSE'

She remembered this being the name of the secret police team her husband had mentioned in Pretoria.

The first file bore the secondary title 'ASKARIS' on the front cover in large, hand written letters and contained six photographs of individual black men with attached notes. One of whom she recognised as the man Dingani Sibanyoni who had come to her house and was a suspect in the murder of her brother – in – law, Johannes du Plessis. Georgina also suspected him of the murder of her husband in Rhodesia, although she had no evidence.

"Bastard," she said out loud.

The other files contained more photographs of various men. She read the attached notes with interest. Most she didn't know, some she recognised as politicians and police officers, some she had even met.

Looking back in the box, Georgie next lifted out a large ledger. Although lacking accountancy skills it didn't take her long to realise that this was the evidence of false accounting that Johannes had discovered and with which he had confronted Hendrik. A separate note book listed the individual payments that had been made and once again the name of Sibanyoni appeared several times.

The last item in the box, that she very nearly overlooked, was a small blue velvet drawstring bag. Teasing open the mouth with her fingertips, she peeped inside before gently tipping the contents out on the table.

"Wow wee," she exclaimed aloud as a dozen large diamonds scattered across the table.

Leaving the sparkling gems where they lay, Georgina sat back in her chair and surveyed the items on the desk for a full five minutes, deep in thought.

Eventually, she leaned forward and picked up the unopened letter, holding it between the tips of her fingers.

Georgina closed her eyes for a few moments before tearing the envelope open and removing the typewritten sheets. Studying the first page she noticed immediately that the missive was not dated.

Cape Town

My Darling Georgie

From the moment Johannes confronted me with the evidence he had discovered of my false accounting, I was aware that I should make some provisions for your safety should all my attempts to rectify the situation fail.

I have always hoped that you would never hear the name 'Slapelose,' but the very fact that you are in London reading these lines proves me wrong.

Having had the foresight to secretly assemble photographic evidence of Askaris and police officers whenever I had the opportunity, I then began filming and tape recording meetings wherever possible. The visit of Sibanyoni to the house was the last straw and forced me to take action. I sent Janet Steyn to London with the evidence I had collected, together with the account books that I had taken from Johannes's office in Loop Street. Although what Johannes has discovered once, he can surely produce again.

Georgina set the letter down for a moment. 'He makes no mention of the murder so all this must have been arranged before Johannes was killed,' she thought.

She read on.

They have told me not to worry and that all will be fine, but I do not believe them. I now realise that I have been incredibly stupid.

"Yes, you most certainly have, my darling." whispered Georgie.

My great regret is that I can give you no further advice, you must use or not use this evidence as you see fit. Should the worst happen and I am arrested it may assist you to bargain for my release or, heaven forbid, protect yourself. It may also be of some consolation for you to know that I am making provisions for your independent financial security should this all end in disaster.

You may trust Janet Steyn implicitly, as you may my two little friends Daize and Weekes. You are probably not aware that before the van Wyks were involved in the legal profession, the family had made their money in diamonds. By bad judgement and even worse luck, on 16th May 1940 my father, with a bag full of South African uncut stones, found himself in the Amsterdam offices of a firm of diamond dealers. With the German army entering the city, the two young English dealers, none other that Mr Daize and Mr Weekes, offered to hide the stones until after the war. My father was dubious to say the least but with no other options open to him, he agreed. No receipt was ever issued for fear of being searched and no name written down. However, the two men requested my father to give them a number that might identify his property. Not wanting to use his date of birth because it appeared on his Passport, he remembered, on the spur of the moment and with the sound of gunfire at the end of the street, the painting that you love to hate. 'The Battle of Blood River' and chose the number 18 12 1838. After the war, to my father's amazement, he discovered 'Daize and Weekes' trading from offices in London. On receipt of the number his diamonds were returned to him in their entirety.

Why their slightly eccentric mode of dress? Apparently, it was what a diamond dealer wore in 1940 Holland and I suppose they see no reason to change.

Are they really brothers? They say not, but who knows.

Now I must finish and leave you to employ your clever

mind to extricate us from this awful situation that arose from my stupidity and greed. I sincerely hope to see you in happier times, either in England or South Africa.

Your loving husband
Hendrik

Georgina threw down the letter and exhaled noisily.

"Well you're certainly right there, lover," she said out loud, "With more money than we could ever spend, a fabulous house and our own good health you manage to get us into this. Then you say you're leaving it to me to sort out. Well thanks a million, darling. What a bloody mess."

Picking up the sheath of documents once more, Georgina read on. The remaining pages were simple transcripts of the audio tapes and descriptions of the content of the reels of Super 8 films. Skimming her eye down the pages, she had to admit that there didn't seem much that was truly earth shattering. Embarrassing for the people mentioned no doubt and possibly even lethal to the Africans in the photographs, but not likely to bring down a government.

She would keep this letter and study it in more detail, but her initial thought was that to leak them to the South African press would do little more than cause a scandal, provoke a denial, a few sackings, a high level resignation or two and then a return to normality. It was simply the case that this evidence was all gathered before the murders took place.

Georgina replaced the letter in its envelope and looked again at the array of objects surrounding the now empty steel box. First, she carefully collected up the diamonds and returned the velvet bag to the box. She didn't need the monetary value they represented and she had a mind, at some time in the future, to give them to Brunelda, the only remaining blood member of the van Wyk family.

She was tempted, but only for a moment, by the gun. Although competent in the use of firearms, she was sure if it came to a shoot out with the South African secret service, there would only be one winner and it was unlikely to be her. She would continue to rely, as she always had, on her own formidable arsenal of social skills.

The files, tapes and ledgers could all remain where they were.

Eventually, the plastic desk was clear except for the envelope and the steel box. Georgina was ready to leave.

Sitting back in her transparent plastic chair she glanced round the amazing futuristic room once more. Was there anything else? She thought not.

Feeling rather foolish she spoke out in the empty room.

"I think I'm finished now, thank you."

Within a minute the entrance door slid open to reveal the now familiar face of Mr Weekes, as he shuffled through the doorway.

"Quite finished are we, young miss?" he beamed, rubbing his hands together. "You know there is no rush, no rush whatever."

"Thank you, you have been very kind," she smiled, raising the envelope. "I would like to take this letter away with me and if it's okay with you, leave the rest of the items in the deposit box for safe keeping."

"Is it okay with us?" laughed Mr Daize, entering the room and standing next to his colleague. "Of course it's okay, that is what we do, tell her Mr Weekes."

"That's what we do." agreed Weekes.

"Couldn't be safer than here." added Daize.

"Quite so, quite so." continued Weekes. "So if you are sure, I will lock the box away and then Mr Daize will show you out."

With that Mr Weekes shuffled off with the deposit box while Mr Daize ushered Georgina from the room.

As they waited in the blue glass entrance hall, Georgina took a last look round. Then, slowly and silently the hugely thick, steel door began to open.

"After you, Miss," said Daize as he stepped back, indicating for Georgina to climb the blue lit steel staircase back to the ground floor.

After the bright modernity of the basement, the ground floor room appeared even more oppressively drab and decaying than she recalled. Turning to face the window, Mr Daize took Georgina's arm as they were joined by a slightly out of breath Mr Weekes who had followed them up the staircase. The three stood at the edge of the room as the rest of the floor slid slowly across to meet them, Georgina feeling the slightest vibration through her feet.

As the floor clicked shut she looked across at her two companions.

"Amazing."

"And unique," smiled Mr Weekes.

"Quite unique," agreed Mr Daize, unlocking the door into the equally drab front room, allowing Georgina to step through.

On seeing Georgina, Bob Simmons, perched uncomfortably on a corner of the desk, bored and eager to depart, jumped to his feet.

She shook hands with the two proprietors.

"It now only remains for me to settle my account," said Georgie, looking from one to the other.

"Madam," replied Mr Weekes with great formality, "The van Wyk account has been settled without fail and on time since 1945, there is nothing for you to pay."

"Without fail, without fail, since 1945," chirped in Mr Daize.

After a final round of goodbyes, Georgina and Bob found themselves back on the pavement, looking at the building.

"You were a long time."

Georgina looked up and down the road.

"Let's walk back down to Kings Cross station and I'll tell you all about."

As they hurried along, Georgina became very animated, describing to Bob the amazing world she had just left. He was suitably astonished and excitedly interrupted her narrative with question after question until Georgina stopped still on the pavement.

"I don't know how it bloody worked, do I?" I just know it bloody did, it was breathtaking."

Georgina noticed that Bob looked a bit crestfallen so as they approached the station she suggested lunch.

"Come on, this place looks okay. I hope you like Chinese food."

"I love it," enthused Bob. The truth was he had never tasted it, but having lunch, in any sort of restaurant with Georgina van Wyk was very high on his current wish list, although his greatest desire, he conceded, was still in the realms of fantasy!

She ordered the meal with practised confidence as Bob basked in the glory of being seen in public with this stunningly beautiful woman. If only his mates could see him now.

He was privately thankful as Georgina took charge of the confusing number of dishes that continued to arrive at the table. She quickly realised that whatever Bob had claimed, this food was outside his experience.

"Hey, shall I fill your plate for you? A selection of everything perhaps?"

Bob nodded thankfully as Georgina explained the nature of the alarming looking dishes.

"Don't worry, use a spoon and fork if it's easier, after all we're paying," she laughed as she wielded her chopsticks with aplomb.

The meal passed remarkably well, Bob decided that he enjoyed most of this strange cuisine as his companion continued to describe the mysteries behind the door of number 3 Dickens Place, Kings Cross Road.

"Look, Bob, I'm going back by cab, I need to think. You get the bike and I'll see you back at the shop."

Georgina paid the bill and as they stepped into the street, she hailed a passing cab. Without any further conversation or a backward glance at Bob, Georgina climbed into the back seat and the cab drove off, leaving him standing on the pavement feeling just a little bit deflated.

The cab driver had at first been reluctant to take the fare as he claimed it was beyond the six mile limit but Georgie was quick to push a five pound note through the communication hatch.

"I suppose that will be alright, miss. You'll still have to pay what's on the meter though."

"Whatever, just get me there." she replied dismissively, slamming the hatch shut as a signal that the conversation was now terminated.

Georgina sat deep in thought for more that half an hour as the taxi edged its way towards Chiswick, until her attention was drawn by the driver tapping on the division.

"Where do you want in the High Road, miss?"

"Pull up there," she pointed, "Outside the café."

Georgina paid the cab, glanced quickly across at Wilding Photography on the opposite side of the road and strode confidently in through the door of the café.

Her nerves were immediately calmed by the look of distress

on the face of the middle aged man sitting at the table in the window. Georgina realised she had the upper hand and meant to keep it.

"Hello," she beamed, walking briskly up to the man's table. "What happened to you? I thought you were following me."

Sitting back in his chair, mouth open in shock, the man stared at her in silence.

"Do us both a favour," Georgie continued, keen to keep the initiative. "Get your bosses to ring me at the shop opposite, any time between ten and four within the next two days and I'll tell them where I've been and what I intend to do. Save you sitting here every day."

With that and before the shocked agent could pull himself together, Georgina turned on her heel and left the café.

"Phheww," she breathed, as she waited on the kerb before crossing confidently through the slow moving west London traffic. Entering the shop, Georgina instantly dropped her air of confidence and calm as she rushed to press her eye to the spy hole in the window screens.

To her great satisfaction the café was empty.

Georgina was about to make her way to her mother's office when Bob came tumbling through the internal door.

"I didn't hear you come in, Georgie, I've only just got back myself. Are our spies still over the road?" He crossed the room to peer through spy hole.

"There was one there when I got out the cab so I went in and spoke to him."

"You did what? You went into the café? Crikey, what did you say?"

"I just told him to get his boss to ring me and I'd tell him where I'd been, save them watching me all the time."

Bob stared in amazement.

"You've got some nerve, Georgie, I'll give you that. What did he say?"

"Too surprised to say anything."

"Do you think he'll come back."

"How should I know?"

Bob looked puzzled as he listened to Georgina. There was so much he didn't understand but thought better of pressing her further. He had never met such an amazing girl and was desperate to remain part of her adventure, whatever the risk.

"Who are these people, Georgie?" he asked, more in hope of an answer than in expectation.

"Is my mother in?" she asked, deliberately ignoring his question.

"Errr…yes, she's in her office."

Without any further explanation Georgina picked up her shoulder bag and swept past, leaving Bob Simmons none the wiser and with only her lingering perfume as company.

Aware that her mother might still be angered by her behaviour that morning, Georgina knocked respectfully on the office door before entering. On later reflection, she was puzzled why her mum's good opinion was increasingly important to her. For all Georgie's wealth and film star lifestyle her mum had become her role model for perseverance and success.

"Hello darling, come in," beamed Joyce Browne, looking up expectantly from her desk. "Did you find it?"

"Yes, we did," replied Georgina with a serious expression, hopeful that she may have regained her mother's favour. "And you were right to insist I took Bob along, he was really helpful, we went up on his motorbike."

"What on earth induced you to get on the back of that contraption, Georgie?"

To her mother's stunned amazement, Georgina explained

how Bob Simmons had discovered that the front of the shop was being watched from the café opposite and the mews entrance at the back was under observation from a car in Mayfield Avenue.

"So that was what all the fuss was about. It sounds absolutely awful at the best of times but the noise he was making this morning was the worst I've ever heard it. I was about to speak to him when off it roared. I had no idea you were on the back though, I thought you must have gone on your own."

Joyce then listened in rapt attention as Georgina continued her narrative of the morning's adventure, not surprisingly reserving her most profound astonishment for the description of Mr Daize and Mr Weekes's establishment in Kings Cross Road.

Georgina concluded her story with the revelation that on her return she had confronted the spy in the café with the suggestion that whoever had ordered the surveillance might do well to speak directly with her. In answer to her mother's pertinent enquiry as to why Georgina had taken this apparently bizarre course of action, she continued.

"Mum, they must be South African secret service, or whatever they call themselves, who else would be interested in me. Remember, Hendrik told these Slapelose people that he had evidence that he might leak to the press if they arrested him or didn't release him from his commitment. Now, think, if they suspect I now have this evidence, why are they still just watching me? Why hasn't your house been burgled?

Joyce put her hand over her face in alarm.

"Why haven't they attacked us here in the shop?" Or burgled my flat or even the offices of Castle and Castle. After all, the evidence could be at any of these locations, couldn't it?"

"This is all too much for me, Georgie."

"These are serious players, Mum. They murdered my

husband, they murdered Johannes and they murdered poor Amos my gardener. So the million dollar question, that is concentrating my mind at the moment, is why haven't they murdered me?"

"Oh my God, Georgina, surely you don't think..."

"As soon as Bob discovered what was going on I started to wonder, what are they doing? Why don't they act?"

"Yes, I'm beginning to understand," responded Joyce, leaning forward across her desk.

"Why are they watching you? Because they think you have evidence that may implicate them in murder. So why haven't they tried to find it?"

"Precisely, Mum."

"So what are you going to say to them, supposing of course that they ring?"

"I'm not sure I'm going to say anything, it's too important for a phone call, I'm going to meet them."

"Georgina, you can't do that," gasped Joyce, putting up her hands in desperation. "You can't be serious, by your own admission you're dealing with murderers. You seem to have this idea that you can do anything you like, that everyone loves Georgina."

"I've been thinking about it, mum," insisted Georgina excitedly, catching one of her mother's hands. "I wouldn't bring them here, of course not, or Staveley Road or even Apollo Court. It would have to be away from here, fifty miles at least, neutral ground, a country hotel perhaps."

'Why can't you just call the police, the Metropolitan Police are very good you know," pleaded Joyce in exasperation. "Why do you always think you know better?"

"Oh great Mum, I can see the police report now, 'South African woman goes unmolested in Chiswick,' I bet they would put their best men on that."

Joyce stared at her daughter in silence.

"You could try 'The Sickle and Scythe' at Henley, I went there with a client a few weeks ago," sighed Joyce in resignation.

"Went there with a client, Mum?" teased Georgie, the faintest smile flickering on her lips. "A male client?"

"Yes, a male client who was accompanied by his wife," responded a shocked Joyce, suddenly aware of her daughter's innuendo.

"Of course."

"How do you know they'd come?"

"I don't know."

"If I could stop you going through with this wild plan I would but as I know you wouldn't listen to me then I'm coming with you."

It was Georgina's turn to shocked.

"Oh no, oh no, I'm not taking you with me, absolutely not…but I'll take Bob Simmons."

"That boy would follow you anywhere, but you can't put him in possible danger without telling him what's going on, he deserves to know."

Georgina thought for a moment.

"Yes okay, but not yet. Let's book the rooms if we can, 'The Sickle and Wotsit' will do. Two nights, I think. It's Monday now, I gave them two days, that takes us to Wednesday so I think Friday and Saturday night with the meeting on Saturday."

"That's a tight schedule," said Joyce, reaching for her address book.

"If they want to talk to me, they'll make it. Make them run around, don't give them too much time to think about it."

Joyce picked up the telephone and dialled the number from her address book.

"You'll be lucky if they have two rooms for Friday and

Saturday at this short notice," said Joyce as she waited for the 'phone to be answered. "It's probably booked with weddings… Hello, is that 'The Sickle and Scythe?' Good, have you two rooms for this Friday and Saturday nights? Yes, I'll hold on."

"Why two nights, anyway?" asked Joyce, with her hand over the mouthpiece.

"Well, I don't want to be turfed out by room service in the middle of the meeting," replied Georgie, raising her eyebrows at her mother's lack of foresight. "I need that room for the whole of Saturday. I…"

Joyce raised her hand for silence.

"Yes, I see, hold on a moment,"

Holding her hand over the mouthpiece once again, Joyce smiled up at her daughter.

"They have a honeymoon suite, very expensive and what they call a 'Grand Double' nearly as expensive."

"Book them," snapped Georgie, clenching her fists in satisfaction.

"I thought you'd say that…Hello? Book them both please… van Wyk, that's W…Y…K. Georgina van Wyk, yes, a London number 994 8234. Thank you, Good bye.

"You were lucky," said Joyce, replacing the receiver. "Mind you, you could buy a small hotel for the price they are charging."

"Great, now we just sit back and wait for their call. I gave them two days, but I suspect they will ring tomorrow."

"Such confidence in one so young."

"Confidence? Maybe, more like a desperate hope."

"Shall I get Bob?"

"There's no point involving him until we know the meeting is on," pondered Georgina, then making a sudden decision. "Invite him home to dinner tomorrow night, Mum, we should know if it's on by then."

"He'll like that," smiled Joyce, going to the door. "And if the meeting is off, then he can sit and look at you all evening."

Bob Simmons was sitting at the reception desk as the two women entered the room.

"Bob, Georgina and I were wondering if you were doing anything tomorrow evening?"

"Errr…no Mrs Browne," he replied with interest. "Is there a job on? I've been reading about night photography."

"Nothing like that, Bob. We just wondered if you would like to come round to Staveley Road for dinner, that's all?"

"Wow…yes please…I'd love to come…thank you," he replied, glancing at Georgina in delight.

"It's a sort of thank you for helping me today," winked Georgie.

Georgina spent the rest of the afternoon in the darkroom watching Bob developing and printing photographs. Clearly in the best of spirits and keen to further impress the boss's daughter with his expertise in all things photographic, any reasonably attentive observer would have realised the young man was, quite simply, showing off. However, it was all to no avail as Georgina's thoughts were wholly concentrated on tomorrow's expected telephone call.

It was the same at home, declining dinner, Georgina sat in front of the television for most of the evening. All attempts by her mother to engage her in conversation met with failure, until at 10pm Georgina announced that she would have an early night.

CHAPTER FIFTEEN

Tuesday 18th February 1969
Chiswick

The next morning found mother and daughter at the shop by 9.30 sharp, Georgina immediately claiming the desk in reception as her own. Next, a check on the spy hole confirmed Bob's announcement that the watcher in the café opposite was indeed back on his boring vigil.

As an act of defiance she opened the front door of the shop and leaning against the door frame, in a suitably sexy pose, blew a kiss in the direction of the café. Back in the shop, she smiled to herself as she settled down behind the reception desk with the Daily Telegraph crossword.

Twenty five minutes later, Bob's proffered tea consumed and the crossword completed, Georgina stared at the telephone, willing it to ring. And ring it did, regularly every few minutes, but to her increasing frustration the calls were from mothers wishing to have their baby photographed, brides of last Saturday ordering prints, bookings for forthcoming weddings and events. All of which Georgina dispatched with a level of politeness bordering on curt.

During the morning, Bob Simmons made several forays into the reception area intent on engaging the object of his dreams in pleasant conversation only to be rebuffed on each occasion with hurtful assaults on his ego such as "Haven't you got any work to do?" and "Can't you see I'm busy?"

"Nothing yet?" asked Joyce, standing in the doorway leading to her office. "It's still not twelve and you've given them until four tomorrow afternoon, it might be a long wait. Of course, there's also a very good chance they may not ring at all and that might be for the best."

"No, they'll ring," replied Georgina defiantly, showing more confidence than she felt. "They will ring today as well, I'm sure of it."

"Maybe, time will tell."

At exactly twelve noon the telephone rang.

"Wilding Photograhy, can I help you?" answered Georgie on the first ring.

"Speaking."

"Thank you for ringing."

"Well, I would have thought the first question would be obvious. Who are you and why are you watching me?"

Georgina frowned as she listened in silence.

"Listen to me, here's the bottom line. I believe you are Operation Slapelose and I also believe you murdered my husband, my brother-in-law and my gardener, for reasons best known to you."

"No, wait till I've finished," she hissed into the 'phone.

"As I know you are aware, I have evidence of your complicity in crime. My husband, fearing his arrest hoped that I would make this evidence available to the press as a lever to ensure his safety. Thanks to you, he is now dead. The decision I have to make is whether I go to the press or not. I don't want to be your fourth victim."

"I've only got your word for that, but I'm not discussing it over the telephone."

"It's Tuesday now, I propose we meet this Saturday at 'The

Sickle and Scythe' at Henley in Berkshire. I have a room booked there so we can talk."

Georgina listened intently.

"No ifs and buts, I need an answer now, are you coming or not?"

"So am I taking a risk, a big risk."

"I'm still waiting, it's an easy choice, a meeting with me or read about your organisation in the newspapers."

"Good, then I'll see you on Saturday at The Sickle and Scythe at Henley, say twelve noon?"

"What name shall I expect?"

"Smith," sneered Georgina, "How appropriate, I shall, of course, use my real name, I'm proud of it."

"Good bye."

Putting down the telephone Georgie hurried down the corridor, bursting into her mother's office without knocking.

"It's on," she shouted across the room. "They've just rung, as I said they would, and they're coming."

"Good Lord," sighed Joyce. Quickly apologising to the person on the other end of her telephone call and promising to ring back, she replaced the receiver.

"Who did you speak to?"

"A man, English accent, said his name was Smith. He seemed a bit taken aback really."

"I'm not surprised," replied Joyce, running her fingers through her hair. "You certainly like to live dangerously."

"How can you say that? All I wanted to do was live in peace with my husband in my lovely home. All I want now is to get these people off my back so that I can rebuild my life again."

"Sorry, darling," replied her mother, regretting her choice of words. "Don't forget we've got Bob to dinner tonight, what are you going to tell him?"

"As little as possible."

Stopping to think for a moment she continued.

"He knows about the murders and I've told him about the evidence in Kings Cross but not what it is. He also knows that Hendrik upset some important people in SA and it's them who are watching me now."

Georgina held her mother's glance.

"He also knows I'm in fear of my life. So perhaps he'd sooner not take a risk with his own."

"I'd prefer neither of you were going on this wild goose chase," exclaimed Joyce, throwing her arms wide in exasperation. "But can you imagine Bob not wanting to go with you?"

"No, I suppose not," smiled Georgie, sitting on the edge of her mother's desk. "I certainly don't want him at the meeting, that would be ridiculous, but I must admit I like having him around. I can see why you employed him. Mum, I just don't want to sit on my own at dinner and can you imagine what it would be like in the bar, all those men trying their luck and offering to buy me a drink?"

Joyce gave a nervous laugh, "You fancy yourself."

"Mum, I don't fancy myself as you so crudely put it," said Georgina crossly. "But it's a fact that I am good looking, I dress well and a single woman like me in a bar or restaurant will attract men. It would even happen to you."

"Even me?" gasped Joyce in mock horror.

Both women laughed.

"Sorry Mum, but you know what I mean. Having Bob with me will save all that and as I said before, I like him. We'll go down in the E.Type and he'll have a good time, I promise."

*

Bob arrived at Staveley Road at precisely 7.30pm, having left his motorcycle at home and walked. From the moment of his arrival it was clear that the evening was of great importance to him and represented a very welcome improvement on his usual evening activities.

Georgina was secretly amused by the great show of ceremony with which he presented her mother with a box of milk chocolates…That, and his astonishment as Georgie snatched them from Joyce's hand.

"I bags the coffee creams," she laughed, taking them off into the kitchen.

Two or three beers did wonders for the young man's nerves and both women were pleased that the alcohol, although clearly easing his inhibitions and loosening his tongue, failed to disclose any underlying and less endearing character traits. He remained polite, amusing and completely sincere, if a little naive.

"Bob, are you doing anything this weekend?" asked Georgina casually, pouring herself another glass of South African red.

"I expect I'll be in the shop on Saturday."

"Well, if you weren't working, I was wondering if you would like to have a weekend away with me?" she continued in a matter of fact manner. "I've arranged to meet these people who are watching the shop, find out what they're doing and what they want. I have to warn you though, it may be dangerous."

Bob glanced again excitedly at his employer and was gratified to be informed he might be spared for the weekend.

"Yes, yes, I want to come."

"Well, if you are sure," teased Georgie. "I had an idea you might, so I've booked a couple of rooms at The Sickle and Scythe at Henley. Mum's been there and apparently it's very good, so at least we'll have a good dinner and a few drinks, if nothing else."

"Fantastic."

"I've booked Friday and Saturday nights with the meeting arranged for Saturday. So I'll pick you up from your place on Friday about two o'clock and we can drive down."

"You can have Friday off, Bob," said Joyce. "Save you rushing."

It would be an understatement to say that young Robert was ecstatic with the invitation.

"Fantastic," he repeated.

At around eleven a very contented and happy Bob prepared to take his leave. He had enjoyed the evening and his behaviour had been impeccable. Joyce felt her decision to employ him had been a good one.

In high spirits and turning up his collar against the heavy rain, Bob was about to step off down the drive at the start of his fifteen minute walk, when Joyce's hand caught his arm, he had no coat and would be soaked by the time he got home.

"You can't walk home in this, Bob and neither of us can drive you as we've all been drinking. You had better stay the night, I'll drop you home in the morning so you can change."

*

Georgina was uncharacteristically quiet and subdued during the next couple of days. Travelling in to work with her mother each day she made herself useful around the office, turning her hand to learning the skills of 'finishing' photographs by touching in tiny imperfections in the prints, preparing mounts and framing. She took her turn to sit in reception and answer the telephone, but all the time her thoughts were on Saturday's meeting.

On Thursday afternoon Richard Wilding accompanied her

to the flat to check that the Jaguar was in good order, after all, suggested Richard, the car had been standing for some time.

To her satisfaction, the big engine started immediately and she was soon piloting the bright red sports car around Chiswick with a delighted Richard Wilding in the passenger seat. Crossing Chiswick Bridge they drove towards Richmond Park, completing a leisurely circuit of the park roads to have coffee in Pembroke Lodge before returning to leave the car next to her mother's Volvo at the rear of the office. She would keep the Jaguar at Staveley Road tonight, ready for Friday.

CHAPTER SIXTEEN

Friday 21st February 1969
Henley on Thames, Berkshire

Georgina was the first to acknowledge that the Jaguar 'E' Type drop head was a spectacular car, she enjoyed driving it, both in England and South Africa. It was the sort of car she was pleased to be seen in. Lean and sexy, she felt it suited her personality exactly, she loved it. However, if it had a fault, she would have to admit that the boot was rather too small for her requirements. So, on Friday morning, by the time she had packed her smart new pair of Louis Vuitton cases and matching shoulder bag in the tiny space, she found there was little room for a couple of dresses to lay on top. Georgina had to sit on the boot lid to get it closed.

"I hope Bob isn't bringing too much kit," smiled Georgie to herself. "Don't suppose so."

Setting off just before two, Georgina drove the mile or so to the other side of the borough where Bob lived. Finding the address, she pulled the car into the large, unkempt front garden that served as a car park, stopping near the front door next to what she guessed to be Bob's motorcycle, carefully protected by a plastic cover.

Locking the Jaguar, she made her way up the decaying flight of stone steps. The shabby front door appeared not to be fully shut, yielding as she gently pushed against it.

Inside the house the grubby magnolia painted entrance hall was furnished with a small wooden side table on which were several piles of letters and newspapers and a wall mounted payphone. Numbers and names were pencilled all over the wall. Next to the telephone was a handwritten list of tenants and their room numbers. Georgina was running her eye down the list in search of the name R. Simmons, when an old lady appeared from a ground floor room.

"Who you looking for dear?" the old woman croaked between coughs.

"Robert Simmons"

"Top floor, room 12, but guests of the opposite sex aren't allowed."

"That's okay," smiled Georgie as she started to climb the staircase. "I'm his sister."

Six flights of stairs and many brown painted doors later, Georgina knocked at room number 12.

"Oh hello, Georgie," said Bob, opening the door. "I meant to be ready and waiting for you down stairs."

"I'm a bit early, so I thought I'd come and find you."

He hesitated for a moment, then pulled the door wide open, inviting her in. It didn't take long for Georgina to realise that she had made a mistake in coming up to Bob's room. He was clearly embarrassed and she was embarrassed for him. The room was dreadful, with sloping attic walls and peeling wallpaper. As she looked around, she noticed three brown stains on the ceiling, indicating where the roof had leaked. The floor was bare wooden boards with a threadbare rug in the centre of the room. Apart from his bed, the only other furniture was a table, an old wardrobe and a chair. A small bookcase against one wall contained Bob's precious collection of photography books and magazines. A portable radio stood on the chair.

Bob avoided looking at Georgie as he picked up some small items from the bed and pushed them into his holdall. She stood in silence, for once lost for words. How could this boy be so full of life, so happy, so enthusiastic in all he did, knowing that at the end of the day he would come home to this.

Georgina knew she had invaded his privacy and was sorry. In all her life she had never been in a room like this. She had never seen inside the servants accommodation of her house in Cape Town, but it was surely better than this.

It was Bob who broke the silence.

"I'm sorry Georgie," he said quietly, giving her a sideways glance. "I know it's awful but it's all I can afford."

Georgie just nodded, not knowing what to say.

"I'm not grumbling, I love my job and Mrs Browne has promised me a rise soon."

"Where do you cook?" whispered Georgie, looking despairingly around the room.

"We're not allowed to cook in the rooms," he explained, still not looking at his visitor. "Though I sometimes make a cup of tea or heat a tin of soup on a camping stove."

"And heating?"

"None, well I've a little electric fire, but the meter takes shillings and they don't last long if I use the fire, so I tend to go to bed with a couple of jumpers on."

Anticipating her next question Bob continued.

"The bathroom is downstairs, you can never get in there in the mornings so I wash and shave last thing at night and then I just clean my teeth here before I come to work."

"I'm so sorry, Bob, I didn't mean to embarrass you, I just didn't know." She stepped forward touching him on the shoulder, "I think you're doing great, so does Mum."

With that, Bob turned and faced her.

"Well, I'm ready," he smiled, lifting up his small holdall.

"We've just about got room for that behind the seats," she laughed, pleased of a chance to lighten the atmosphere. "The boot's completely full of my stuff. Come on, let's go."

Walking back down the stairs in silence, it wasn't until they stepped out of the front door that Bob suddenly erupted back to his usual self as he caught his first glimpse of the red Jaguar.

"That can't be yours," he shouted in delight.

"Oh can't it? I thought it was," said Georgie, laughing at his antics, as Bob ran fully three times around the car before stopping to stroke the bonnet.

"Come on, Georgie," shouted Bob, pulling his camera from his holdall. "Just one photo, with you leaning on the bonnet, the light is just right."

After a full five minutes and half a roll of film, Georgina called a halt to the impromptu photographic session.

"It's stunning, I didn't even know you had a car."

"I've got this one and another exactly the same in South Africa." It was odd the effect the Jag had on men, she thought, remembering her cousin's excitement when she let him drive it home from the Italian restaurant in Cape Town.

Unlocking the car and getting in, Georgina leaned across and opened the passenger door.

"Get in, throw your bag over the back of the seat, the boot's full."

Bob climbed in, stowed his bag and sat in awe as Georgie started the engine, easing the big sports car back out of the parking space and then, engaging first, edging out of the front garden onto the road where, to her passenger's delight, she gave the car a little more acceleration than was really necessary.

As they waited at a red traffic light, Georgina glanced across at Bob.

"Look Bob, we don't know what's going to happen tomorrow but let's enjoy ourselves this evening."

"Fantastic."

Within ten minutes they were on the M4 Motorway to the west and Georgina began to give the big sports car it's head. She smiled to hear Bob's opinions on the relative benefits of a fast motorcycle, compared with her Jaguar.

"Of course my Gold Star would be faster up to 60," opined Bob with sage like authority. "But after that, I suppose the Jag would start to catch up."

Georgina had no idea, all she new was that the E.Type was fast enough for her and she certainly didn't want to dent his pride again.

"Your bike's great, I'll give you that. But this keeps me dry and warm and I don't have to wear a helmet.

Bob laughed.

"How fast are we going, Georgie?"

Hands at ten to two on the steering wheel, she glanced down at the instruments.

"One hundred and ten," she laughed. "I'd better slow down, I suppose. I don't want to be stopped by the police."

"Fantastic, Georgie, you certainly know how to drive, I'm really impressed, Is there anything you can't do?"

"I can't fly a 'plane, like my mum, that's my next project."

The miles raced past in a similar manner and they were soon turning off the motorway and following the signs for Henley.

Fifteen more sedate minutes later, Bob suddenly sat forward in his seat.

"There it is Georgie, on the right, there's the sign, The Sickle and Scythe, looks good."

"It's only taken us forty five minutes," he said, looking at his watch.

Georgina nodded her agreement, the engine roaring as she change down into third and flicked on the right hand indicator. With a break in the traffic, she changed down again, turning right to follow a white painted sign entitled 'Customer Parking and Reception.' Passing through the entrance gates, the cars tyres crunched over the gravel surface as she drove slowly across to a pair of double glass doors.

Bob and Georgina got out of the car and looked around. The Sickle and Scythe was a handsome old coaching inn resplendent in pristine white paint that highlighted ancient black timber beams. Two low floors nestled under roofs that were a mixture of russet coloured tiles and well maintained thatch. It looked comfortable and inviting.

Walking round to the back of the car, Georgina opened the boot. Taking the small shoulder bag, she made her way to the hotel entrance and pushed open the door.

"Make sure you don't crease my dresses," she called back, as she entered the hotel, the doors closing behind her.

Bob, realising that Georgina's verbal advice was the only assistance that was likely to be forthcoming, set about carrying the luggage. With his own holdall over his right shoulder and with one of her cases in his left hand, he managed to hook the hangers of her two dresses on to the top pocket of his jacket. Slamming the boot lid shut he picked up her second case in his right hand before staggering in pursuit of the object of his dreams.

Georgina was by now standing at the reception desk in the far corner of a large and comfortable lounge and bar. Bob, loaded down like a pack horse, waited patiently behind her as she signed the register.

"Rooms 101 and 103 on the first floor and I hope you enjoy your stay. Will your husband be joining you later, Mrs van Wyk?" enquired the puzzled receptionist.

"I very much doubt it," replied Georgie, raising her eyebrows, "One other thing, get someone to park my car, it's the red E.Type Jaguar."

Before the astounded clerk could object, Georgina slid her car keys across the desk and walked off towards the lift, with Bob dutifully following behind.

"Bong" sounded the lift microphone, heralding their arrival at the first floor. Stepping into the corridor, a polished wooden sign in Tudor script indicated that rooms 101 to 109 were to the right.

"Here we are," said Georgie, turning the key in the door of Room 101, "This is mine."

Pushing the door open, the two companions entered the room, Bob quickly depositing the luggage on the huge double bed.

The Honeymoon Suite consisted of a very large bedroom area, dominated by a four poster double bed with 'Tiffany lamps' on tables at either side. A large wardrobe, dressing table and chest of drawers, all in carved mahogany, completed the principle furnishings.

A door led to a spacious and well appointed bathroom.

At the far end of the bedroom area were three steps leading to a comfortable lounge with a large coffee table, surrounded by four leather Chesterfield armchairs.

The walls and ceilings of the suite continued the style of the hotel, being finished in white, interspersed with the ubiquitous black beams. Underfoot was a thickly piled dark red carpet.

The suite was lit by two, small lattice windows affording views of the extensive gardens.

Once again, Bob was amazed. This sort of luxury, commonplace to Georgina, was a revelation to him.

"Georgie," he gasped, running his hand over the back of a leather armchair. "This is really fantastic."

"I agree, it's just what I'd hoped for," she replied as she strolled around, opening and closing all the doors and drawers in the suite.

Further conversation was interrupted by a knock at the outside door. Georgina looked on as Bob responded. A hotel porter swept into the room and crossed the bedroom to the lounge area, where Georgina was sitting. He placed a bottle of Champagne in an ice bucket in the centre of the coffee table, together with two glasses.

"The compliments of the management, we hope you enjoy your stay."

"Thank you," smiled Georgina.

Without any further ado, the porter swept out closing the door behind him.

Bob picked up the Champagne with a puzzled look at Georgie, who had started to laugh.

"Oh, I get it," he said in amazement. "This is the Honeymoon Suite, and they think we are married."

"I think so," agreed Georgie, continuing to laugh. "Get it open then, I could do with a glass of Champagne."

With continuous advice from Georgina, Bob removed the cork with a satisfying pop. Carefully filling the two flutes, he handed one to his companion.

"Cheers, wife." he laughed.

"No chance," she replied, taking the glass, the suggestion of a smile flickering on her lips.

"Grab your bag," said Georgina, taking a sip, "Let's see what your room is like, 103 isn't it?"

"It's just across the corridor, I saw it as we came in."

Georgina, Champagne glass in hand, led the way out into the hotel corridor, standing aside to allow Bob to unlock the door of room 103, immediately opposite.

The room was similar to the Honeymoon Suite though perhaps a little smaller. Lacking the raised lounge area, two small armchairs and a coffee table were situated near the bed. After her now established fashion, Georgina inspected the room, opening and closing all drawers, doors and cupboards. All seemed to meet with her approval.

"I think you will have enough room for all your clothes," she laughed at Bob's expense, glancing at the small nylon holdall laying on the bed.

"Come on, it's gone four," said Georgie, looking at her watch, "One more drink and I've got to get on."

Back in the Honeymoon Suite, Bob refilled their glasses. The Champagne was working it's magic and Georgina was unrestrained. He listened attentively to her opinions on the Champagne, the hotel and the quality of the curtains, her grave concerns over the absence of a dressing table light and her regret at forgetting to pack a favourite pair of shoes.

For his part, Bob was in paradise, sitting in an expensive hotel room, drinking Champagne with the most beautiful and exciting woman he had ever met. He had completely forgotten his earlier embarrassment, when Georgie had seen how he was forced to live, what was more important, so apparently had she. A whole wonderful weekend stretched ahead of him. As he sipped his wine Bob determined to be cautious in his behaviour, he was aware that his loyalty had been tested in the last few days, by both Georgina and perhaps more importantly, by her mother, his boss. He would not be found wanting and he would not fall foul of his companion's mercurial temper. He had seen her moods change in an instant, the privilege of rich and beautiful women, he supposed.

"I cannot believe it's five o'clock," exclaimed Georgie, staring at her wristwatch in horror, "Out, now, I've got to get ready. I've booked a table for eight so give me a knock at seven thirty, all bright eyed and bushy tailed."

Bob got up to go.

Georgina refilled his glass as he left.

★

At seven thirty precisely, Bob Simmons stood outside the door of Room 101. Dressed in his best, and only dark blue suit, a newly purchased and matching shirt and tie, shiny black shoes and smelling of 'Brut 33,' he gathered his thoughts and knocked.

Opening the door, Georgina completely ignored him as she hurried back to the dressing table, fiddling with an earring.

"Zip me up." she commanded.

"What?"

"Zip me up, you idiot," she glared, turning her back towards him, "I can't reach the zip."

Hurrying forward, Bob saw that Georgina's short, black dress was open to the small of her back. Taking the tiny pull between his fingertips and being careful not to touch her skin he gave a gentle pull. It would not move, all he achieved was to pull at the whole dress.

"Hold the bottom and then pull it," she hissed, quickly losing patience.

Now encompassed in her perfume, Bob was acutely aware that the zip bottom was perilously close to Georgina's delightful bottom, but orders were orders, so dutifully grasping the bottom of her dress in his left hand, he pulled with the right, the zip gliding up to the top of the dress. She looked marvellous and Bob manfully resisted his urge to kiss the back of her neck.

"Let's have a look at you," said Georgie, turning and giving

Bob an appraising glance, "Not bad, remind me to buy you a decent suit."

Bob looked a little crestfallen.

Slipping on a pair of black high heels, she picked up a small bag from the bed.

"You can buy me a drink. Put everything on my room number, but you might need this." She slipped some bank notes into Bob's top pocket.

As they walked into the hotel bar, Bob was surprised but delighted, as Georgina slipped her arm through his. He was aware it was only role play, but nevertheless he felt enormous pride at the appreciative glances their entrance drew from the other guests. He felt like shouting out, 'I'm Bob Simmons and this is my girl.' He restrained himself and on Georgie's instructions, they found a small table. Going to the bar, he ordered a gin and tonic for her and a beer for himself.

As they chatted over their drinks he basked in the envious glances of other men. Georgina, of course, appeared oblivious to the stir she was causing.

At around eight they made their way to the restaurant and enjoyed an excellent dinner with attentive service. Bob was now feeling sufficiently confident to order the meal and wine with only a few prompts from Georgina. The conversation continually reverted to the expected meeting the following day. Bob was keen to know more, but Georgina evaded his attempts to probe Hendrik's political activities in South Africa. It was clear to her that he had no knowledge of South Africa and she was disinclined to educate him. With the exception of whoever she would meet tomorrow, nobody had any real idea of what had been going on. The fact was, she had very little firm knowledge herself. Hendrik had tried, until the very last, to withhold the full story from her. The dossier she had recovered from Daize and Weekes, upon which he had placed such reliance, was old and prepared before any of the murders had taken place. She secretly thought it was of little use, but Georgina would need all her intellect to convince her pursuers that she was a key player and held vital information, while at the same time convincing them that she was ready to cut a deal to protect her own skin. Bob could not be involved in any of this.

Georgina, for all her bravado and high spirits, felt deeply frightened and alone. Her husband had only been dead a week and still awaited burial, she feared for her own life. As a widow, her lack of grief was almost indecent, it shocked and amazed everyone who knew her. It shocked Georgina herself.

"I enjoyed that," sighed Georgina, glancing first at her watch, then at Bob, "It's a quarter to ten and we've a big day tomorrow, I suggest we get one last drink from the bar and take it upstairs, then an early night."

Back in the Honeymoon Suite they sat in the comfortable armchairs, sipping their drinks. There was little conversation, Georgina lit a cigarette, blowing a cloud of smoke into the room.

"I think I'll say good night and turn in then," said Bob, diplomatically.

She smiled at him as he passed her chair catching hold of his tie and pulling him towards her.

"I should have thought my bed was big enough for both of us."

Bob stood stock still, he couldn't believe his ears, her husband had only died last week for Heaven's sake.

Keeping hold of his tie, Georgina stood and gently kissed him.

Bob's heart was racing as he felt her hand slip behind his neck, pulling him towards her. She kissed him with more passion. This time, he returned the lingering kiss, breaking off only to bury his face in her neck, kissing her throat and ear before returning to her mouth. He felt her slender body pressing against him as his hands explored her form through the silky feel of her close fitting dress.

Georgina kissed him again and he felt their tongues caress. His hands continued to explore her exquisite body with increased urgency, feeling the contours of her perfect bottom.

"Unzip me," breathed Georgina, turning as she pushed him away.

Slithering out of her dress, Georgina continued to hold Bob away from her as she pulled off his tie and quickly unbuttoned his shirt. Slipping a hand inside she began to push him back towards the bed, her other hand pulling at his trouser belt.

Bob fell back onto the bed with Georgina on top of him. Once again he buried his face in her neck, his senses overwhelmed by her wonderful closeness, her warmth, her smell. Holding her tightly to him, Bob rolled over, supporting himself on an elbow, he looked down at her, kissing her shoulder, then onwards to her small but perfect breasts, her flat stomach and beyond.

Rolling away, Georgina was suddenly astride him, her bra now discarded she bent forward. Bob, lifting his head from the bed, desperate to kiss her open mouth, was shocked as a sudden pain shot through his lip. Georgie's beautiful white teeth nipped his lip again, before her face slid across his cheek. He felt a series of sharp pains as she bit his ear lobe, his neck, his shoulder. Her perfectly manicured nails tore down his chest.

Bob had never experienced anything like this, he had never known a passion within him like this. He had never known a woman like this. He had never desired a woman like this.

For the life of him he had no idea how, but they were

both naked. Even now at the height of his passion, Bob felt apprehensive as he moved to consummate their love making. However, he abandoned all restraint as he felt her body move to receive him, a hand urgently directing him. Her lips brushing his face as she breathed obscenities in his ear.

He could not help himself as he gasped, "I love you, Georgie."

She laughed.

Both still only twenty years of age, their lovemaking continued into the early hours. Alternating between kisses and whispers and awesome sex, Georgina smoking too many cigarettes. It was nearly 4.00am before they drifted off to sleep, still in each other's arms.

Saturday 22nd February 1969

Bob opened his eyes. It took him a moment to remember where he was and as the realisation of what had occurred only a few hours previously came pouring back, he felt Georgina stir. Her beautiful face rested against his shoulder, he could feel her warm breath caress his chest. He leaned across and placed a gentle but lingering kiss on her cheek.

"It's eight o'clock, Georgie," he whispered in her ear, "You wanted an early breakfast."

He kissed her again.

Opening her eyes, Georgina lay still for a few moments. Lifting her head she looked at him without expression, before rising and crossing to the bathroom without comment, closing and locking the door behind her.

Bob collected his clothes and opened the door onto the corridor, checking he was unobserved, he hurried across to his own room.

It was just after 8.30 as Georgina and Bob made their way down to breakfast. At the entrance to the restaurant, leaning against the head waiter's dais, was a large sign announcing PLEASE WAIT TO BE SEATED. In compliance, an elderly couple waited patiently for the waiter, who was fully occupied serving another table. Georgina glanced at the sign with disdain as she swept past into the dining room, selecting a table for two in the conservatory area. Bob followed.

Having completed his serving duties, the waiter continued to ignore the elderly couple and hurried across to Georgina's table.

"Madam, did you not see the sign? It is my duty to seat you personally."

"For what purpose?" sneered Georgie. "My friend and I require breakfast, here is a table set for two and we are sitting at it. Please take our order as we are busy this morning and need to get on.

"I need to tick your room number off my list." he replied reproachfully.

"Room 101 and tell me, do you collect train numbers on your day off?"

"Can I take your order, please?" he enquired, pressing on with his duty and sensibly deciding to ignore Georgina's insult.

"You can bring a pot of tea and then perhaps you'd do well to seat that elderly lady and gentleman, before they fall down," smiled Georgie sweetly.

Smarting from her unfair criticism, the waiter hurried away to attend to his duties.

Surprised by Georgina's confrontational mood and aware from recent experience that he was no match for her sarcasm, Bob was cautious not to provoke his companion. The order was eventually taken and served and he contented himself with wondering how such a small and petite frame could consume a half grapefruit, a full English breakfast, five slices of toast, marmalade and two pots of tea.

Still blissfully conjuring memories of the previous night, Bob was disappointed that all attempts at conversation were met with monosyllables.

"Finished? Let's go," said Georgina.

Not waiting for an answer, Georgie left the debris strewn breakfast table, walking quickly towards the stairs, ignoring the waiter's enquiry as to her satisfaction with the meal.

"Very nice, thank you," replied an embarrassed Bob on her behalf.

Back in the hotel room, Bob made a further attempt at conversation.

"How are we going to deal with this chap when he arrives?" asked Bob, brightly, clapping his hands together hopefully.

"How are we going to deal?" snapped Georgina, stressing the word 'we', "What do you mean, we? There's no we, Bob."

Bob was confused, what had he said? Whatever it was had met with Georgina's scorn.

"Well, I thought we were a team, you and me."

"Team? Don't make yourself sound more stupid than you already are. Us a team? You're not even in my league."

Bob was shocked, he could not believe what she was saying. It was incomprehensible.

"Georgie, what's wrong, what have I said?" Why are you being like this?"

"Like what?"

"Georgie, please, stop it, I love you, just tell me what I've done."

"You love me," she sneered, hands on hips. "You love me. What's that supposed to mean? You think it's some password, you only have to say 'I love you Georgie' and you have some special claim over me."

Georgina was fast losing her temper, spitting out her words vindictively.

"Love me, do you? Well that's your problem, it's nothing to do with me, you're nothing to me, you're just a nobody, a pathetic nonentity."

"You didn't say that last night, did you?" he blurted out in desperation, his temper rising, his pride hurt.

Georgina had lost control, shouting at Bob, she continued. "Don't you dare mention last night, don't you fucking dare. If anyone ever finds out what happened, I'll destroy you, everything you value, all your hopes, I'll tear them down. You'll wish you never crossed me."

"I haven't crossed you, Georgie, we're friends," he pleaded, in horror at what was happening.

Bob stepped towards her, holding out his hands but she was uncontrollable, her temper was terrifying.

"Here," she screamed, taking some bank notes from the back pocket of her jeans and throwing them at him. "Take this, get a cab to the nearest station and fuck off back to your grotty little room, you creep. Don't think your travelling home in my car."

Angry and frustrated, Bob Simmons struggled to find the words to defend himself against Georgina's vicious and totally unwarranted attack, but he knew he was no match for her. All he could do was leave with a much dignity as he could muster.

A moment later, Bob was sitting in the silence of his room across the corridor. He struggled to come to terms with what had just happened. It was so unfair, he knew that Georgina had an explosive temper, he accepted that, even made allowances for it. His stomach churned, all he had dared to hope for lay in ruins. As he sat there, the revelation dawned on him that it was all pointless now, there could be no going back, it was finished.

He was engulfed in an immense sadness. What to do? How to get home? He had the money Georgina had given him the previous evening, he would not touch that. He counted out three pounds of his own. He resolved to walk to the station and travel as far as his money would take him and hitch the rest, but he kept returning to the thought that as soon as he left this room, he would be walking away from her.

Back in her room, Georgina sat at her dressing table. Her temper now subsiding as quickly as it had risen, she stared blankly into the mirror at her own reflection. What had she done? Her temper had got her into trouble before and now it had lost her someone she liked and enjoyed being with. Someone who had been loyal to her, someone who had done nothing to deserve her dreadful tirade. Deep inside, she new the reason for her outburst, guilt, guilt at seducing Bob when Hendrik still lay unburied.

Bob, delaying his departure for a few more pointless minutes, lay back on the bed, he knew he would have to go soon. His brain continually racing through the events of the last few minutes, desperately trying to make sense of what had happened.

He was suddenly roused from his thoughts by a soft knock at the door. Opening it, his stomach turned a cartwheel as he came face to face with Georgina. Barefoot in blue jeans, she looked like a waif.

Without speaking he stepped back into the room.

"Were you about to leave?" she asked in little more than a whisper.

"Yes, I'm going," replied Bob with a sigh. "I obviously got it all wrong, I'm sorry to have been such an idiot."

Georgina entered the room allowing the door to close behind her.

"You didn't get anything wrong, it's me. Last night was my fault, it shouldn't have happened."

"Georgie, it was wonderful, you were wonderful and I don't regret for a moment what happened, but I was happily going back to my room when you stopped me. You're hard to resist."

"I know," she conceded, shrugging her shoulders.

Feeling emboldened by Georgie's quiet, reflective manner, Bob continued.

"I know my room is awful and I know I'm not rich and clever like you, but I'm getting there. I love my job and I'm saving like mad, I'll get a better place soon, maybe a small flat. I was happy until you came along and turned my life upside down. When I said I loved you, I meant it. I don't want a special claim over you, I just want to be with you, near you."

Georgina smiled.

"Bob, I've come to apologise, I don't apologise often and I'm not very good at it, but I am apologising now. You didn't deserve any of the abuse I gave you, it's just I have a problem with my temper, I say things I don't mean, I can't help myself. You have been a real friend to me and I treat you like this."

"But Georgie, the things you said, I…"

"…Please don't go Bob, I need you, I'm frightened and I need you," interrupted Georgina, sitting on the edge of the bed with her hands covering her face.

Bob's head was still spinning from this roller coaster of emotions he had experienced during the last hour. He listened to what she was saying and desperately wanted to believe her, but was she just using him? He hoped with all his heart she was being honest.

"There's no need to say anymore, if you want me to stay,

then of course I'll stay," he replied, looking across at her. Whatever happened, at least he hoped to be spared the sad and lonely journey home he had been about to embark upon.

On her feet, Georgina took a step towards him, then hesitated.

"Thank you," she smiled, disarmingly. "Come over when you're ready."

"Wait, I'll come with you," he replied, picking up his money from the bed.

Back in her own room, Georgina's usual confidence slowly returned.

"Look at the time," she gasped. "I told him to arrive at twelve, it's gone eleven now… Bob, what I would really like you to do is go downstairs, get yourself a beer and find a seat in the bar as close to the reception desk as possible, okay?"

Bob nodded, eager to be of use.

"Read a paper or something. Keep an eye on people coming in and when a Mr. Smith asks for my room, see if he's with anyone, listen to everything that's said, it may be useful."

"But will you be alright up here on your own?"

"I hope so, but hey, it's too late to change anything now."

"Right, it's 11.20, I'd better get going, you never know, he or they might be early, to give them the element of surprise."

As Bob opened the door to leave, Georgina caught his hand, pulling him back towards her, she kissed his cheek.

"I'll make things right with you, I promise."

Smiling back at her, Bob hurried off down the corridor to do her bidding. Common sense dictated that he should not be here, or at least should still be angry, but in truth he was delighted to be back on Georgie's team, on any terms.

Returning to her dressing table, Georgina hurriedly changed out of her blue jeans and into a smart grey skirt and white sweater. Looking in the mirror she flicked up her hair with the tips of her fingers, applying the smallest amount of make up.

"That will have to do," she muttered to herself, slipping her feet into a pair of black leather boots before surveying her completed ensemble in the full length mirror. Just a final dab or two of perfume and that was it.

Moving to the coffee table she placed two glasses with two bottles of mineral water, one still the other sparkling.

"Cigarettes, ashtray, lighter, paper and pencils, ballpoint pens." Talking quietly to herself she checked the items off on her fingers. She would order some coffee and sandwiches later, depending how the meeting progressed.

Now it was a simple matter of waiting. It was a quarter to twelve but there was no guarantee her visitor would arrive on time, if at all. It might be a long wait. Georgina sat in one of the armchairs and her thoughts immediately reverted to her unforgivable attack on poor Bob. The real cause of which was her disgust at herself for seducing him and a seduction was what it was. He was telling the truth, they'd had a great evening and he had been happy to return to his own room. But Georgie wanted more, she always wanted more, she wanted to possess all she saw.

Her reflections were interrupted by the ringing of the telephone.

"Yes, I am expecting him," she said, as calmly as she could manage. "Please send him up."

Georgina could feel her heart pounding in her chest as she glanced one final time in the mirror. Smoothing down her skirt with both hands, she stood facing the door. This was it, had she done the right thing? Was she about to die, the victim of an assassin's bullet?

The knock, although expected, made her jump, but that was nothing to her surprise on opening the door to see the identity of her visitor.

"Mr. Meyer," she gasped, as she surveyed the immaculately dressed South African.

"Mrs. van Wyk. As soon as I received the message that you wanted to see one of our officers, I was determined that the pleasure should be mine."

"Surely you haven't come all the way from South Africa?"

"Of course, may I come in?"

Quickly recovering her composure, Georgina invited Meyer into the room, directing him to an armchair.

Sitting in the proffered leather Chesterfield, he glanced around the room.

"Charming, quintessentially English."

"Mmm…I suppose so."

"There was a charming young man in reception paying great attention to my arrival," he asked affably, steepling his fingers. "A friend of yours?"

"Ah…you saw him," stumbled Georgina, aware that she had got off to a bad start. "He works for my mother, I brought him along to save me being bothered by men in the bar and restaurant, it happens to single women in hotels."

"A wise precaution, and pleasant company I should imagine."

Georgina felt herself blush.

"He's okay, he has a room along the corridor."

"Of course he has."

This was bad, Georgina was already on the back foot and the meeting was still in it's opening pleasantries. Meyer was clever, she must strike back as quickly as possible.

"I take it that you are not really the Chief Immigration Officer for the Pretoria area?"

Meyer laughed.

"I thought it better not to disclose my real interest until now."

"Oh, I knew who you were a few moments after our interview at Wonderboom, my aircrew had seen you getting out of a police car."

"Ah, well," he smiled.

Georgina's confidence began to return.

"Mr. Meyer," she asked without any sign of emotion. "Why did you have my husband murdered?"

The directness of the question caused even the urbane Meyer to raise an eyebrow.

"My dear Mrs van Wyk, quite simply, I didn't. Neither myself nor any of my colleagues were directly involved in the murders of either your husband, your brother – in – law or for that matter your gardener."

"Not directly involved? Then how about indirectly."

Meyer thought for a moment before answering.

"Not directly involved insomuch as the real murderer was one of my informants but he was acting without my authority."

"So Sibanyoni was a member of Operation Slapelose?"

Once again, Meyer pondered the question while staring at Georgina.

"He was an informant controlled by me, certainly, but hardly a member."

Georgina sat forward in her chair as she opened a new line of questioning.

"My husband told me that he held money to pay your informants as your operations were 'ultra vires' and could not, therefore be funded through normal police channels. Is that not correct, Mr. Meyer?"

"Our purpose was to infiltrate the activities of the banned

African National Congress, particularly their military wing, the so called Umkhonto we Sizwe, the MK, the Spear of the Nation. To do that, we created a network of informants. Forewarned is forearmed when dealing with terrorists, dear lady."

Now Georgina felt she was getting somewhere, but she had to play her hand carefully.

"And my husband funded this?"

"He would invoice the department for legal services he had not provided, enabling payment to be made that would then be used to pay Sibanyoni, whom he employed, at our request, as a messenger."

"If that's the case you have clearly lied to me," challenged Georgie, secretly delighted to find herself with the upper hand in her cerebral contest with this clever man, "Much more importantly, you have lied to my husband about the purpose of Operation Slapelose."

"What advantage have I in lying?"

"Mr. Meyer, I have little knowledge of detective work but I would imagine that every police force in the world employs informants. So I am sure that few politicians or members of the public anywhere, let alone South Africa, would take exception to the funding of a universally acceptable means of crime detection. If my premise is correct then why the need for a clandestine arrangement for payments? They could simply have been recorded, quite reasonably as 'payment of informants'."

Meyer listened silently to Georgina's onslaught, blinking like a rabbit caught in the headlights of an approaching car.

"Logically, therefore, I have no alternative than to surmise that you are involved in some activity that is not universally acceptable," continued Georgina, stressing the point with a stabbing index finger. "Some activity that if known about by the public, or in government circles, could not be guaranteed to be met with approbation. Something that must be kept secret. So what are you up to Mr. Meyer? You may have satisfied my husband, but not me."

She sat back in her armchair, confident of being in the ascendancy over this shadowy opponent.

For his part, Meyer was aware he had once again underestimated this beautiful young woman. He stood up and walked to the window before sighing and returning to his chair.

He looked at Georgina as she sat poker faced, returning his stare.

"May I smoke?" he asked, taking his pipe from his pocket.

"By all means."

Meyer silently filled his pipe from a small leather pouch, all the time studying Georgina as he tamped the tobacco down with his thumb. Having completed the procedure to his apparent satisfaction, he struck a match and lit the pipe with infinite care and precision, exhaling clouds of aromatic smoke into the room.

"Before I answer you Mrs. van Wyk, I must enquire if you are wired?" He sat back in his armchair awaiting a reply.

"Am I what?"

"I mean have you a microphone hidden in your clothing?

Without speaking, Georgina stood and in an instant pulled her sweater off over her head, shaking her hair back into shape. As she reached behind her back to unclip her bra, Meyer jumped to his feet.

"Mrs. van Wyk, please. That really is quite unnecessary, it was only an enquiry, I'm quite prepared to take your word."

"Oh, it's no trouble, Mr. Meyer, I can be naked in a moment," she smiled, secretly delighted to have him on the back foot once again.

Meyer held up both hands in a posture of surrender as a

victorious Georgina replaced her sweater, taking a few moments to attend to her hair, before eventually returning to her chair. She lit a cigarette and sat back in anticipation of his reply.

Meyer puffed on his pipe for a few moments before commencing to speak.

"Because of our internal affairs, South Africa has few friends in the world. This situation is inexplicable when one considers that we represent one of the last bastions of democracy against the inexorable advance of African communism. However, the world seems more interested in censuring us over our treatment of convicted terrorists and our banning of the African National Congress and the South African Communist Party."

He paused for a moment as Georgina gave a slight nod of acknowledgment.

"We believe that the aspirations of the ANC are receiving sympathetic attention from many governments and organisations around the world. It may surprise you to know, there are ANC offices in many capital cities. The truth is, Mrs. van Wyk, they are gaining legitimacy while we are being increasingly vilified. Our government is concerned that this policy of diplomacy may continue. Fortunately, the activities of Umkhonto we Sizwe tend, in the eyes of the rest of the world, to reinstate the ANC as terrorists. The world doesn't like to hear over it's breakfast of dead civilians."

Mr. Meyer got up and walked once more to the window. After looking into the gardens for a few moments he turned to face Georgina.

"So in the eyes of the rest of the world, every peaceful meeting in a foreign capital increases their reputation, every terrorist atrocity decreases it."

Georgina stubbed out her cigarette.

"So where do you come in, Mr. Meyer?"

"I was asked…"

"…Asked by whom?"

"That doesn't matter. I was asked to form a department…"

"Operation Slapelose?"

"…Yes, Operation Slapelose, to see if it would be possible to use some of our informants in a more…how shall we say?… proactive manner…"

"Proactive?"

"Quite simply, if we thought that 'Umkhonto we Sizwe' were not…er…quite active enough then we would commit the occasional outrage on their behalf, affording them full credit in the newspapers, of course."

With raised eyebrows, Georgina whistled quietly through her teeth as she sat back in her chair.

"Now I understand," she said in amazement. "That would need special funding, I agree. Unbelievable. Let me get this straight, you, the police, Operation Slapelose committed atrocities and then blamed the ANC?"

"In a nutshell, yes."

"And my husband funded it?"

"Not really. Occasionally Sibanyoni and his gang would be instructed to attack a commercial premises and any proceeds would be passed to your husband to hold, as I described earlier, for future payments. Weapons, explosives, that sort of thing, would be supplied by the South African Defence Force free of charge."

"Kind of them," she smiled. "The purpose of all this, I take it, was to undermine the reputation of the ANC by showing them to the world with blood on their hands. So what went wrong?"

"Nothing really," said Meyer, resuming his seat and placing his pipe on the table. "Nothing until your husband's brother-in-law, Mr. du Plessis discovered the false accounting in the company's books. Your husband came to me in a great panic, saying he wanted nothing more to do with 'Slapelose'. He feared it might ruin his company."

"What did you say to him?"

Meyer sighed.

"I told him, in all honesty, not to worry. His brother-in-law was hardly likely to go public and risk damaging his own firm. I suggested he explained to Mr. du Plessis that the money had been used for his political activities or some such story, your husband owned the company after all. Then promise it would not happen again…matter closed. For our part, it was a nuisance and meant our activities would need to be suspended while we found some other means of holding and paying out funds, but that would not have been too difficult to arrange."

Georgina's suspicions were immediately aroused, that statement was a little too glib. She felt sure that her husband's demands to be free of the operation must have caused more concern than Meyer was admitting. She unscrewed the top of a bottle of mineral water and poured two glasses.

"So how was Johannes murdered, I assume it was that creep Sibanyoni?"

"Yes, we are sure it was Sibanyoni and so is the detective in charge of the case…"

"…Captain Adendorff, does he know about 'Slapelose'?" asked Georgina, now on the edge of her chair.

"No, Adendorff is just a good detective, he knows nothing of our activities, except that I am a senior officer he occasionally encounters at police HQ. But you refer to our suspect Sibanyoni, of course you have met him, haven't you?"

"Certainly I've met him and what an unpleasant introduction it was."

It was Meyer's turn to sit on the edge of his chair as he listened to Georgina's description of her meeting with Sibanyoni. How, clad only in a bikini she had opened her Cape Town front door one Saturday morning to be confronted by the man's leering attentions, how she had tried to eavesdrop on her husband's meeting with him and how she had later confronted Hendrik in his office about the purpose of Sibanyoni's unwelcome visit. Georgina concluded her narrative with the assertion that this event marked her first inkling of her husband's links with 'Operation Slapelose'.

Leaving his armchair, Meyer paced up and down the room several times before standing behind his chair, looking intently at Georgina.

"What you have said, Mrs. van Wyk, is very interesting, I had no idea of the unfortunate nature of your meeting, it may explain a report we have received from the police in Rhodesia."

He remained silent for a few moments, considering whether to disclose the information he had. Deciding in the affirmative he continued.

"I have received, or I should say the investigating officer has received a report from the British South Africa Police up in Salisbury. They are, as you are aware, the lead investigators into your husband's murder. It seems that Sibanyoni was tracked to a settlement in one of the African Purchase Areas near Gokwe. The BSAP believe they only missed him by a few hours when they discovered the hut he had been occupying. Little useful evidence was found except..."

Meyer coughed as he stared at Georgina, clearly still hesitant whether to continue.

"Mrs. van Wyk, the BSAP report that behind a curtain they discovered a wall papered with dozens of photographs of..."

"Of what, man?"

"Of you, Mrs van Wyk. The whole wall was covered with pictures of you."

"Oh my God," gasped Georgina, staring at Meyer in horror. Holding a hand to her mouth, she was unable to prevent a visible shudder.

Meyer, showing genuine concern, took a step towards her.

"Do you think we could take a break for a few minutes, Mr. Meyer?" asked Georgina, hurriedly taking another cigarette, clearly shocked.

Georgina made a supreme effort to control her emotions as she struggled to maintain her sang froid.

"I think I need a coffee, and a sandwich, will you join me?" Georgina picked up the 'phone.

"Thank you, yes," replied Meyer, still showing gentlemanly concern.

Georgina gave instructions for lunch and replaced the telephone before returning to her seat.

"I'm really glad it was you who came to see me."

While they waited for lunch to arrive, Meyer continued to explain to Georgina the patently obvious. Sibanyoni was obsessed with her following their acrimonious meeting. For her part, she didn't need telling how serious this disclosure was for her safety if she returned to South Africa. As long as Sibanyoni remained free she would always be at risk.

A welcome break followed as a splendid cold buffet lunch was served. As Georgina listened to Meyer's polite conversation, the thought occurred to her that both Johannes and Hendrik's murders would have been the stock in trade of Operation Slapelose. If that were true, the obvious scapegoat to be framed would be Sibanyoni. The ANC had already been spectacularly blamed in the press. Quite a coup for the charming and cultured gentlemen with whom she was sharing lunch and of course, any risk of denouncement would have been eliminated.

The meal completed and sitting back with their coffee, Georgina resumed her offensive.

"So why did Sibanyoni murder Johannes?"

"Well, we haven't been able to find him to ask. But I suspect that when we suspended 'Slapelose' activities, he was suddenly short of money. We know that apart from working for us, he was a powerful gang leader in the townships. His authority was based on the money and equipment he was able to divert to his own use from our operations. I turned a blind eye to this as it was useful to have a paramount gang leader in our pocket."

Meyer took up his pipe from the table, attending to it's refilling as he continued his explanation.

"We know that your husband refused to give him money, that was the purpose of his visit to your home. Mr. van Wyk may have unwittingly mentioned that Mr. du Plessis had discovered the false accounts. Whatever was said, Sibanyoni visited your brother-in-law, he was allowed in as he was a company employee. He may have demanded the books but more likely he wanted money. The rest we know."

Or perhaps you simply ordered him to kill Johannes, thought Georgie.

"But why the dramatic nature of the killing? It was almost ceremonial, that was Hendrik's description," queried Georgie, now back on the edge of her chair and hanging on Meyer's every word.

"Two reasons, I think," he continued, lighting his pipe. "To create panic within your family, for I think it certain he intended to try again to obtain money from your husband. Also to give a warning to his power rivals in the townships, who by now, due to his lack of funds and equipment, were snapping at his heels.

Don't forget, he is a Zulu and the assegai and knobkerrie are the traditional weapons of his race. That would be a signature to those who understood, that he was still a power to be reckoned with."

"And my poor gardener?"

"Your gardener was also a Zulu and I think Sibanyoni expected his support as he tried to enter your house, either to search for money, to murder your husband, or both. However, your gardener was loyal to your family and paid for it with his life."

"And then used the poor old man's body to replicate Johannes's killing and further terrify us?"

"I think so," smiled Meyer, apologetically. "You all, quite understandably, went up to Pretoria and unfortunately we lost all track of Sibanyoni. Clearly he followed you by some means or other. Your husband, following these murders had totally convinced himself that we would never release him from the operation. The contrary was the truth, but we could not convince him. To this end he arranged a meeting with a senior government minister up in Pretoria. Don't ask who, if you don't know already, I won't tell you."

Georgina smiled and remained silent.

Fortunately, this minister was aware of our activities and again assured your husband of his grateful thanks and released him from the operation. That should have been the end of it. Your husband seemed convinced, but warned our minister that he was in possession of incriminating evidence that he would release to the papers should we renege on the agreement. That worried us somewhat, but by then, of course, you were in London."

"Okay, I understand all that, I think," resumed Georgina, pouring another coffee. "But why did you have me stopped on the way to the airport and why all the subterfuge at Wonderboom. Chief Immigration Officer, I ask you?"

For the first time during their meeting, Meyer laughed out loud.

"I was intrigued, Mrs. van Wyk, as simple as that, I was intrigued. My people had been observing your movements since your arrival in Pretoria and the reports I was receiving suggested that far from being cowed and terrified by the frightening events with which you were confronted, you seemed to be enjoying life immensely."

"That's only half the truth."

"I must confess to being a little provocative when I had your taxi stopped," smiled Meyer, eyes sparkling with amusement. "But when I received the report from our bruised and indignant Sergeant Wessels, I could hardly conceal my delight. You certainly lived up to my expectations."

"Glad it amused you."

Ignoring Georgina's mild rebuke, Meyer continued.

"I felt I just had to meet you. You must understand that in my line of work much depends upon intuition, so I invented my little subterfuge. You were truly a delight, witty, intelligent and confrontational. I could see how you must have destroyed my sergeant. I think your best reply, one that I will always treasure, was when I challenged you about the amount of money you were taking to Rhodesia. 'Just about right for a weekend' you said, 'depends on one's standards.' Priceless, Mrs van Wyk."

Georgina smiled as Meyer continued. She was forced to concede to herself that although still harbouring grave suspicions as to Meyer's complicity in her husband's murder, she nevertheless admired this man.

"It was then that I formed the opinion that whatever happened you would not be driven by a desire for revenge. You clearly wanted to get on with your life. I hope and believe I was right. So I let you go, after all, you had done nothing wrong, although you did take me by surprise when you ducked out to Nairobi and on to London. That's when I set up the surveillance in Chiswick."

"But your men took no action. You knew I had access to my husband's file of incriminating evidence, but you took no action to retrieve it."

"To be absolutely honest with you, I doubt whether your evidence amounts to very much. What would have been the point in burgling your apartment, your mother's house, her office? The files could have been anywhere and any provocative action by us might have panicked you into going public. I was more interested in what you were going to do. You are a charismatic figure and anything you said would be headline news, especially in South Africa. Were you meeting journalists or politicians? If you were, you could have caused us real problems, but it didn't seem so. I was pleased to see that you were just getting on with life. My hunch was right."

"I lost your men on the back of that motor cycle though, didn't I?" grinned Georgina.

"A true 'Georgina' moment," laughed Meyer, "You continued to live up to expectation."

Meyer suddenly became serious as he continued.

"But I was not prepared for the murder of your husband. The BSAP believe Sibanyoni travelled up to Victoria Falls on one of the trains taking the miners back to Zambia from our gold mines. As the men have no right of access into Rhodesia, the trains are sealed and do not stop until they get to the Zambia border. They believe he escaped while the train was being checked by Rhodesian immigration officers. Why did he murder your husband? I think he was fearful Mr. van Wyk was going to make a public statement about 'Operation Slapelose.' He was desperate, a lose cannon, he knew that we were in pursuit of him, but if the ANC became aware of his treachery he would not have survived long. Who really knows what was going through his mind?"

Or was it you who was fearful of what Hendrik might do, she mused.

Lighting another cigarette, she stood in front of the seated Meyer. For all his charm and logical explanation to her questions, she was increasingly suspicious he had ordered Hendrik's murder.

"So what do you intend for me, Mr. Meyer?"

"That depends on your intentions," he replied, looking up at her from his chair.

Georgina now embarked on the performance of her life, speaking with determination, her eyes sparkling.

"I accept what you have told me and given a chance, I just want to get on with my life. I am a very rich woman, but I am aware that the world sees me as a parvenu, I intend to become even richer by taking over Hendrik's company, which I now own in it's entirety. I intend to diversify into family law. Before I'm finished there will be a van Wyk solicitor in every high street in South Africa, then, perhaps Europe. I also have a mind to enter the air transport business, I believe it has a great future."

Georgina warmed to her subject.

"I will be internationally known. A welcome visitor in Downing Street, the White House, the Elysee Palace. My photograph will be everywhere and all the time I intend to be an ambassador for South Africa. Wherever I am invited, South Africa travels with me."

"I have no doubt you will succeed, but have you no doubts about our policies?"

"I am not a political person, Mr. Meyer, nor am I a very moral one. I think that apartheid will continue to cause us problems, but it is not my direct concern. Since you've asked, I believe that most importantly, it will restrict our industrial development,"

"How so?"

"Simply, that our industries, to develop and be competitive with the rest of the world, must keep pace with modern technology. I believe that we may be dropping behind already and the need for huge numbers of unskilled labourers will be replaced by a shortage of skilled labour. In that respect, the so called Colour Bar Act that protects white workers by prohibiting blacks from holding skilled jobs will, I think, cause problems. So will the Group Areas Act, I cannot see industry relocating to the sources of labour in the homelands. I think we may need to create a black middle class. But as I say, it's not my problem."

"Perhaps," smiled Meyer. "You make some interesting points. I am sure you would have a brilliant career in politics, should you ever choose to take that path."

"What, like my husband?" answered Georgina with a wry smile. "I think not. I'll just stick to spending my money and making more and leave the politics to someone else."

"Wise words, Mrs. van Wyk, as I would have expected from you," said Meyer, rising and holding out his hand. "I've thoroughly enjoyed meeting you and I'm confident you will be brilliantly successful. Please be assured that providing you keep your word, you have nothing to fear from us. We will catch Sibanyoni and he will go on trial for murder, if someone doesn't kill him first…"

"…Wouldn't that be best for all of us?"

"…Again, perhaps," responded Meyer with another smile. "I look forward to following your glittering career and if I can ever be of assistance to you, here is my card."

Georgina accepted the offered credentials.

"Major General Orlando Meyer, South Africa Police," read Georgie, smiling, offering hers in exchange.

With that, ignoring Meyer's offered hand, she stepped forward and to his surprise, kissed him full on the lips.

"I shall return to South Africa as soon as possible. You can trust me to remain silent and thank you."

Quickly recovering his calm demeanour, Meyer placed his hand gently on Georgina's shoulder.

"When you are back in Cape Town, perhaps we could have lunch together?"

"I would like that," she whispered. "You have my number."

Georgina considered for a moment, without any emotion, that it might be necessary, at some time in the future, to sleep with this man.

"If Sibanyoni is still at large, we will do our utmost to protect you."

"Thank you again."

The interview ended, Georgina experienced a huge feeling of relief. She was confident that she had won.

Bob Simmons leapt to his feet as he saw Georgina enter the reception in company with Major General Meyer. Seeing his alarm, Georgie quickly subdued his fears with a smile as she waved him back to his seat. Meyer smiled with amusement.

At the door to the car park, they shook hands and Meyer was gone. Georgina returned to Bob's table as he looked expectantly towards her. She raised both her hands.

"It's okay, I think I've won. Come on, I need some fresh air."

As they strolled around the hotel gardens, Georgina explained a very little of what had transpired during the interview. Bob, never having fully understood what was going on anyway, was content that Georgie was happy and he, once more, was with her.

Suddenly tired of the hotel, Georgina suggested a change of scene. So that evening they drove into Henley and found a quiet restaurant for dinner. By 10.30, content, but exhausted they were back in their separate bedrooms. Laying in bed, Georgina went over in her mind the meeting with Meyer. Regardless of her personal dislike for Sibanyoni, she was now convinced that he, her husband, brother – in law and gardener had all been victims of Operation Slapelose. Sibanyoni was probably already dead, that would explain why Adendorff couldn't trace him and as for the BSAP finding his hut full of her pictures, well that would do very nicely in outraging white South Africa over it's breakfast. Of one thing she was certain, Meyer's version of the murders would appear in the press when it suited him and Georgina knew that she would remain silent, whatever was said.

Why was she still alive? Simply, because a police major general was infatuated with her. Well, she could cope with that and perhaps use it to her advantage.

She fell asleep with a smile on her face.

Across the corridor Bob Simmons was finding it difficult to sleep. He was delighted to be back on good terms with Georgina, that was paramount above everything, but from the bottom of his soul a doubt kept niggling at him, spoiling his happiness and refusing to go away.

Less than two weeks ago he was riding on the crest of a wave, he had a wonderful job, his boss was great and the future was all green lights. True, his room was awful, he had been embarrassed for Georgie to see it, but he would be gone from there soon. It wasn't important. Above all, he was comfortable with himself. Then the boss's daughter exploded into his life.

Put simply, he adored her. She was stunningly beautiful, funny, exciting to be with, clever and rich, yes very rich. He could only imagine the lifestyle she was used to. The cars, the houses, the men. Clearly he didn't stand a chance, as Georgie had said, she was out of his league. But she kept him on a string. The thought he kept returning to was the lack of equality in their relationship. He would always bend to suit her moods. Every time her outrageous behaviour offended or humiliated him, when he should have stood up to her with some masculine pride, what did he do? He let her win, anything to stay on good terms, to remain one of Georgina's friends. The truth was, his happiness now depended on pleasing her. And she used him, he knew she used him. The unpalatable truth was, he didn't care. He needed to stay close to her, in any capacity. He was acutely aware of being seduced by her on Friday night. Wonderful it was, but it shouldn't have happened like that. By seducing him she had emasculated him. He would do anything for her, however she treated him and she knew it. But did any of this matter? Of course not, he was in love with Georgina van Wyk and on her terms.

CHAPTER SEVENTEEN

Sunday 23rd February 1969
Chiswick

Bob and Georgina excelled themselves at breakfast on Sunday morning, eating everything in sight. Georgie settled the bill, as Bob loaded the car and by 11.00am they were on their way home, both still in high spirits.

As they sped down the M4 towards London, Georgina glanced across at Bob.

"Why don't you give up that horrid room of yours and come and share my flat?"

Bob's head spun round to face her, jaw open in astonishment.

"Don't get too excited," she laughed, glancing in her mirror before accelerating past a slower moving car. "I shan't be there, well not often."

"I didn't even know you had a flat," he gasped in amazement.

"I didn't know either, my husband bought it for me, it's in Barrowgate Road, two bedrooms, very nice, but I'll need someone to look after it when I go back to SA."

Bob's high spirits were dented by the thought of her inevitable departure from his life.

"I couldn't afford the rents in Barrowgate Road."

She waved his protest away with her hand.

"Just come and look, we can pop in on the way back."

They drove on in silence as Georgie continued to cast amused glances at Bob's frowning expression.

After less than an hour they pulled up outside Apollo Court.

"Come on," called Georgie, as Bob trudged reluctantly behind her. "Just have a look."

Georgina showed Bob around the immaculate, newly decorated apartment. She could see he was clearly impressed, but retained his fixed expression.

"Well, what do you think?"

Bob sunk his hands deep in his pockets.

"It's not fair, you're just teasing me, you know I could never afford this."

"Here's the deal," she continued, laughing at Bob's dejection. "You pick one of the bedrooms, either one, I don't mind. The other one is mine. Nobody goes in there except you, to do a bit of vacuuming. Apart from that the place is yours, you can have your pals round, do what you like, but no parties. I expect you to keep on good terms with the neighbours. Open all the mail, even if it's addressed to me, I'll set you up with a cheque book, so you can pay all the bills. I don't suppose I will ever stay here, but you never know, so keep it tidy. The 'phone, TV, heating, everything is yours to use, free of charge. You can even keep your bike in the garage. Any problems then ring me, I'll give you all my numbers. How does that sound?"

"It sounds like charity, I'll manage on my own."

Georgina's smile faded from her face.

"I don't do charity, I'm not a very charitable person," said Georgie, angrily. "What I get is free property maintenance that would cost me a fortune if I went to an estate agent. I think it's a good deal for both of us, but it's your choice Bob, think carefully, as I'll not make the offer again."

Bob thought for a few minutes while darting furtive glances at Georgie, who stood hands on hips looking out of the window.

He knew that in taking this fantastic offer he would be in Georgina's pocket for as long as she wanted him. The alternative was to walk away and out of her life and perhaps out of his dream job as well, he had no doubt she could be that vindictive if she chose. But as he realised last night, did he care? No, not a jot, he loved her and on her terms, on any terms she chose. He contented himself that, in her own words, she was not a bad person.

"I'm sorry, Georgie, I didn't understand. If you put it like that I'd love to live here, thank you, but I have to give a month's notice."

"Great, that's decided then, you can give a month's notice, but you don't have to live there. You've done me a real favour. I'll take you home now and tomorrow after work I'll borrow Mum's Volvo and pick up your stuff. You haven't got much kit, have you?"

Monday morning found Bob at work in the dark room of Wilding Photographic. He should have felt elated about his imminent departure from his attic bedroom, but his thoughts were clouded by Georgina's absence.

It was stupid really, but her previously regular presence at the shop had led him to consider her as a fellow employee, but of course, her reason to be there was her fear of being alone. Now free of that fear, she had no need of his companionship. Bob felt the hopelessness of his love as the chasms of wealth, aspirations, opportunities, life styles, even continents, opened up between them. These thoughts dogged him all day and were noticed by Mrs. Browne.

At 4.30 his gloom was shattered as Georgina erupted into the office.

"Come on, Bob." she beamed. "Let's get you moved."

Georgie could not resist a smile at the meagre size of Bob's pile of possessions in the back of the big Volvo estate as she set off towards the flat, Bob following on his bike.

Moving in was just as simple and soon the couple stood facing each other in the lounge.

"Thanks, Georgie, I really appreciate this," he said, still with some embarrassment, "Can we have a drink tonight?"

"No, I don't think so," she replied, avoiding eye contact. "I have to pack, I'm flying back to SA tomorrow."

"Tomorrow, so soon," he gasped in panic, "Take me with you, please."

Expecting him to be upset by news of her imminent departure, she was nonetheless surprised by his outburst.

"Absolutely not. You've a job here, you're needed and I have a lot to do when I get home. Don't forget I have to bury my husband and you, of all people, cannot be with me for obvious reasons."

Georgina stepped forward and put her arms around her crestfallen friend, resting her head against his chest.

"You have my telephone numbers," she whispered tenderly. "Ring me any time, don't worry about the bill. If I'm there I'll always speak to you, if I'm not, I'll get back to you, I promise."

"I love you, Georgie," he gasped.

"I know you do. Listen, it's your 21st birthday soon isn't it? Book a table for two at a really good restaurant and I'll be there."

"You'd come back from South Africa for me?"

"You're important to me, I'll be there." she smiled and kissed him.

"I'll see you in the morning?"

"No, I'll be gone in the morning, I'll see you soon," replied Georgie as she gave him a lingering kiss and left.

To be continued.

ACKNOWLEDGEMENTS

Over the last few years I have developed a fascination for the history of southern Africa and in pursuit of this interest have assembled an eclectic collection of books. I would like to mention two.

'The Last Trek', the erudite and authoritative autobiography by F.W. de Klerk and our friend Karl Greenberg's 'The Gokwe Kid', recounting his short but hilarious career in The British South Africa Police. It is quite simply one of the best and funniest books on southern Africa I have ever read.

I recommend them both.

Of course, huge thanks to my wife Linda for her unwavering support as the story took shape. For the long discussions, heated arguments and much laughter as she attempted to keep Georgina's outrageous behaviour within bounds.

The better side of Georgina's personality, many of the characters and some of the less sensational events in the book are biographical of Linda's early life, particularly Joyce Browne, Bob Simmons, the photographic studio and life in Chiswick in the late 1960's.

Sadly however, references to the heroine's great wealth are purely fictional for the benefit of the story.

Thanks next to our friend Jenny Gardner for thinking of the title of the book. For her great patience and good humour in contending with my long and rambling e.mails. One of her funniest responses I quote:

'Dear Rob, If you insist on e.mailing in Afrikaans please include an English translation'.
To which I replied, 'I thought you could speak Afrikaans?'
Her one line reply was, 'I can, you plainly cannot!'
Priceless.

My appreciation to Jenny's sister, Diana Botha, for seeking out and advising on 1960's Cape Town locations in a twenty – first century city.

Jan Saxelby, Carla Smith and my daughter, Celia Castle in England together with Richard Heath in France helped enormously by cheerfully agreeing to interrupt their busy and successful lives to undertake the onerous task of proof reading. Thanks also to Linda's cousin Robert Gardner for his knowledge of Rhodesia and his permission to use the photograph of Linda.

I must also commend my elder daughter, Liz Parker for her patience, as I grappled with the intricacies of the plot.

Finally, I must mention the one person without whom this book would have been impossible to write – the outrageously delightful heroine, Georgina van Wyk. She has been my constant companion for over a year and although she may be to you, my reader, a character of fiction, she is real to me. I saw her recently, getting out of a cab in Piccadilly, I know it was her as she waved to me.

I hope you enjoy the book, meanwhile I will keep taking the tablets.